THE LETTER

by

Charna Ainsworth

To my beloved muse, who inspired this novel.

Acknowledgements

A very special thank you to:

Charles Burkhalter: My dad, who helped to shape and mold The Letter from its beginning.

Barbara Burkhalter: My mom, who cheerfully read and reread the book after editing.

Charlotte Henley: My sister, who is an excellent proofreader.

Susanne Ford: A new friend, who greatly helped me during the final edit.

And to you, the reader: Thank you. I am honored that you would read this story that is so dear to my heart.

Chapter 1

Did the world stop spinning when a stranger walked in the room and sat down beside me? Unknowingly, she took my breath away, without even saying a word. It was as if her blue eyes spoke an inaudible language that only I could understand. Now, it's only a memory but I keep going over and over it in my mind, beginning from the very first second I saw her. Then I move forward, moment by moment, trying to figure out what this girl has done to me.

She was shy as she said her name. I repeated, Tiffany Crenshaw, and she quietly answered yes. It was the distance in her voice that drew me in. Like she had a big secret and my mission was to reveal it. I wanted to introduce myself by saying, I'm Steven Cross, and I want to be your man. Instead, I extended my hand introducing myself. Then she turned to face me. Long red hair cascaded over slender shoulders as she said it was nice to meet me. As our hands touched her crystal blue eyes captivated me, maybe, for a moment too long. She turned her head suddenly, as if in shame. I wanted to reach out and hold her face still, to stare deeper into the windows of her soul, but I didn't.

When my brother Blake started waving his hand in front of my face, he brought me out of my dreamland. Then my best friend Brad pulled me off the tailgate of my truck, reminding me it was Saturday night and time to party. The music was so loud I could barely hear him tell me about the headlights coming up the road. When I turned around all I noticed was how the bon-fire lit up the tall pine trees. It seemed like I was still in a dream-like-state and then I realized, that everyone was having fun, except for me.

My mind continued to race with thoughts of Tiffany and I knew I needed to stop reliving the moments of yesterday. The possibility of seeing her tonight was almost non-existent. There was no way she could know about the 'bog'. Even if she knew about it, she probably wouldn't come to a place like this. But still, I silently made a wish, that somehow I would see her again. When I opened my eyes, Amber was standing right in front of me.

"Hi, Steven."

"Oh, hi, Amber."

"I was hoping you'd be here tonight, there's something I need to ask you," she said sweetly, touching my arm.

"What is it?" I asked, looking away. My heart skipped a beat when Tiffany and Victoria walked out of the shadows of the forest.

"Who is that?" Amber asked.

"Steven," Victoria yelled. She ran toward us, out of the darkness, with Tiffany behind her.

"Did ya'll walk all the way here?" I asked, walking toward them.

"Yes," Victoria answered, out of breath.

"We meet again," Tiffany said, looking surprised to see me.

"Yeah, I was just thinking about you," I said, smiling. Victoria walked past us, looking to see who else was here.

"I was thinking about you too, country boy."

"Everyone who comes to our party must have a drink," Brad said. He had a six-pack in his hand and started handing them out to the girls.

Amber stared Tiffany up and down, with a strange look on her face and asked, "Who are you?"

"I'm Tiffany. Nice to meet you…"

"I met a girl named Tiffany once but she didn't look anything like you," Amber said sarcastically, ignoring Tiffany, reaching out for my hand. "Aren't you going to open this for me?"

"Sure." I took her beer and as the top opened, beer spewed out everywhere.

"Steven! You got beer all over my sweater!"

"I'm sorry," I said, putting the beer in her hand. Victoria and Tiffany started laughing and I couldn't help but laugh too. Amber looked into my eyes, dropped the beer at my feet and ran to her car.

"Does she think she's going to melt?" Tiffany asked.

"Of course she does, darling. Don't you know? All witches have the ability to melt," Victoria said, sinking toward the ground, laughing louder.

8

"No, really, what's her problem?" Tiffany asked seriously.

"She's Stevens' ex-girlfriend," Victoria replied, looking at me.

"Oh, I know all about ex's. I got one back in California."

Brad turned up the music and Victoria grabbed Tiffany's hand, pulling her toward the fire. When they started dancing, Tiffany didn't appear to be the same girl I met yesterday. She closed her eyes, shutting out the world, as her body matched the rhythm of the beat.

Then suddenly, she turned and slowly danced up to me. I didn't even try to tell her no. My body just started moving, trying to match her rhythm. Everyone was staring but I didn't care who was watching. I kept catching glimpses of Tiffany's blue eyes and no one else's eyes mattered.

When the song ended, I put my arm around her waist and we walked back to my truck where Amber stood waiting.

"When did you learn to dance like that, Steven?" Amber asked, fists firmly on her hips, glaring at me.

"I don't know. Was I any good?"

"You were great," Tiffany said, putting her arm around me, pulling me closer.

"You are just full of surprises tonight," Amber said, abruptly turning around and stomping away.

"I bet she'll become an actress someday," Victoria said, pointing at Amber.

"Why do you say that?" Tiffany asked.

"Look at her. Have you ever seen anybody act like that? She'll probably win awards someday for that crap."

Tiffany climbed up on the tailgate of my truck and said,"I'll be the one winning awards someday. As soon as I'm eighteen I'm moving back to California to become an actress."

I could hear Amber starting her car and her friends begging her to stay. And then I could hear her driving away but I didn't even turn to look. Instead, I moved closer to Tiffany and whispered, "I'm glad you're here tonight."

"Me, too."

"Steven, can you take us home when you leave?" Victoria asked.

"Of course, we'll take ya'll home," Blake answered, turning up the radio. In every direction, headlights were shining, doors were slamming and motors were turning over.

"Everybody is going over to Amber's house. I told them we might be there later," Brad said.

"Cool! We got the place to ourselves. Dance with me, Brad!" Victoria yelled, running toward the fire.

"Here I come, baby," Brad said, following her.

Tiffany sat down beside me and I watched their bodies move erratically, wondering what I must have looked like earlier. She touched my hand and I turned to look in her eyes. There were so many things I didn't know about Tiffany but still, I felt incredibly close to her.

"So, why did ya'll move to Natchez?"

"I guess Dad thought if we're far enough away from California we'll forget about Mom."

"Where is your Mom?"

"She took off for New York. She said she had to 'find herself', whatever that means." Tiffany said, standing up to face me.

"And what's the story on your ex-boyfriend?"

"Oh Alan, he was my first love, I mean is my first love. We've known each other since first grade."

"Are you still together?"

"It's hard to be together when he's in California and I'm in Mississippi."

"Well, I'm glad you moved here," I said, suddenly wishing I'd kept my mouth shut because of the look on her face.

"Then you would be the only one," she replied sarcastically.

"I'm sorry, I just…"

"That's alright, Steven. I'm just mad and it has nothing to do with you. I mean, how can a mother just leave her family without even saying goodbye?"

She walked away suddenly and I almost got up and followed her. I didn't know what to do or say so my eyes followed her every move, looking for direction. She opened the ice chest, took out two beers and walked back over, sitting down beside me.

After a few awkward moments of silence, Tiffany gently took my hand and led me back to the fire. Then she did the strangest thing. She placed my hands on her waist and put her hands around my neck. The song that was playing had a fast beat but she moved slowly. Tiffany leaned on my chest and I pulled her close. Before I knew what I was doing, we were kissing and kissing and kissing and kissing.

****

"Blake! Wait up!"

"What is it, Steven? I'm going to be late for class!" He yelled over the sound of a crowded hallway.

I caught up with him, asking, "Have you seen Tiffany today?"

"No, she wasn't in homeroom this morning."

"Then where is she?"

"How would I know, I'm not her keeper," he said, walking away throwing his hands in the air.

"Have you seen Victoria?"

"No!" he yelled, over his shoulder.

Everything that happened Saturday night seemed like a dream to me. Only when I could see her face again would it become reality. Knowing Victoria, she talked Tiffany into skipping today. That girl would do just about anything to get out of going to school. I knew I had to get out of here so I went to see the school nurse.

Within a few minutes of seeing the nurse and a phone call home, I was walking out the door to my truck. After leaving the school parking lot, I debated on which direction to go. I doubted they would be at Victoria's so I went by Tiffany's house and knocked on the door. No one answered so I drove by the lake in their subdivision to check it out.

As soon as I saw the water, I could see Tiffany's beautiful long red hair waving in the wind. So I parked the truck on the shoulder of the road and walked over to surprise them.

"Victoria, you are so bad! I can't believe you talked Tiffany into skipping school today."

"Steven! How did you find us?"

"It wasn't that hard to find you. All I had to do was look for trouble."

"Why do you think skipping was her idea?" Tiffany asked.

"Because I know her, that's why. So, what are you two drinking?"

"It's some of my momma's wine. Want some?" Victoria asked.

"Sure. Let me get a cup out of my truck."

"Hey, Tiffany, Steven has a truck. Let's get out of here," Victoria said. She picked up the bottle of wine and started walking.

"We can't go anywhere. We're supposed to be sick," Tiffany said, stepping backwards.

Victoria turned around, slinging her long brown hair over her shoulder. She walked back toward us and said, "Get real, girlfriend.

This is the reason we said we were sick, so we could go somewhere and have some fun."

"Aren't we already having fun?"

"We're leaving with or without you. Come on, Steven," Victoria said, pulling me forward.

I reached out for Tiffany and she took my hand. I pulled her as Victoria pulled me and said, "I promise I'll bring you back in one piece."

"You know if you make a promise, you have to keep it," Tiffany said, looking in my eyes.

"I know," I said, pulling her up to walk beside me.

She looked so beautiful that I had the overwhelming urge to reach out and touch her soft skin. Tiffany's full red lips spoke untouchable words that could inspire me to write a million poems. Her body was perfect in every way, except it was not in my arms.

There were so many things I wanted to ask her and so many things I wanted to say. But all of those words had to be held back for a more private moment. I jumped in the drivers' seat and Tiffany got in the middle.

"Where are we going?" Victoria asked, as I pulled onto the road.

"To the falls."

"Cool. I can't wait for you to see them, Tiffany."

She just smiled, saying nothing so I turned up the radio. It was a short drive and I parked the truck on the side of the road. As we got out, I grabbed a blanket, following the girls down to the woods.

Tall pine trees and brush lined the path on both sides. As we walked, flowers would pop into view in shades of yellow, white and pink. My eyes watched every move she made, trying to be inconspicuous, but I was completely mesmerized by Tiffany's natural beauty. As soon as we walked over the last hill, we could hear the water. It dropped nearly twenty feet before slamming against the rocks.

"Wow!" she exclaimed, running over to the edge.

I had seen it all of my life but it seemed even more beautiful with the expression on her face. I looked back and watched the stream spilling over into the large pool of water. Then quietly, without turning to look at her, I asked, "Do you like it? It's one of my favorite places."

"It's so beautiful, Steven. I need a camera!" Tiffany exclaimed, walking closer to the falls.

"I can bring you back, anytime you want. Just let me know when…"

"Let's come down here tonight and party," she said, turning to look at Victoria.

Shaking her head from side to side, Victoria said in a low voice, "Nobody comes down here at night."

"Why?"

"The bog is better for night time," I said, throwing the blanket up in the air to spread it out on the ground.

"Come on, you guys. How come no one comes down here at night?"

"You tell her, Steven. You tell the story better than I do," Victoria said as she lay down.

Tiffany lay down on her side, facing the falls and I sat between them. I didn't want to tell the story. I didn't want to spoil the beauty she was seeing. But if Tiffany wanted to know, I would be the one to tell her.

"It happened in nineteen fifty-seven. A woman named Shelia had recently given birth, to her first child, a boy. It was a difficult birth; mother and child were still in the hospital a week after delivery."

"Suddenly, Shelia's blood pressure bottomed out. The nurses, fearing the worst, called the family to come to the hospital. But no one could find her husband. The family gathered in her hospital room discussing where her husband could be. All of a sudden, Shelia sat up, demanding they all leave at once."

"The nurses checked Shelia's vital signs and she seemed to be stable. As soon as they walked out of her room, she took the I.V. out of her arm and left the hospital."

"Shelia went home but her husband was no where to be found. As her anger grew, she walked out to the shed picking up an axe. She walked into the woods and then turned and started walking in the opposite direction. It has been said, that she could hear a voice calling to her."

"When Shelia approached the waterfalls, she heard strange noises. She crouched down in the bushes and watched her husband with his lover. They were naked, standing on rocks, under the falls."

"Sheila entered the water by crawling into it. She swam behind his lover then in one quick motion stood up and swung the axe. The woman fell back on her, pushing Shelia down into the water. She scrambled to find the axe as her husband grabbed her by the hair. She pushed him, fighting to break free from his grasp and he fell off the rock. As he was coming up out of the water Sheila swung the axe over and over again, while screaming, die, die, die!"

"Later that day, a neighbor found Shelia and rushed her back to the hospital. When they arrived, the nurses told her the terrible news. Her son had died while she was gone. Shelia never shed a tear but instead, asked the nurse to call the sheriff."

"In great detail, Shelia told the Sheriff what had happened that day. When he said he would have to place her under arrest, she told him that wouldn't be necessary. Her heart stopped beating at that very moment."

"Over the years, many people have claimed to see the naked lovers under the waterfall and others have only heard voices. Personally, I have never seen or heard anything, and I don't want to."

"I can't believe something so tragic happened in a place so beautiful," Tiffany said, rolling onto her back, looking up at the sky.

"All kinds of strange things have happened in this town. That's only one of the stories I could tell you."

Victoria got up and walked over to the water's edge. She knelt down to pick some flowers as I looked at Tiffany. "Do you want some more wine?"

Tiffany replied slowly, "No. I want you to lie down beside me so I can look into those brown eyes."

"Okay," I said softly, taking a deep breath and lying down.

"Look up at those clouds, aren't they beautiful? That one is shaped almost like a heart," she said, moving closer, pointing up.

The little cloud looked like a misshaped heart but I could still see what she saw. "Tiffany?"

"Yes," she said, turning toward me.

"Are you and Alan still together?"

"We still talk and stuff. Why do you ask?"

"Well, I wanted to ask you out for Saturday."

"Where would you take me?" Tiffany asked, rolling over and putting her chin on my chest.

"Wherever you want to go. We could go out to eat, to the movies, anything you want."

"Anything I want? Now that's an offer I can't refuse, Mr. Cross," she said, lying back on the blanket.

I had a strong desire to kiss her. I rolled onto my side and put my head in my hand, where I could look into her eyes. "Anything."

"That's not fair! What are you two doing? Why didn't you bring Brad with you?" Victoria whined.

"He didn't know I was leaving school today." I acknowledged her question with words only because I couldn't stop staring into Tiffany's blue eyes.

"Well, let's go get him," Victoria said, walking toward the path.

I took my time getting up and folding the blanket because I wasn't ready to leave. Victoria was already walking up the path yelling for us to hurry up. Tiffany could sense the way I was feeling and ignored her command too.

Once Victoria was out of sight, Tiffany pulled me close and kissed me softly. As we walked back to the path, hand in hand, my heart was racing. I could hardly believe, in just a few days, we would go out on our first date.

****

"Hi, I'm Steven. Is Tiffany home?"

"Tiffany! Your date is here!" the girl yelled, walking back into the house.

The door was open so I walked inside and saw Tiffany coming down the stairs. She looked angelic and all I could do was stare at her.

"For me?"

I nodded yes, handing her a single rose. When our fingers touched, I got lost in her eyes with thoughts of kissing those beautiful lips. So lost that I didn't hear or see her father walk into the room.

"Hi, Steven, I'm Henry Crenshaw. Nice to meet you," he said as he reached for my hand. "That was Cheryl who answered the door, Tiffany's sister."

"I thought that's who it was."

"She's not very happy about our move to Natchez."

"I sure am glad you moved here," I replied, nervous and excited at the same time.

"To be honest with you, Steven, I'm a little surprised Tiffany is going out with you. She was even more upset than Cheryl about moving here."

"Dad."

"Well, it's the truth. Her and that boy Alan were begging and pleading with me to stay out there."

"Okay, dad, we're going to go now..." Tiffany said, pulling me toward the door.

15

"Alright Steven, take care of my baby girl. Don't drive too fast and have her home by ten-thirty."

"Yes, sir."

"Love you, dad," she said as we walked out the door.

We drove through the winding, curving roads in the darkness. As I turned onto a dirt road that led into the peach orchard, Tiffany looked surprised. The contrast of the pale pink flowers against the night sky made the little trees stand out. The dew was falling, which seemed to trap the wonderful smell of the peach blossoms. Fresh peaches smell good but the flowers have a very unique smell of their own. It was as if you could almost taste the sweetness by breathing in the air.

I parked the truck outside the old abandoned brick building, asking Tiffany to bring her rose. The door was the only thing that looked sturdy from the outside. Even the windows had little or no glass. As I opened the door, I was surprised she hadn't asked any questions. There was no roof on the old building, no interior walls, just a dirt floor with grass and weeds.

I walked around the room lighting candles then started a fire in the old fireplace. The blanket we laid on at the falls was on the ground with several large pillows. I watched Tiffany, standing silently, looking up at the night sky. I walked up behind her putting my arms around her waist and looked up too.

I took the rose from her hand and laid it on a pillow. Then I turned on my boom box and the music began to play. We were dancing slowly when I put my hand on the back of her neck. Kissing her tenderly, our breath became intertwined as I gently picked her up. Everything felt so natural as I laid her down and slowly began to unbutton her shirt. She started breathing harder and suddenly I realized what we were doing.

"Do you want me to stop?" I asked, kissing her neck.

"Yes. No. Just touch me," she said, pulling me down against her.

It had never been hard for me to stop before but that was before Tiffany. The object of my every desire laid before me and there was no fighting my feelings anymore. Every touch of her fingertips made my heart beat faster and the anxiety I felt, melted away. I closed my eyes and pretended this had happened a million times before and I knew what I was doing.

We took our time, touching and kissing for what seemed like forever. Never in my wildest dreams did I think we would make love to each other tonight but as the minutes quickly passed, I found myself unable to resist being one with Tiffany.

I had never felt so utterly content and happy as I held her in my arms, as close to me as possible. She was hugging me so tightly that she made it hard for me to breath. I tried to move, to look into her eyes but she wouldn't let go.

"Don't worry baby, I'm not going anywhere."

"I have to tell you something, but I'm scared," Tiffany whispered.

"You can tell me anything."

"I'm a virgin. I mean, I was a virgin."

"Why didn't you tell me that, Tiffany?" I asked, leaning up to look at her.

"I just did."

She stared right past me, into the starry sky. I felt so small because I couldn't take my words back and it was too late to change the tone of my voice. The damage had been done unknowingly, even though all I wanted to do was make Tiffany feel secure.

I made her look at me and said, "It's okay. I just wish I would've known before we did it. I didn't hurt you, did I?"

"No, you didn't hurt me. I know I'm not experienced like you, but I do know something about sex. It is nineteen eighty-nine, you know," she said, pulling away from me.

"It just seemed like you knew what you were doing. Remember, I didn't know this was your first time."

"Well it was. Do you think I would lie about it?"

"No. I don't think you'd lie about anything," I replied softly, gently kissing her cheek. But I didn't know what to believe. When I thought of virgins, I thought of ignorance. How could Tiffany be a virgin and make love to me like that? There was little evidence that she was telling me the truth, except for the look in her eyes.

"Please don't be upset, Tiffany," I said, gently caressing her face. "I have to ask you something important."

"Ask me anything and I'll tell you the truth," she said defensively.

"It's not that kind of question. I want to know if you'll go with me."

"Sure, we can go out," she said.

"I bought you something just in case you said yes," I said, reaching over to get my coat.

"What is it?" she asked, sitting up.

"Well, you'll just have to open it and see."

Her slender fingers opened the tiny box slowly. "Steven! You bought me a ring. Is that a real diamond?" She asked, taking the ring out, holding it up to the candlelight.

"Yes, it's real. I know it's not much but it means a lot to me," I said, taking the ring from her fingers. "Tonight only makes this promise stronger. I give you this ring with a promise to always be here if you need anything and also as a symbol of our friendship," I said, slipping the ring on her finger.

"I love it," she said, putting her arms around my neck, kissing my cheek.

We laid back down and looked up into the sky. At the same time we pointed up and said, "Did you see that shooting star?"

"Tiffany, I need to tell you something important."

"What is it?"

"I'll be moving to New York in the fall to start college. My grandparents live out there."

"That's ironic, isn't it? That's where my mother lives," she said, reaching for her clothes.

"You don't have to get dressed. It's not time to leave yet."

"I'm getting cold," she said in a distant voice.

"Stay right here. I'll put some more wood on the fire. So, why did your mother move to New York?" I asked as I put my pants on.

"My mother was a dancer before she met my dad. She got tired of playing mother and wife, so she moved back to New York to play dancer again," Tiffany said.

"I bet she's good if she dances anything like you," I said, kneeling to put more wood on the fire.

"I wouldn't know, Steven."

I turned toward her, still on my knees and said, "I'm sorry, Tiffany. I didn't mean to…."

"It's okay. Just drop it," she said, as she walked towards me and kneeled down.

"Okay, let's change the subject, beautiful. Tell me what would you like to do tomorrow? Can I see you tomorrow?"
****

Tiffany and I spent practically every day together after our first date but we had to do a lot of sneaking around. My mother was against us dating and dad took her side. My ex-girlfriend, Amber, persuaded

18

everyone she could to hate Tiffany. We ignored the complaints of my mother and the talk we heard about us around town. I knew they were all jealous and their rumors were just lies. I was so in love with Tiffany that nothing could keep us apart.

When I couldn't be with her, I would write her poetry in one of my journals. She gave me two that looked just alike so we could exchange them every time we saw each other. Occasionally, Tiffany would write a tiny note at the bottom of a poem she liked. I savored every kind word she ever wrote to me.

Before I knew it, the time had come for me to leave for college. I begged Mom and Dad to let me go to a university nearby. My mother would not listen. She had it made up in her mind that Amber and I would be together, if Tiffany wasn't in the picture. There was absolutely no way she was going to let me stay in Natchez.

I had one last day, to spend with my beloved and we went to Carter's Trail. Being alone with her in the forest, surrounded by nature, made me feel a little better. There's a special way the sunlight beams through the pines trees here. One day as we were walking, Tiffany stopped and stood directly in a ray of sunlight. It was one of those moments I don't think I'll ever forget. So today, I had to be here with her one last time.

We spent the entire morning reminiscing about the past and making plans for our future. One moment we were happy and the next we were sad. But it didn't matter how we felt, we could not be apart.

On the way back we walked slowly and I picked her every wildflower I could find. We stopped in the woods before reaching the parking lot and I kissed her softly. Tiffany started to cry and I gently raised her hand to my lips. She was wearing my ring and I kissed her finger over it.

"Don't forget what I promised you, Tiffany. I meant it," I said, seriously, wiping her tears away.

"I won't forget," she said, looking into my eyes.

We left Carter's Trail and drove to the city park. She jumped out of the truck running and I quickly ran after her. Tiffany lay down on the merry-go-round, asking me to push. The harder I pushed, the louder she laughed.

"Stop! Stop, Steven! I can't take anymore," she yelled.

"Come on! Just a little bit faster," I said, pushing harder.

"Stop this merry-go-round right now or I'm going to jump," she threatened, trying to stand up.

I slowed it down, with the palm of my hand, until it stopped. Tiffany was stumbling toward me as I reached out for her and asked, "Are you hungry now?"

"I could eat a little something. Can we put the blanket on the ground, under the big oak tree?"

"Sure, I'll go get everything."

I unpacked our lunch as Tiffany walked around the old oak tree's roots. She seemed so content, with no concern about tomorrow. All I wanted was to hold her in my arms forever but how could I escape my future?

We ate our sandwiches in silence then she laid her head in my lap. I sat there gently stroking her hair, wishing this day would never end. But we had to go and get ready for our last night together.
****

It was seven o'clock when I rang the doorbell and surprised her with a dozen yellow roses. Then Mr. Crenshaw surprised me when he said I didn't have to bring Tiffany home until midnight.

Our dinner reservations were for an expensive restaurant that she and I had never been to. As we parked, she asked if I was sure the place was open because there were hardly any lights on.

When we walked inside, it was richly furnished and candles were glowing from each table. Tiffany smiled at me as the hostess took us to our table. I sat across from her and even though there was only candlelight, her eyes sparkled like diamonds.

The minutes flew by as we pretended that I wasn't leaving tomorrow. Even though we had spent so much time together, we still had so much to talk about. I had never realized how many interesting things had happened to me in my life. And I never knew how much I could care about what another person had done and seen.

When we finished dinner, we got into my truck and I took her hand. I raised it slowly to my lips while looking in her eyes and kissed it softly. She would never know, at that moment, I felt like the luckiest guy in the world.

Somehow, I had to keep my feelings locked up inside, so I moved over and started the truck. Tiffany moved over beside me and I put my arm around her. One of our favorite songs, When I See You Smile by Bad English started to play and we both started to sing along as I drove back toward our neighborhood.

For some strange reason, tomorrow felt so far away. The only reality we knew was in this very moment. Few words were exchanged as we got closer to home but I knew exactly how she felt. We both had a lot of anticipation about tonight and there was no way of hiding it.

"Why did you pull the truck over?" Tiffany asked.

"You are just full of questions tonight, aren't you?" I asked, teasing her with every word.

"Come on. Give me one hint," she said, holding her finger in front of my face.

"I have something I want you to wear."

"Is it red?"

"No, it's black."

"Is it going to make me look sexy?" Tiffany asked, looking deep into my eyes.

"Some people think they're sexy. Some people just think they're useful."

"Do you want me to change in the truck?"

"No. I want you to close your eyes."

"Come here, I want you to kiss me first."

I kissed her softly, I kissed her passionately then said, "Turn around and close your eyes."

"I trust you," she said softly.

"I know you do," I said, putting the blindfold across her eyes.

She turned around, touched the blindfold and said, "I guess you really don't want me to know where we're going?"

"I want you to use your other senses," I said, kissing her again.

"Please don't stop," she begged, pressing her lips against mine.

"We'll be there in just a few minutes," I said, sliding over and starting the truck.

"Do I look sexy?"

"You always look sexy to me, baby," I said as she moved closer. I put my arm around her and drove quickly to our destination.

When I turned the truck off, she asked, "Can I take my blindfold off now?"

"Not yet," I said, opening the door. "Here, take my hand." I led her down the path, telling her where to walk. She took each step carefully as the leaves crunched beneath our feet. My heart raced with anticipation, wondering if she would like her surprise.

"Wait, I hear something," Tiffany said.

"What is it?"

"I think I hear water."

"Come on, baby; watch your step," I whispered, pulling her hand.

"Steven," she said softly, stopping me. "Are we at the falls?"

"Yes."

"Can you hear them yet?"

"No, I can't. I want to carry you the rest of the way." I quickly took her in my arms, which made her giggle.

"I bet you're glad you've been lifting weights."

"I could carry you a thousand miles if I needed to," I said seriously.

"I bet you could, Steven Cross; I bet you could."

I carried her the rest of the way and gently laid her on the blanket. Lifting her head, I moved the pillow and touched her face softly. Then I lit the lanterns and turned on the music. Tiffany smiled as she heard our song I'll be There for You by Bon Jovi, begin to play.

Kneeling down beside her, I reached over and touched her hand. Her body jolted from my unforeseen touch and I quickly took my hand away. Opening a bottle of wine, I poured us both a glass. A bouquet of white daises lay on the other side of her body. Still on my knees, I leaned across to reach out for the flowers.

Tiffany moaned as our bodies touched and softly asked, "When are you going to take this off of me?"

"Just one more minute, I'm almost ready." I quickly opened the flowers and put them around the edge of the blanket.

"What are you doing?"

"Okay, it's time for you to sit up." I knelt down behind her and carefully untied the blindfold.

"It's beautiful, Steven! I can't believe you did all this for me," she said, picking up a daisy. She broke the stem off and put the flower behind her ear.

"You are the only thing I see around here that is beautiful."

"I love you."

"I love you, too. More than you'll ever know."

"You've always told me we couldn't come down here at night. What changed your mind?"

"I don't know what I've been afraid of all these years. All I know, is when I'm with you, I'm not scared of anything."

"I feel the same way. That's why I can't believe you're leaving tomorrow."

"It doesn't seem real, does it? What are we going to do without each other?"

"I don't know," she said, holding her glass out for more wine.

I wanted to lie down beside her but being too close hurt my heart. My mind was racing, dreading the inevitable tick of the clock. Tiffany would never know how desperate I felt because I wouldn't let it show.

"Steven," Tiffany said in a sultry voice.

"Yes," I said, looking down at her as she turned toward me.

"Don't you want some TLC?"

"You know I do."

"Then come over here."

I lay down, holding her in my arms and asked, "How did you get your middle name?"

"My mom did it. Her best friend from high school was named Tiffany. Love was because she said she fell in love with my dad all over again when I was born."

"It's the perfect name for someone as beautiful as you, Tiffany Love."

She leaned up and said, "Just think, if we get married someday, my initials won't even change."

Pulling her closer, I kissed her lips, pressing them hard against mine. As we quietly undressed each other, the stars shined brightly in the sky. I felt the chill of night and covered her body with mine. We lay there, softly kissing for a very long time. We started making love and I could feel Tiffany trembling beneath me.

The longer we made love, the harder we kissed. I put my hand behind her head and pulled her closer. It felt like I was a river and she was the ocean. I could no longer feel where my body ended and Tiffany's began.

I kept my eyes closed because I couldn't look into her eyes. Never had I experienced such pleasure with so much pain. My tears began to fall and Tiffany had to feel them as they dropped. I finally opened my eyes when she began to cry. It was hard to believe we were both crying or that making love could be so bittersweet.

We lay there, listening to the water and held each other close. It was past time for us to leave but I hoped Mr. Crenshaw would understand. The only person in the world that mattered to me right now was safe in my arms. But when Tiffany started to fall asleep, I told her we had to go.

On the drive to her house, Tiffany tried to act like she was okay. I could tell she wasn't, but neither was I. She looked lost, like a homeless child and I felt helpless.

It was one a.m. when we pulled up and her father was at the front door waiting. She kissed me goodbye and I sat there watching as Tiffany ran to the door. I drove away knowing I would see her one last time, in the morning, before I left.

****

My bags were in the truck and I told my family goodbye. I drove to Tiffany's house in complete disbelief that the day had finally come when I had to leave her here alone. She and Victoria were waiting for me as I pulled up in the driveway. They were holding hands and I could tell Tiffany had been crying. I stepped out of the truck and Victoria walked over, pulling Tiffany behind her.

"Don't worry; I'll take care of her," Victoria said as we hugged.

"Thanks," I whispered.

"Well, I'll be right over there, if you need me," Victoria said as she squeezed Tiffany's hand.

"Good luck, Steven."

"Thanks, Victoria. Take care of yourself."

I wrapped my arms around Tiffany and buried my face in her long red hair. When I started to speak, I couldn't and had to wait a second before saying, "I don't want to go."

"I've been up all night thinking about it. I think we should just run away. I have almost seven hundred dollars saved up. We could just go somewhere and be together," Tiffany said, with tears in her eyes.

"I wish we could do it. I wish we could be together all the time," I said, putting my hands on her waist, pulling her closer.

"Why can't we do it? I could pack some stuff and you could come get me," Tiffany pleaded, hugging me harder.

No matter how much I kissed her beautiful face, I couldn't stop her tears from falling. "I'll come back for you. I promise."

"Why do you have to go?" she asked, stepping back. Suddenly, she seemed angry but her tearstained face told the truth.

"Are you going to be okay?"

"I just can't believe you're really leaving me. Why is it, when I need people the most, they're just gone?"

"Please don't cry, baby. I don't want to leave you here. I would never choose to be away from you, not even for one day," I said, taking her by the shoulders, looking into her blue eyes. I could feel the tears filling my eyes and I pulled her closer.

"Please don't forget me. Promise me, you'll never forget! Promise," she cried in anguish.

"I could never forget you, Tiffany. You are light to me. Always remember this, without you, I am in eternal darkness."

"Write to me, Steven. No matter what happens, write to me. Let me know what is going on in your life. I need to know if you're okay. This is going to be so much harder on me if I don't know you're okay. Do you understand what I'm saying?"

"Yes, I understand. Don't worry I won't stop writing to you. I'm not going to move to New York and just leave you behind. How in the world do you think I could ever forget about you?" I asked, looking deep into her eyes.

When I realized what I'd said, I felt weak. Her own mother had done the exact same thing. She looked so much like a child at that moment; it broke my heart into a thousand pieces. For the first time, I understood her rebellion. I understood the wildness about her. This time when I looked in her eyes, I understood her pain.

"Forgive me baby, forgive me, please forgive me."

Tiffany fell into my arms and whispered, "I love you."

"I love you, too," I whispered, then pulled back to look her in the eyes and said, "You know it's not like we're never going to see each other again. I'll come home for Christmas and Spring Break. You can come see me too."

"I know, but it won't ever be the same," Tiffany said, looking down as her long red hair fell over her shoulders.

"Maybe you can go to college in New York too. It will only be two years until you graduate," I said, stepping back.

"We'll just have to stay in touch the best way we can," she said sadly.

Tiffany took my hand and we walked over to the truck. It was so hard to remember that I had to do the right thing. All I could think about was grabbing her and running as far away from Natchez, Mississippi as possible. I felt like if Tiffany was with me I wouldn't need anyone or anything else.

We stood there hugging for a long time before I finally got in the truck. She leaned forward and kissed me softly through the window. She looked defeated or perhaps broken and I'm not sure which one hurt me more. All I ever wanted was the chance to love her and make her happy. I never once considered how much I could hurt her.

Backing slowly out of the driveway, it felt like I had left my heart in Tiffany's hands. I blew her one last kiss and she tried to smile. My leg felt numb as I pushed the gas pedal and looked in the rear-view mirror. Nothing I had ever done in my life was harder than driving away from the one I loved.

2
Chapter

As Steven backed out of the driveway, I followed him into the street. Then all I could see was his hand waving goodbye. The same hand that held mine, that gently caressed my skin and dried my tears. A beautiful strong hand, tanned by the Mississippi sun that belongs to the one I love. And before he was out of sight, I had to turn and walk away. I couldn't bear to watch him leave.

If I'd been able to convince him to run away with me, then my heart would unclench itself with hope. However, the floodgate had opened, as my emotions came in wave after wave like an angry sea. Inside, I wanted to stop because I didn't want Victoria to see me this way. But how could I stop the unbelievable pain of reality?

"It's going to be okay, Tiffany."

"But you don't know how this feels. You can't know because it's happening to me."

"It sounds to me like we need to go out and party. It's the only thing that's going to cheer you up," Victoria said, pushing the hair out of my face.

"Going out is the last thing on my mind."

"Look, if hanging out helped you get over Alan that quick then that's what you need to do to get over Steven."

"I'm just so sad. I miss him already."

"Having fun is better than sitting around being sad. Come on let's go in, start getting ready and see how you feel."

We went inside and she picked out some clothes to wear. She helped me get dressed and then did my hair and make-up and I felt a little better. A friend of Brad's was having a keg party so she called him and asked if he would come get us.

We got in Brad's car and I stared out the window, trying to contain myself. It was only a ten minute ride but it seemed much, much longer.

The little house was crowded but I had never felt so alone. Several guys tried to talk to me and I pretended to listen. But all I could think about was Steven and why he wasn't here with me.

When I couldn't take it anymore, I went to the bathroom, to get away from the people and the noise. Washing my hands, I looked into the mirror. As I felt the bass from the stereo shaking my body, I stared into my eyes. Kissing Steven was all I could think about. My heart felt faint as I grabbed the counter. I looked around the dirty little bathroom and washed my hands again. Wiping away my tears, I opened the door and went back into the living room.

Victoria was putting on a show for everyone, dancing in front of the stereo. All the guys were asking me to dance with her, almost demanding it. I walked right pass them, ignoring their pleas and opened the front door. Closing it behind me, I looked up into the sky. I wished on a star that Steven was looking up too. After all, it was the same sky. A single drop of rain fell upon my forehead and I began to walk home in the misty rain.

****

Fall started to turn into winter and I spent a lot of time alone. The only thing I could do to feel better was go to all our favorite places. It wasn't the same but somehow I felt closer to Steven when I reminisced about the time we spent together. He would always tell me that I was never alone. It's strange how before he left, I didn't understand, but now I do.

Victoria and I remained friends after Steven left for college. I often wondered if she was tired of the melancholy world I had become a part of. She did everything she could to get me to go out and sometimes I went. But as much as I could, I convinced her to just hang out in my room.

Dad knocked on my door and Victoria jumped up to answer it. He handed her the envelope and gave me the same strange look again. He didn't want me to be sad either but it was something I couldn't help.

Victoria handed me the envelope and lay down on my bed. It was addressed to me with Steven's return address. I sat beside her and held it close to my heart before opening it, to read it aloud.

My love,

I am searching endlessly for the light that lovingly shines in your eyes. Whenever you look at me, wherever we are, I feel it burning so deep inside. When I seldom see you, I have absolutely no pride. The ties that bind us have no boundaries of time; everything simply stops when I look into your eyes.

Wasn't yesterday the last time I saw your beautiful face? If time has passed us by, I fail to find a trace, of evidence that points truly to a deeply dreaded ill-fate, that somehow our time was up and you never truly got to see me. Because there is light in my eyes shining back at you, time can never change what we have, it is forever just between us two.

In my memory, there you are again, running by the water's edge, walking slowly in the rain. I see you not, yet I see you still… everyday. Your hair blowing in the wind… it's you, kissing me again. Do you remember our last day in the park? You laid down on the merry-go-round and I pushed as your laughter filled the air. Tiffany, sometimes, I still hear it in my heart.

Forgive me baby, I just got lost in the memories. I can hardly wait to make more of them with you. Think of me and I will think of you… in long white dresses with flowers in your hair. What longing I feel for you. If I could only touch you on the rainy days, then I might be okay. But the sun continues to shine, which only reminds me of you.

My precious gift from heaven, you are a dream come true. If only I could stay in that dream forever, but it cannot be that way. Please darling, don't you think I know, I'm too far away? Still, my heart… it only knows your name. I pray, my beloved, that your heart feels the same. I will wait for you, until the earth is at an end. Then I will wait for you again and again.

Love,
Steven

"Why is Steven going to college to become an engineer?" Victoria asked, rolling over to look at me.

"I don't know. Why do you ask?"

"He should be a writer."

"Hey when you write him back this time, tell him I said hello."

"I haven't written him yet."

"Girl, you better write that boy! How many letters has he already sent you?" she asked, as we walked to the kitchen.

"I know, I know. I'll do it tonight."

"You can't do it tonight. Remember, we're going to Kenny's house for a bon-fire."

"Then I'll do it tomorrow night."

"We're going to Jeremy's tomorrow night," she said sarcastically, putting her hand on her hip.

"Well, I have to do it sometime," I said, handing her a glass of tea. "It really sucks his mom decided to go to New York for Christmas. She just didn't want Steven to come home and see me."

"Forget about her, Tiffany. Steven is the only one who really counts." Victoria smiled nervously, like she wanted to change the subject.

"I just wish I could understand why she hates me so much."

"I hate to tell you this, but you never had a chance with her. Mrs. Cross decided a long time ago that Amber was the only one for her little boy."

"I guess she'll see how much he cares about Amber the next time he comes home."

"What do you mean by that?"

"Oh nothing. But I know whose door he'll be knocking on, and it won't be Ambers."

"When is he coming home?" she asked, sitting down at the table.

"He'll be here for spring break. You just watch and see."

Even though I sounded sure to Victoria, my mind was racing with questions. What was Steven doing in New York? More importantly, who was he doing it with? If I could look into his eyes, I know I would feel all right. But his mother made sure I wouldn't get the chance any time soon.

3

Chapter

Living in New York began a whole new lifestyle for me. The apartment, that I share with roommates, is only six blocks from the university. There is concrete and asphalt when I am use to the woods and dirt roads. And the parties we had down at the bog didn't compare to these city parties. It seemed like every night someone wanted me to go somewhere. But I still found time to be alone, just to think about the most important girl in my life.

All my hopes of seeing Tiffany during the Christmas holidays were shattered after a brief phone conversation with my mother. When Blake told Tiffany I wouldn't be coming home, he said she seemed upset. But I couldn't stop the feeling that she was slipping far, far away from me.

"He didn't even hear us walk in," Tommy, my roommate, said.

"Did you get the mail?"

"There was nothing for you," Scott answered.

"Are you sure she has your address?" Tommy asked, laughing.

"Maybe she doesn't know how to address an envelope," Scott said.

"Real funny, guys. Maybe you two should become comedians," I said, thinking that coming to New York was a huge mistake. I had only been here a few months and it was already hard to live with them.

"I don't know about you Tommy, but I'm beginning to wonder about Steven. He hasn't had a date since he got here," Scott said, giving me an accusing glance.

"Me too. He wouldn't even give Lisa the time of day and anybody could see she was hot for him," Tommy said, making strange gestures with his hands.

"I don't want Lisa. She's not my type."

"Well, she'd be better than nothing. I'd go out with her," Scott said, looking me up and down.

"Then go for it, Scott! She's all yours."

"Man, you don't have to get pissed off," Tommy said, plopping down on the couch, opening a beer.

"Neither one of you can understand how I feel about Tiffany. All that you see in girls is what you can get from them," I said, wondering what kind of people I was living with.

"Oh, like you weren't getting any from Tiffany?"

"That is none of your business, Tommy. Besides, it was more important to me what I could give her than what I was getting."

"Well, surprise, surprise! Your girl isn't here. But there are hundreds of fine babes right here on campus," Scott said, checking his perfect black hair in the mirror.

"You can have my share of the babes."

"What kind of crap is that, Steven? That girl is probably partying her butt off and here you are waiting for the postman," Tommy said, picking up the mail and throwing it across the coffee table.

Anger rushed through my veins as I walked back to my room. I could hear my roommates laughing, even after I closed the door. Admitting to them that I am worried was something I would never do. But the reason I hadn't received a letter from Tiffany yet, was constantly on my mind.

Chapter 4

"It's time to go, Tiffany. We'll be late for our appointment," Dad said, jingling his keys.

"Why do we have to get pictures taken today?"

"Your sister is moving to New York and this could be my last chance to take a portrait with everyone in it."

"Everybody won't be in it, Dad. Mom won't be in it!"

"I know that, Tiffany. Do you think I don't know she isn't here anymore?" dad asked, pointing at himself.

"Yes sir, I know you know she isn't here. I'm sorry. I just don't feel like myself today."

"I'm sorry, baby. Don't cry. Please, please don't cry."

"It's okay, Daddy," I said as we hugged.

"I want you to stay home for the next few days. You're not in trouble. I'm just worried about you. I think you've been hanging out with your friends too much lately."

"Okay," I said, looking into his eyes, wishing my mom was here.

Dad turned to walk out the door and I turned off the lights. We got in the car and I wanted to say something, anything to make him feel better. But as we began to drive, all I could think about was Steven. Where was he, when I needed him so badly? Today it seemed he was just too far away from me.

****

"Hello," I said, answering the phone.

"Hey. Is your dad going to let you out of the house tonight?" Victoria asked.

"Not yet."

"Well, you need to tell him it's cruel and unusual punishment to keep you held prisoner."

"I know, but it'll give me time to write Steven a letter."

"You haven't written him, yet," Victoria said, like I had committed a crime.

"No, I haven't. I got my pictures back and I think I'm going to send him one."

"What does it look like?"

"I have my red dress on that I wore to the Christmas party and I'm lying on a white chase lounge. My dad only got the proof because he said I looked too grown up. Do you think I should send it?"

"Of course." She said slowly, then paused before saying, "I bet Steven is having so much fun in New York."

"Yeah, he probably is. Sometimes I wonder if he even thinks about me."

"You know he does, or he wouldn't send you those mushy love letters. But, he's still probably doing his own thing."

"I guess you're right. We haven't seen each other in a long time."

"I think you should go out with somebody new."

"Do you think he's going out with other girls?"

"I would think so. Did he tell you he wouldn't date anyone else before he left?"

"No, because he didn't want me to promise that I wouldn't date other guys. He said it's too much to ask of me."

"Well for once he's right. You're supposed to be having fun, not promising some guy a million miles away something you can't keep anyway."

"He is not just some guy."

"You know what I mean."

"Okay I hear you. I'm going to let you go. Have fun tonight."

"I will. Kirk's band is getting together to jam."

"Sounds like fun, but don't you think Kirk is a little too old for you?"

"He's only three years older than Steven."

"And that makes him five years older than us. He doesn't even look like your type with that long hair."

"I know he's wild, but I like it. It's better than dating some of the guys we go to school with," she said, directly aiming her comment toward Steven.

"I just think he's trouble."

"Don't worry about me, chick."

"Okay, I'm going to let you go."

"I'll call you tomorrow, bye."

"Bye."

I sat down at my desk and took out some paper. No matter what it sounded like, I was determined to write Steven a letter. And I had to send him a picture as soon as possible so he wouldn't forget about me.

Dear Steven,

I hope you're okay and you like college. Victoria says hello. I wonder if you're happy there. I'm sending you a picture I had taken recently. We went to get a family portrait and dad let Cheryl and I get our picture taken by ourselves. It's the only copy because it's a proof. I hope you like it. My dad said I looked too grown up so he wouldn't buy any copies.

I've been going to school and I'm passing all of my classes. And I can hardly wait to graduate so I can move back to California. I have been trying to find out where I can go for the best acting classes. And I am trying to get a part in every play around Natchez for experience. That way, by the time you graduate from college I will be a successful actress. Then you can move to California and get a job as an engineer.

I wish you could have been here for Christmas but you didn't make it. I got some new clothes and make-up. I wonder what you got? I'm sorry I haven't written to you yet. Victoria and I go out almost every night. Do you go out a lot up there? I know we didn't promise not to see other people but I'm scared I'm going to lose you forever. Part of me wishes we had never made love. Then being without you would be so much easier. But I know I will be okay.

I like getting your letters. Please don't ever stop sending them to me, no matter what happens. The words you write are so beautiful. Have you ever thought about writing for a magazine or the newspaper? I think you would be good at it. Please take care of yourself. I miss you and hope to see you in the spring.

Love,
Tiffany

5
Chapter

It felt like eternity would come to pass but finally the day had come. As I read the return address, my stomach felt like it was Nadia Comaneci's body at the Olympics. Even her handwriting made my heart beat faster. Each step I took became quicker then I quickly opened the door and sat down on the couch.

It was obvious why her dad didn't buy any copies of this picture and it made me wonder what she was thinking when the photographer took it. I lifted it to my lips and kissed her image. My heart ached to see her and my body ached to hold her in my arms again. If I could, I would fly to her right now and I'd be the one begging her to run away with me.

Even though it felt like my heart was failing, in my hands laid the proof that she missed me too. As I sat studying every curve of her body, the front door suddenly opened. I jumped up quickly, putting the picture and letter back in the envelope.

"Did you finally get a letter?" Scott asked as he and Tommy walked through the door.

"Yes."

"Are you going to read it to us?"

"No, it's personal," I said, sitting back down.

"Come on, man. Let me see it." Tommy said, sitting down beside me, grabbing the envelope.

"Give it back!"

"Who's the red head?" Tommy asked slowly.

"Who do you think it is, bonehead?" I asked sarcastically, taking back the letter.

"Hold on, let me have another look. Man, she is fine. Does she have a sister?"

"Yes but they don't look anything alike. And Cheryl's personality is completely opposite of Tiffany's."

"Can I see?" Scott asked, looking over Tommy's shoulder.

"Here, man. Take a look at this little number," Tommy said, handing her picture to Scott.

"She's beautiful. Now I see why you didn't want to go out with Lisa," Scott said.

"Tiffany's looks are not the reason I didn't go out with Lisa."

"Well, fill us in on the details."

"I think I'll keep that information to myself, Tommy."

"I bet every guy in your hometown is knocking on her door. Do you think a girl that looks like that is being faithful to you? Wake up, Steven."

"Our relationship is not like that." I walked over to Scott, looked back at Tommy and wondered why he seemed so angry.

"When is she coming to see you?" Scott asked.

"I don't know. She's sixteen and her dad probably won't let her come until she graduates."

"That girl is only sixteen years old? Now the real story is coming out," Tommy said, looking at me like he was a detective.

"What's wrong with that? I'm eighteen."

"Can you imagine how fine she's going to be when she grows up," Scott said, looking at her picture again.

"Yes, I can. I just hope I'm still around."

I took the picture out of his hand and turned to go to my room. I wanted to read her letter again and prepare to write her back. Just having her picture and letter made me feel like I had a part of her here with me. It was something Tiffany had touched, she had written and put in the mailbox. As I opened the envelope to read it once again, I felt like the happiest man in the world. Then I took out a piece of paper and poured out my love for her in ink.

My darling,
No words can describe the excitement that your words brought to

me. No matter how much I search, the words do not exist to describe the beauty of your image on paper. The red of your dress, the blue of your eyes, they remind me that I am still alive. These gifts you give to me from your soul, could never be repaid. There is not enough money, nor diamonds or gold. Not even if the world was mine, and it could be sold.

The days I spend without you my beloved, are like centuries I spend searching for something precious that almost feels lost. I once wished I could see you Tiffany, but this you never knew. I was the most surprised, when my wish came true. It was the first night that I ever kissed your lips. I think of it often and the feeling it brings is bliss. I dream of you now, because it is all I can do. Seeing you in every way, reliving the moments, savoring the days. When will I hold you again?

These arms of mine are empty without your love. If I told you that I am desperately wanting to kiss your lips once more, would you be there to open the door? Tell me, would your face have a smile or would there be tears?

I shall take a journey in spring, to bring you wildflowers and anything; you want. The only desire, that fills my soul, is to see your smile. My departure will barely be soon enough to save my heart. Please know that now and forever I will be true. It is the beauty of your soul that will never keep us apart.

If you have found a new life without me, still; let me see you. No one else sees you the way I do. Their eyes are blindfolded and I have tied the knots. Only to protect you from evil you need not see. If God would grant me wings, I would fly to you tonight. The miles are just our imaginations... you are with me, each breath I take...every moment, every second...always.

Love,
Steven

Chapter 6

When I got home from school I found a letter from Steven on my desk. Victoria and I took our usual places on the bed and I quickly opened the envelope.

"Victoria, that means he'll be home for spring break!"

"Sounds like it. I can't believe the way he writes to you," she said, rolling over to look at me.

"I know."

"What are you going to do with Shawn when Steven gets here?" Victoria asked, standing up.

"What do you mean what am I going to do with Shawn?" I asked, following her to the kitchen.

"It looked like you two were getting pretty close last night at Kirk's party."

"I wouldn't even know Shawn if you weren't going out with Kirk. When are you going to break up with him?"

"I've almost got my walking boots on, chick. If Leigh doesn't stop hanging all over him, I'm out of there!" Victoria exclaimed, slamming her hand on the counter.

"You put up with a whole lot more than I would."

"I know, but he's the first guy I've dated for this long."

"I just hate the way he treats you." We looked at each other and I could tell she was upset. I opened the refrigerator, looking for a lemon, wondering if I should have said anything.

"Have you even told Shawn about Steven? And what about Alex, has he called you lately?" she asked, changing the subject.

"I don't have to tell Shawn anything and Alex called yesterday."

She looked at me and smiled, playfully asking, "So, what are you going to wear tonight?"

"I think I'm going to wear my black mini skirt with black boots and my new red sweater."

"I was going to wear your new sweater," Victoria said, teasing me.

"Not before I wear it," I said, running down the hall, into my room.

"What are you doing, Cheryl?"

"What does it look like I'm doing?"

"Those are my letters! How could you come in my room and read my letters?"

"Here, you can have the stupid things," Cheryl yelled as she threw them on the floor at my feet.

"You are just like Momma, Cheryl! Your life is so empty and meaningless...."

"Let me tell you something, Daddy's little girl," Cheryl said, grabbing me by the collar, "if it wasn't for our mother you wouldn't be alive."

"Get out of my room! I can't wait until you go away for college."

"Go kiss up to her, Victoria. You do it so well," Cheryl said, giving us one last mean glance before slamming the door.

I fell to the floor on my knees and looked up at Victoria. "Why?"

"She's just jealous of you. Are you sure that you're blood sisters?" Victoria asked, kneeling down beside me.

"My mother is mysterious, but I think she would have told us if we weren't real sisters."

"What is your mother like? You never talk about her."

"When I was a little girl, I wanted to learn how to read minds. I thought if I could, then I would know what mom was thinking but most of the time she was just silent. Silence is deadly, Victoria. Do you know that?"

"My parents have never talked to me. At least you have your dad," she said, picking up my letters.

"I don't know what I would do if he left too."

"Your dad isn't going anywhere. You don't have to worry about that. Hey, why don't we go to the mall and I'll buy you a box with a lock, to put your letters in."

"Okay," I said, hoping she was right.

She hugged me tightly and said, "You know I love you, don't you, Tiffany?"

"Yes, I know, I love you too."

****

The months flew by but I thought of Steven everyday and wondered if he thought about me. Of course, everything had changed since the last time we'd seen each other but I hoped when he got home he'd still want to see me.

Last night I had a dream that he was at a big party with lots of girls sitting around him. He was telling a story and they were intently listening to his every word. It was all I could think about this morning. And it made me wonder what Steven was doing in New York and what my dream meant. So when I saw his brother, Blake, sitting alone during break, I had to ask him a few questions.

"Hi, Blake."

"Hey, where's your sidekick?" Blake asked, looking behind me.

"Oh, Victoria skipped school to hang out with Kirk."

"Is she still going out with that guy?"

"Yes, but I think she's getting tired of him."

"She needs to go out with a guy that's nice, like me," he said, smiling, as his brown wavy hair was tossed by the wind.

"You know she only goes out with older guys," I said, reaching over to touch his arm.

"Yes, she's just like you."

When he looked at me, I could see the resemblance to Steven and it took me a moment before asking, "Is Steven coming home for spring break?"

"He'll be here Saturday. I talked to him on the phone last night. He asked me how you're doing."

"What did you tell him?" I asked, looking into his dark brown eyes.

"I told him you seemed to be doing fine," he said, sounding irritated.

"Blake, do you know if he's dating anyone?"

"He hasn't mentioned anybody. Why?"

"I was just wondering. It's been a long time since I've seen him."

"Well you don't have to wait long now," he said, picking up his books as the bell rang for class.

It was hard to believe it would only be a few more days before I saw Steven again. Not even a year had passed but it seemed like it had been a lifetime.

****

My plan for Friday night was to get everything ready to see Steven. Nothing else was more important to me. My nails had to be painted and my hair needed deep conditioning. And of course, I had to figure out what to wear. Everything had to be perfect for Saturday night.

Just when I began to relax in a bubble bath, Victoria called. I told her no but she kept insisting that I go with her to Alex's party. But as usual, I gave in and told her to come pick me up in an hour.

"It's your turn," Victoria yelled over the music.

"I'm going to make it this time," I said, picking up the quarter and closing one eye to aim at the glass. But I missed again and drank the shot of beer.

"I love playing quarters with you. You're so much fun when the game is over," Shawn said, taking my hand and pulling me toward him.

"Let go!" I said, pulling away from him, walking into the crowd. "Hey, does anybody know where Alex is?"

"I think he went out back," Terry said, touching me on the shoulder.

"Can you help me find him?"

"Sure, come with me," he said, reaching out for my hand.

He guided me through the couples dancing in the living room. And we walked out the backdoor, I yelled, "Alex. Where are you?"

"I'm over here darling, come sit on my lap," he slurred.

"Man, you've got to teach me how to make the quarter go in the glass. I can't do it."

"What?"

"Will you teach me?"

"I'll teach you anything you want to know," he said, kissing the back of my neck.

"Stop, that tickles," I said trying to stand up. "Where's your girlfriend?"

"She had to stay home and get her beauty sleep," he said, pulling me back.

"Please stop, everybody is staring at us," I said, trying to sit up.

"Tiffany! Tiffany!" Victoria called as she walked out the backdoor. "Look who found us."

"Steven, I can't believe you're here," I said, pulling away from Alex's grasp and running to jump in his arms. He turned round and round, hugging me tightly. As my feet touched the ground we stopped to look into each other's eyes. All I wanted was to kiss him, right there in front of everybody.

"I think she might have had a little too much to drink. We were playing quarters and you know she can't play very well."

"I can see that, Victoria. Thanks for your help."

"He knows I can't play quarters worth a flip," I said taking his hand. "I thought you wouldn't be here until tomorrow."

"I couldn't wait to see you."

Steven put his arms around me and I felt safe once again. I put my head on his chest and said, "Let's get out of here."

"Hey man, where are you taking her?" Alex asked, grabbing me by the arm.

"It's none of your business where she's going," Victoria said, grabbing his hand.

"Don't tell me what to do. This is my party and I want her to stay."

"Maybe she doesn't want to stay at your party."

"I tell you what, Victoria. I think it's time for you to leave. And take your sleazy boyfriend with you."

"Fine, Alex. Your party sucked anyway."

"Come on, baby. Let's go," Steven said, reaching for my hand.

"I can't believe your leaving with him," Alex said, shaking his head.

"Well at least he's not a jerk like you," I yelled, walking away, pulling Steven with me.

"I'm sorry, Tiffany. I didn't mean to start a fight."

"Don't worry about it. I didn't want to be here anyway. Where's your truck?"

"It's right down there."

"I'm so happy to see you. When did you get here?"

"About thirty minutes ago."

Steven opened the passenger door, helping me get in and I asked, "Where are we going?"

"Anywhere with you is good for me," he whispered in my ear.

While Steven drove through the maze of cars, I spotted Victoria, Kirk, and Shawn. When Victoria saw me, she started waving for us to stop. I looked at Shawn and he was looking right at me. Then I saw the look on Kirk's face. Victoria looked at me and turned around to look at Kirk. The second she saw his face, she put her arms around him, trying to hold him back. He pushed her down, out of his way and started running toward us.

"Go, Steven! Get out of here now!"

"Who is that?"

"It's Kirk and Shawn, Victoria's boyfriend and his friend," I said, crawling over Steven to lock his door and then turned to lock mine.

"What the hell's going on, Tiffany?" Shawn screamed as he hit the side of Steven's truck.

"Is that your boyfriend?" Steven asked.

"No. He thinks he is, but I don't like him," I said as I turned around in the seat to look back at Victoria. The three of them were walking toward her car and she and Kirk were arguing.

"How old is he?"

"He's twenty-two but he acts like he's fifteen. I'm sorry about your truck," I said, turning around to sit down.

"Don't worry about this old truck. I'm just glad you're okay."

He reached over and took my hand. He squeezed it gently, smiling at me. It felt so good to finally see him again. "Where have you been, Steven Cross? I've been so lost without you."

"I have been right here," Steven said as he touched my chest.

7
Chapter

Slowly, I drove through the countryside. I knew exactly where we were going but I didn't say anything. Tiffany laid her head in my lap and I gently rubbed her back. Finally, all of the worry and anxiety were gone. She still wanted to see me and I had the living proof within my grasp.

We pulled up to the old building and I opened my door. The rich smell of peach blossoms flooded the air. It was hard to believe an entire year had passed since our first night here together. As I got out, I gently moved her head to the seat of the truck.

"Don't leave me."

"I'll be right back," I said, leaning over to kiss her cheek.

I grabbed my sleeping bag and a blanket and walked toward the old building. It brought back so many memories that I had to stop for a moment. Kneeling down, I unzipped the sleeping bag then folded the blanket for a pillow.

Walking back to the truck I started gently caressing Tiffany's arm. She crawled over to me and I lifted her into my arms then stepped back, closing the door. Carrying Tiffany inside, with our bodies so close, I didn't want to put her down. I held her for another moment before laying her on the sleeping bag. Then I gently took her shoes off, tucking her feet inside and kissed her cheek softly.

Within seconds, Tiffany fell back asleep and I got in and zipped us up. Tears filled my eyes as I listened to her breathe and strained to see her face. I could only see the outline so I closed my eyes because I could see her better that way.

Matching my breath with hers, we began to breathe in unison.
Tiffany rolled onto her stomach and I reached over and put my hand
on her back. Then I had the overwhelming urge to do something
I could have never imagined wanting to do. It was strange and I
almost stopped myself from doing it. But after I did it the first time
with hesitation, the second time felt really good. I don't know how
many times I did it before I fell asleep. I used my index finger, as an
imaginary pen and wrote my name on her back again and again and
again.

"Good morning, beautiful," I softly said, watching her wake up.

"Where are we?" she asked, stretching her arms out to hug.

"We're at the peach orchard. Did I get you in trouble?"

"No. I was suppose to spend the night with Victoria."

"Did you sleep okay?"

"Yes, but I had the strangest dream. I was in a foreign country,
and I was an actress, making a movie. It looked kind of like Italy or
Greece. We were filming on a real steep hillside near the ocean and
the wind was blowing so hard, the camera crew was having problems
keeping the cameras steady. We kept doing the same scene over and
over. Every time we would break for a few minutes, I was looking
around trying to find someone. I think I was looking for you but I
couldn't find you no matter how hard I tried. It was the worst feeling."

"Don't you worry about a thing, baby. I'm right here."

"I know, but you're so far away."

"Shhh," I said, moving forward to kiss her lips.

Never losing our embrace, Tiffany crawled on top of me. I
unzipped the sleeping bag and she stood up. Pulling her shirt over her
head, she threw it on the ground. She unbuttoned her mini skirt and
dropped it on my chest. Then she wrapped her arms around her back,
to take her bra off but I stopped her.

"Come here," I said reaching up to touch her, "I want to hold
you."

She dropped to her knees, unbuttoning my shirt while kissing my
neck. It had been so long since I'd touched her body and I could hardly
wait any longer. We were kissing hard, with built up desire, but I had
to stop her again.

"Tiffany, I have to tell you something."

"It can wait."

"No, it's really important."

"Then tell me."

She rolled onto her back and looked up into the sky. I turned and leaned toward her until my face was next to hers. She stared at me and for the first time, I realized how much she didn't understand about me.

"I love you, Tiffany."

"I know," she said, pulling me toward her, kissing me harder than before.

Hours flew by as we searched for new ways to give each other pleasure. We made love like no time had separated or passed us by. I knew her body and she knew mine. The whole world just seemed to melt away, whenever we were together.

With her head on my shoulder, we laid side-by-side, looking up into the sky. Puffy white clouds floated by slowly, against a perfect background of blue. A feeling of serenity and peace surrounded me. I closed my eyes, wishing we would never have to leave, but of course we did.

Chapter 8

In my mind, I could see the brightness of a beautiful afternoon. It feels like hot June weather but we're lying in the shade. A cool breeze gently blows my hair and Steven stops mid sentence to stare into my eyes. His lips are drawn to mine as I move forward to receive his kiss. He moves slowly down to my neck then even more slowly up to my ear. He whispers something beautiful but the words are almost too faint for me to hear.

"Will you pass me the suntan oil," Victoria asked, bringing me out of my daydream.

"Where is it?"

"Right there. Oh, and while you're up, will you turn up the radio?"

"Sure. Anything else, madam?"

"Yes, one more thing," she said, sitting up to look at me. "What do you think about Joel?"

"He's nice."

"He's a little too nice. I mean, I like hanging out with him but he's just so c-a-l-m all the time."

"I like the way he's laid-back. It's better than dating somebody like Kirk. You never knew what that guy was going to do."

"That's true, but at least he was fun."

By the tone of her voice I knew I had offended Victoria. Joel would be good for her but she didn't care. When it came to guys if it wasn't a bad boy, she didn't want him. It wouldn't be long before Joel was history and I almost wanted to warn him. But she is my best friend, so I pushed the thought far from my mind.

To keep the peace, I excused myself and went to the bathroom. Besides, I wanted to be alone to read Steven's last letter again. I washed the suntan oil off my hands and leaned back against the counter.

My angel,

I am certain you have invisible wings. What earthly creature could make a man feel this way? You have made my soul take flight to greater heights than I have ever known. You did it without saying a word, not even a glance. It was your tender kiss I felt as we laid under an open sky. When your heartbeat was so incredibly close to mine.

I see you now, in summer days. How I want to be there and not so very far away. I know I will see you yet again, when jolly ole' Saint Nick calls out to Dancer. Until that moment in time, my darling, you are in my thoughts. I look up at the sky, and you are there. I look at the water and I see the blue of your eyes. I see flowers waving in the wind and it reminds me of your beautiful face.

The days we spent together on my journey past, my only regret is that they could not forever last. The morning I made love to you, felt like it would have no end. When I told you I loved you, I wanted to say it again and again.

I hope for you safe things, no harm in your way. I wish for you wonderful blessings that will always stay. I pray that God is watching over you as you live. I want to tell you something now, so you'll never forget.

I remember you Tiffany, I hold on to your memory with all of my might. I remember you sitting in the back of a room one fateful night and I remember how you look in the early morning's light. No matter what! I will remember you...

"What are you doing in here?" Victoria asked, startling me.

"What? Oh, I was reading his letter."

"Speaking of guys we need to forget."

"I can't believe you would say that. I thought you and Steven were friends."

"Well, you know how life is, we grew up together. I mean he's cool to be around, but he isn't here anymore. Plus I thought it was real crappy for him to leave me at Alex's party when he saw Kirk push me down."

"I don't think he saw that."

"Well maybe he didn't, but if he did, that really sucks."

I couldn't believe she was attacking Steven just because she was mad at me. The look on her face gave away her jealousy. I followed her back to the pool and she started packing her bag so I did the same.

We walked to the car in complete silence and all the way home we barely said a word to each other. It was almost like it made her mad that he was still sending me letters. I was beginning to wonder if she didn't have a secret crush on him. Of course, I had talked myself out of the idea by the time we reached my house.

I opened the car door and asked, "Do you want to stay for dinner?"

"No, I have to go home and get ready. Call me," Victoria said as she put the car in reverse.

"I think I'm going to call Shane and see what he's up to tonight."

"Have fun," Victoria said, quickly backing out of my driveway.

I had never seen her this upset before. Could I have offended her this much over what I'd said about Kirk? Maybe it was because I said Joel is a nice guy. After all the rumors and lies Steven's ex-girlfriend, Amber, had spread about me, Victoria was my only friend. There were plenty of guys who wanted to hang out with me but she was just about the only girl. If I lost her friendship, I would be alone in this miserable little town.

As I walked through the door, my emotions were running wild. I tried to calm down, but I just didn't know how to feel. Lying across my bed, I read Steven's letter again savoring every word. Holding it close to my heart, I thought of the last time we were together. My desire to touch him made me feel like I was going to lose control. No one on earth understood me like he did. I laid my head down and closed my eyes so I could see his face in my mind, then drifted off to dream.

9
Chapter

"What are you doing out here, man?" Scott asked as he walked up to our apartment building.

"I just thought I would get some sun."

"I can see what you're doing, Steven."

"Is it a crime to sit outside and get some sun?"

"It is when there's a pool around the corner."

"Stop giving me a hard time," I said, looking away, putting on my sunglasses. I was hoping he would go inside but no such luck.

"Here he comes. The man you've been waiting for."

"I wasn't waiting for him," I sighed, turning my head.

"Good afternoon," Scott said, greeting the postman.

"Good afternoon," the postman replied, walking inside.

Scott followed him and came out a few minutes later smiling, then said, "Well, let's see what we have. Here's a letter for you. It's not exactly what you wanted but at least you got mail."

"So, what are you going to do this afternoon?" I asked, trying to control my anger. It had been too long since Tiffany had written me and I needed to know what in the hell was going on with her.

"You and I have a date with destiny my friend," he said pulling me up out of my chair.

Scott and I went to the pool that afternoon and met several girls. One named Linda and her roommate Sophia invited us to a party at their place. We went home, took a shower and headed straight over so we could help cook dinner.

By nine o'clock, there were eight girls, Scott and I, and a guy named Matt. Sophia and Scott were in their own little world so I decided to ask if anyone would like to hear a story. Linda sat down beside me and the other girls gathered around. Matt sat down on the ice chest and I told them the story about the falls.

When I had finished Linda turned on some music and all the girls started dancing. Scott and I sat down to watch them but none of them would have that. I couldn't remember the last time I had felt like dancing but for some reason I didn't resist at all.

After a while I sat back down on the couch and Linda came over, sitting down on my lap.

"That was so much fun. Let's dance again," she said, putting her arm around my neck.

"Okay," I said, feeling awkward.

We stood up and a slow song came on. I put my hand on her waist and pulled her gently toward me. She looked into my eyes and for a moment, I held my breath. I closed my eyes and turned my head.

"What's wrong?"

"Nothing. Nothing's wrong. It's just, I haven't slow danced in a long time," I said, trying to control my voice.

"We can stop if you want to," she said, stepping back.

"No," I said, taking her hand.

"Do you have a girlfriend?"

I hesitated to reply and she looked at my face for the answer. I looked away and said no but she could tell there was somebody I was thinking about. I just pulled her closer and closed my eyes.

Soon after the song ended, Matt and the other girls left and it was just the four of us. Linda and I stayed in the living room talking and Sophia and Scott went to her room. Linda kind of reminded me of Tiffany with her reddish-brown hair, blue eyes and slender frame. But of course, she wasn't Tiffany.

Scott and Sophia really hit it off and it seemed like almost every day they planned something for the four of us to do. We began going out with Sophia and Linda to movies, dinners and parties more often then I would have cared to. I guess you could say I got tired of being alone and waiting for the postman.

Before long the leaves started to change colors and there was a chill in the air. The more I got to know Linda, the more I knew she was nothing like Tiffany at all. But her company did take away some of the loneliness I felt. I knew she cared about me, but I could never give her the affection she wanted. It was all because Linda's touch was not the touch I longed for.

10 Chapter

Every morning, when I wake up, I have to go over this again in my mind. Sometimes, I feel like I'm doing something wrong and I have to remind myself that I'm not.

Then I think of how nice it is to have a guy to take me out. It doesn't even matter where he takes me. I think it's just knowing someone wants to spend time with me is what feels good.

Shane tries so hard to make me happy and sometimes I feel that way. But there is something I can't stand about going out with him. Whenever he kisses me and I close my eyes, the only thing I see is Steven's face.

Today, I got to school early so maybe I could see Shane before class. I walked to the courtyard, to our usual spot and he was standing alone, waiting for me.

"Hey, I've been thinking about you all morning."

"You have," I replied.

"Where were you last night?"

"I was with Victoria. She came by and wanted to go riding around. Are you mad at me?"

"No, I just thought we'd do something together last night. I called but your dad said you'd already left."

"I've already told you, Shane, I can't handle spending every night with you."

"I know, I know. You have told me that a thousand times."

"Well when you pressure me, it only makes me want to see you less."

"Okay, no more pressure," he replied, reaching out to take my hand.

I pulled my hand back and started walking away right before the bell rang. The day had just begun but I could hardly wait to go home.

All day long I thought about Shane. What in the world was I doing? I needed someone to spend time with and it was nice to be with someone who cared about me. But everything was moving too fast and getting way too serious for me to ignore. A guy like Shane has a reputation to protect. He had already taken a lot of crap since we had started going out because of Amber and all of her friends.

When I got home from school, the first thing I did was check the mail. Somehow I knew there would be a letter from Steven waiting for me. I ran inside and quickly walked to my bedroom. I lay across my bed before opening his letter to read it aloud.

My Beloved,

I have turned the hourglass over a million times since I last beheld your beautiful grace. Yet, it feels like yesterday I held you in my arms. I can see you walking toward me, with a look of innocence on your face. I remember brushing your hair after a hot bath and so many kisses we secretly shared. Life has had to carry on, yet my thoughts of you still remain strong.

I had a dream, several nights ago. I could see you, and I could see me. We were sitting under that old oak tree. My new friend Scott started to walk our way. I quickly got up and went to greet him halfway. We turned and looked back at you. Then we looked at each other. I said to him, look at her, isn't she beautiful. Then you smiled. You had overheard what I said. The next morning, when I awoke, I felt so good. And even though I didn't know exactly why, I think I understood.

If only we could visit each other every night in our dreams. Then the miles would seem like such a small thing. I'm with you when you look into the sky. I'm with you when you close your eyes at night. I will see you soon my Love, when it is Christmas time.

Love,
Steven

****

Letter after letter arrived as the days slipped by and I read each one aloud. Sometimes it felt like he was writing to some other girl.

How could *I* mean that much to him after all of this time? And the reason why I was unable to write him back was something I didn't understand. Part of me just didn't feel worthy of someone like him and the other part felt like he and Amber would eventually be together anyway. Then the guilt of seeing other guys made me feel bad about myself. Regardless of what my thoughts were each time I would sit at my desk to write him back, every page would end up crumbled and thrown into the trash can.

When we first met, my life was a total mess. Between mom leaving us and moving away from California, I was barely myself. Sometimes, my imagination led me to believe Steven had fallen in love with a different person. So much had changed since he had moved away. It had to be a version of me that doesn't exist anymore. And even though I tried to convince myself of this, I still longed to see him everyday.

Christmas was only a couple of weeks away when dad surprised me with a gift. He bought tickets to fly to New York for the holidays. He wanted to see Cheryl and said I needed to spend time with my mom. I tried to act happy but certainly he could see the sadness in my eyes. He obviously ignored it and I never said a word. Only behind closed doors did I let the pain come out. I was so angry with my dad for not knowing how much I needed to see Steven. But how was he supposed to know something I never let show?

Sheet after sheet of paper was ripped to shreds as I tried to explain my absence to Steven. How he could always write the perfect words to make everything better, I'll never know. My frustration drove me to the point of telling dad I just wouldn't go. Of course, there was no way I could do that so I choose to call Blake instead. Just to let him know that if Steven were still here on New Year's Eve, I'd get to see him before he left.

"Hello."

"Hey Blake, this is Tiffany."

"Hey."

"I was calling because my dad decided that we're going to New York to see my sister for Christmas."

"Okay. Thanks for calling to tell me that," he replied strangely.

"I was calling so you could tell your brother."

"I'll tell him," he answered shortly.

"Just tell him that I'm going to New York for Christmas, but I'll be back on New Year's Eve."

"I'll do it."

"One more thing. Please tell him I said Merry Christmas, Merry Christmas to you and your dad and mom, you know, the whole family."

"I'll tell him."

"Okay, thanks."

"Bye."

"Bye," I said, hanging up the phone.

As I sat down on the edge of my bed, I had the strangest feeling. Blake had almost made me feel like I shouldn't be calling. I couldn't understand why he would treat me so coldly. I had never done anything to make him mad at me that I knew of. Was I just overreacting? But still, the nagging feeling in the center of my chest would not go away. Then I thought, maybe it's because Steven doesn't actually live there anymore.

Chapter 11

"Welcome home, Steven."

"Thanks, Dad," I said, putting my bags in the back of his truck.

"Good to see you, son," he said, patting my shoulder.

"Good to see you too. Where are Mom and Blake?"

"They're at home. How's New York treating you?"

"It's alright. But I still want to come back to home."

"Well, you're here now."

My dad looked older and as I gazed at him I could see parts of myself. My hands looked just like his, strong, not a stranger to hard work and tanned by the Mississippi sun. His hazel eyes had lost a little of their sparkle and I wondered if mine would look the same when I was his age. Then I pondered an unusual question. Did he ever love Mom the way I love Tiffany? Then I thought maybe no one has ever loved anyone as much as I love her.

The moment we walked through the door I wanted to leave. I needed to see Tiffany and nothing else mattered to me. I knew it was just the anticipation that had been building up inside but I would have done anything just to see her.

It wasn't too hard to convince Blake to go for a ride. He had just got his license and the truck he always wanted, a completely loaded, dark blue 1989 Chevrolet Silverado 4x4. How he talked Mom and Dad into buying it, I'll never know.

The only problem was getting him to help me find Tiffany. I knew he would have other destinations in mind but I could only think of one thing, finding my beloved.

"Man, I am glad to get out of there."

"You just got here, man," Blake said as we got into his truck.

"Where is everybody partying these days?"

"They still go down to the bog sometimes," he replied strangely, putting the truck in reverse.

"Come on, it's Christmas. Somebody's got to be having a party."

"Let's go to the bog and see if anyone is down there first."

Blake punched the gas as the force pulled our bodies back against the seat. As I sat there while my brother tried to make small talk all I could think about was where Tiffany could be. If I had my truck I would drive around all night long if that is what it took. Natchez, Mississippi is not that big of a town to keep me from finding her.

"Hey, did you hear what happened to Brad?" Blake asked, laughing.

"No, what happened?"

"He got kicked out of college. They say it was like a date rape thing. Brad says the girl is a liar. He swears she begged him for it."

"Where is he now?"

"His mom sent him to his grandpa's house. Do you know where that is?" he asked, turning on the high beams to see down the tiny dirt road.

"I think it's in New Orleans."

"Doesn't look like anyone is down here."

"Not unless they're sitting in the dark. So, have you seen Tiffany lately?"

"Yeah, I see her around sometimes."

"Is she dating anyone?"

"She's going out with Shane Patterson. Do you remember him?" he asked, turning the truck around.

"The guy with blonde hair and glasses?"

"He wears contacts now."

"Are they serious?"

"He hasn't bought her a ring like you did, if that's what you're asking."

"I was just making conversation. Can't I talk to my kid brother?" I asked, hitting Blake on the arm.

"Hey man, I'm driving!"

"Tell me how she's doing and I'll leave you alone."

"She called yesterday."

"She called you?"

"Yes she called me, but not for me. She called so I could tell you something."

"Well, when were you planning on telling me?"

"Do you want to know or not?"

"You better tell me."

"She said she decided to go to New York for Christmas to see her sister. And she might make it back before you leave and she might not."

"Did she say when she would be back?"

"No she didn't."

"Is that all she said?"

"Yep, that's all she said. Where else do you want to go?"

"I'm ready to get back to the house. I'm tired."

"I knew I shouldn't have told you. Come on, I thought you wanted to go out and party," he said sarcastically.

When I knew there was no way I could see her, I felt like a balloon after a pin is stuck in it. All the excitement and anticipation, just to be let down again, had drained my body of energy. The only thing I wanted was to crawl in bed and sleep for a long time. During the entire ride back to the house, I prayed and prayed for rain.

My parents wanted to talk but I was unable to carry on a conversation. I went to my room with the lame excuse of being tired. This entire holiday season would be full of the hope of seeing her again if only for a moment. The waiting had already consumed me and I felt like I couldn't wait any longer. The thought of another week was just too much to bear. I needed to see her now, right now, but fate had to have its way.

If only I had stayed in New York, she would be in my arms this very second. My body ached to hold her as I squeezed my pillow. The only way to ease my pain was to make a promise to myself. There was absolutely no way I'd return to New York, until I had kissed her lips again. I closed my eyes and heard the faint pitter-patter of rain upon the roof.

The time passed by slower than a snail crawling across the desert. I spent time at all of our favorite spots, remembering all the things we had done in the past. And I did manage to find out where all of the New Year's Eve parties were going to be. My best bet to see Tiffany, if she made it home, was Tony Naples's party. So, I made sure to drop by and pay him a visit.

New Year's Eve had finally arrived after all of the waiting. I was probably overdressed but everything had to be just right. As I looked at my reflection, I imagined what it would be like to see her. I had bought Tiffany a blank card and wrote a poem on the inside. I put it in my jacket pocket hoping I would have the chance to give it to her tonight.

****

"Steven, I can't believe you're here."

"Victoria, how are you girl?"

"Good. Happy New Year," she exclaimed, hugging me close.

"Happy New Year. Can you believe it's almost 1992?"

"I know, it's strange, isn't it?"

"I'm glad to see you. I hardly know anybody."

"Well, it's been awhile since you've been home. So, how is college life treating you?"

"When I get that degree, it'll be worth it."

"You're going to be an engineer?"

"Yes."

"I think you should be a writer. Oh my gosh, those letters you send to Tiffany, they're so beautiful."

My heart felt like it had cracked open and a piece of me was leaking out. I couldn't believe Tiffany let Victoria read my letters. I felt nauseous as I sat back down and asked, "Do you know where she is?"

"I'm not sure but she should be here tonight."

"I need to see her before I go back to New York."

"When are you leaving?"

"Tomorrow night. How is she?"

"Why don't you ask her yourself, here she comes."

"Steven, I'm so glad you're here. I was afraid I'd miss you," Tiffany said, leaning over to hug me.

When she let go I stood up and said, "Let's try that one more time." I hugged her body close to mine and when I started to let go she held on.

"Here you two go again. Are you ever going to get over it?" Victoria asked, pulling us apart as she put her arms around our shoulders and led us into the living room.

We were in the noisiest room at the party but I didn't mind too much. It meant I had to be close to Tiffany to talk to her. The moment I was back in her presence, I never had a doubt. Even the pain of her letting Victoria read my letters seemed to fade away. The miles and the tick of the clock may separate us but we always pick up right where we left off. But it was strange how home didn't feel like home anymore, unless I could see her face.

I think we could have talked all night but Shane found us and interrupted our conversation. Tiffany politely excused herself and asked me to wait there for her. She said she would be back in fifteen minutes.

I waited thirty and went to look for her. Forty-five minutes passed and I sat alone in the corner. I didn't know how to feel, worried, mad or sick. I think I felt all three at the same time. Just when I was about to lose my cool, she walked up.

"I'm sorry it took so long."

"I looked everywhere for you. I thought you left without even saying goodbye."

"I said I was sorry. I'm here now," she said softly, sitting down.

"Is Shane your boyfriend?"

"Not really. We hang out a lot but I wouldn't call him my boyfriend."

"What are you doing tomorrow?"

"Nothing. What about you?"

"I'd like to see you before I leave, if I could."

"Of course. I was afraid I wouldn't get to see you at all."

"I would have waited, until you got back from New York, even if it meant missing my flight."

"You would?" she asked, surprised by my response.

"You know I would, Tiffany," I said honestly, taking her hand.

"What do you want to do tomorrow?"

"I don't know. What about going to the park for a picnic?"

"Don't you think it's a little cold?"

"I'll keep you warm," I said, staring deeply into her blue eyes, trying to find a trace of love in them for me.

"Okay, it's a date. What time will you pick me up?" she asked, pulling her hand away and looking down to open her purse.

"About ten-thirty, if that's not too early?"

"Come by for what?" Shane asked, walking up.

"Oh nothing. Are you ready to go?" Tiffany asked, standing up quickly, obviously nervous.

"I've been ready, just waiting on you."

Tiffany leaned over and whispered, "I'll see you in the morning."

"Are you ready to go now, Tiffany?" Shane asked, pulling her away.

"Yes I am," she said, shaking loose from his grasp. "Have fun tonight, Steven. Don't stay up too late."

She walked away, never looking back. It hurt me so bad that I took the card out and tore it up. I didn't want her to read such words of longing when she could so easily walk away.

Tomorrow, when Shane is nowhere in sight, will she act differently toward me? My heart felt so heavy as I slowly walked out of the house. I wanted to follow them and plead with Tiffany to spend this precious time with me. But after all the waiting, I didn't have the strength or courage to beg her now.

****

"Tiffany, Steven is here."

"I'll be down in a minute, Dad."

"Have a seat, Steven. Tell me, how is the Big Apple treating you?"

"Its okay, Mr. Crenshaw but I wish I was a little closer to home."

"Why don't you move back?"

"My mother's parents live in New York. That's why Mom sent me there."

"The truth is she just wanted to get you away from me," Tiffany said, walking into the living room.

"Now I don't think that's true, baby. I'm sure she was thinking about his education. So what are you kids going to do today?"

"We're going on a picnic," she said, putting a pink scarf around her neck.

"You might want to change your plans. It's really cold out there," he said, helping Tiffany with her coat.

"It doesn't matter to me what we do," I said, standing up.

"When will you be heading back to New York?" Mr. Crenshaw asked.

"Tonight, around five-thirty."

"It was good to see you," he said, shaking my hand.

"It was good to see you too, sir."

"I'll be back later, Dad," she said, kissing him on the cheek.

"Okay, be careful and have fun."

We decided instead of a picnic to go to a restaurant where it was nice and warm. We took our time as if we had nowhere else to be and nowhere else to go. I let Tiffany do most of the talking, because she had so much to say.

After lunch, she wanted to go to the park and just sit in the car for a while. We were talking about the first time she and I came here together and all of the sudden she got out of the car. Tiffany ran and I quickly jumped out, running after her. She put her gloved hand on the old oak tree's trunk and hung her head down to watch her step. I started following her like we were playing Follow the Leader.

"I love to walk around on its roots."

"I know you do."

"It's almost like I'm dancing with it."

"Then I bet the tree likes it too."

I reached out and touched her waist. Tiffany stopped walking and leaned back against the tree. As I turned to stand in front of her my foot slipped, making me lean closer. She put her hands on the front of my coat and pulled me toward her. We looked into each other's eyes and kissed passionately.

"I still love you, Tiffany."

"I love you, too."

I knew she was telling me the truth but there was sadness in her eyes that I could not deny nor forget.

Chapter 12

It was only a few days after Steven left that I received a letter. I wanted to be alone so I took the keys to dad's car and walked out the door. Once I was in the drivers' seat, there was only one destination in mind. And even though it was cold, I drove straight to the falls.

It hardly looks the same here in winter. The trees lose their leaves and there are no flowers in sight. I closed my eyes trying to remember what it looked like in spring, the way it was the first day Steven brought me here.

The path seemed longer this time or maybe it was just because my heart felt so heavy. Steven had never seen me with another guy before. And even though we didn't talk about it, I could tell it bothered him. That's why I just had to break up with Shane. Besides he wasn't really my type. And I was tired of all of the rumors Amber and her friends had started about us.

After I sat down on the ground, I took a deep breath. Whatever he said, however he feels now, I'll find a way to understand. I closed my eyes; fighting back the tears then opened the envelope to read his words.

My love,

I am here again, far away from you. Could I drive a thousand miles, to stop this eternal burning? What is this pain that fills my heart with such longing? Why do the miles seem stretched farther than ever before? Perhaps it is because we only shared moments instead of days. My love would have spilled over, but time was the bay.

I have recited I don't need you, a million times to my dense little head. I am immensely numb from stopping my heart. My faint lies, it refuses to truly believe. The days I live without you, they almost feel like sin. I long for the certain day, our life will begin. I see it so real, when I look into your eyes. I have tried to hide it, when you look into mine. Will I be able to walk far enough away, to stop my dreams of you that come all day? I have planned a billion faraway trips, like the scenery could change my mind. I am left, only knowing, that my feeble feet, so unhappy, could never find what they need. If I became a runaway, desperately running, would it stop my love for you that is growing?

You, my love, are the star that all evenings await. We are innocent my darling, this feeling is not a mistake. I think now only of you in spring. When that moment arrives, I will see you again. These are wasted days and lonely nights until I take flight. I shall think of you by day and dream of you at night. When the sun shines, I will see your hair. When the wind blows I will hear your voice. When the rain falls I will feel your heartbeat with mine.

Love forever,
Steven

****

Letter after letter arrived as winter turned to spring. Each one gave me a deeper understanding of the way he feels. There are no borders or boundaries for two people like us. When I was silent, I could hear his words in my heart. Sometimes it made me angry to need someone so much that is too far away. And knowing that he felt the same way didn't make anything better. There were even moments I felt angry. After all, he did leave me behind when I begged him to run away with me.

We only had a few more weeks of school left and everyone was ready for summer. I knew school was the last place I wanted to be today. I looked out the window as the sunrays beamed down through the clouds and noticed the azaleas were in full bloom. It felt like it was almost warm enough to lay out in the sun and I longed to be outside.

The first bell rang and I picked up my books. Victoria must have felt the same way today because I couldn't find her anywhere this morning. But unlike me, she always found a way to skip school. As I walked down the hall toward the classroom, I walked right pass the door, heading for the nurse's office. Just as I turned the corner, Victoria was walking toward me.

"Guess where we're going for spring break?"

"Where?"

"Florida! Mom and Dad said they would pay for our hotel room if we wanted to go. Isn't that great?"

"Yes, but I have to ask my dad first."

"Aren't you excited?"

"I know we'd have fun, but Steven is suppose to come home."

"You can always see him, but spring break in Florida. Girl, we're going to party our butts off," she said, dancing around, snapping her fingers.

"Maybe we could come home early so I could see him before he leaves."

"If we're not having too much fun," she said as the bell rang.

Victoria ran in the other direction even though she was already tardy. I stood there watching her as I contemplated what she had just said. I knew we'd have fun but then my heart ached when I thought about going. It had been too long since I'd seen Steven. Spring break was the time I'd been waiting for. That and his letters were the only things that had kept me going lately.

****

We drove to Panama City and checked into the hotel. After unpacking the car, we got ready to cruise the strip. Victoria could hardly wait to go out and have some fun. I wanted to be as excited as she was and except for the thought of Steven coming home and me not being there again, I was.

We drove up and down the strip, waving at all the cute guys. Two guys, named Chad and Tommy pulled us over and Victoria asked them where everybody went to have fun. They told us about a bar named Coconuts and Victoria said we'd follow them.

"One! Two! Three!" Victoria yelled, before we took another shot of tequila.

"I think it's time to dance now," I said, sitting the shot glass down and taking Victoria's hand.

"Come over here, let's dance on the platform."

We climbed up and I closed my eyes and let the music move my body. I was in my own little world as the lights swirled and the beat banged in my head. There were so many people around us that I almost didn't feel someone tug on my pants.

"What?" I asked, leaning over. "Help me down, I can't hear

you," I said, putting my hand on his shoulder. The man took my other hand and I jumped down. He led me to the back of the bar, near the bathrooms, where it was a little quieter.

"I like the way you dance."

"Thanks. Is that why you dragged me over here?"

"No, it isn't. I'm Ron Taylor," he said, handing me his business card.

"So you're from Los Angeles?"

"Yes, I've lived there for fourteen years."

"What are you doing in Panama City?"

"I was born here," he said proudly.

"And you teach acting?"

"Among other things," he said, raising his eyebrows.

"Well, that is so weird. I've been thinking about moving to L.A. after I graduate."

"Have you ever thought of becoming an actress?"

"Yes, that is what I'm going to be when I grow up," I said, looking into his eyes.

"Well you certainly you have the look."

"I do?"

"Yes. And I could teach you the rest. What is your name, beautiful?"

"Tiffany."

He gave me the strangest grin saying, "Tiffany Starr. Yes, Tiffany Starr, I like it."

"No, it's Tiffany Crenshaw. Actually, it's Tiffany Love Crenshaw. You know, TLC, tender, loving care."

"Tiffany Love Crenshaw," he said slowly, "No, no, no, Tiffany Starr is much better."

"What are you talking about, Mr. Taylor?"

"Please, never call me Mr. Taylor, its Ron," he said, shaking his head from side to side while pouting his lips.

"Okay, Ron."

"Where are you from, Tiffany?"

"Natchez, Mississippi."

"You don't have much of a southern accent."

"I just moved there a couple of years ago. I grew up in Santa Maria, its north of Los Angeles."

"I know right where it is. I have an aunt who lives there, been there several times."

"Well, that's the reason I don't have a southern drawl, unlike my friend," I said, seeing Victoria on her way to the bathroom. I grabbed her by the arm, saying, "This is Victoria."

"Girl, I didn't even see you. Hi! What's your name handsome?"

"Ron," he said, raising her hand to his lips.

"I like him, Tiffany. Can we keep him?"

"I guess so."

"Mr. Ron," Victoria said, smiling and touching his arm.

"It's Ron, just Ron. Would you ladies do me the pleasure of cruising down the strip with me?"

"Let's go, Tiffany," Victoria said, pleading with her eyes.

I pulled back from instinct and asked, "Are you sure you don't want to just stay here?"

"Ron, you'd think the girl could chill out during spring break."

"Okay, let's go," I said, walking ahead of them.

We walked out the door and Ron snapped his fingers. I turned to look at him, as if to ask why, but he walked past me. I looked over at Victoria and her brown eyes widened. A long, shiny black limousine pulled up to the curb. The driver quickly got out and opened the door.

"Ron, is there any way I could like you more?" Victoria asked, climbing in.

"I don't know, maybe."

"I know a way," she replied, teasing him.

"Tell me," he said as we pulled away from the bar.

"Make me a shot of tequila and open the sunroof and I'll be in deeper."

"I can do that. Anything for you, Tiffany?"

"No, thank you."

"Where to, Mr. Taylor?" the driver asked.

"Down the strip and to the boat."

Ron opened the sunroof and Victoria was the first to stand up. He encouraged me to join her and I didn't resist. I couldn't remember the last time Victoria or I had received so many compliments but obviously riding in a long shiny black limo makes you look really good.

When we arrived at the marina, we went onboard his boat. It was bigger than any boat I'd ever seen and was beautifully decorated. As he took us on the tour, I felt better about coming here with him but I was still nervous. I knew Ron Taylor wanted something from me. I just wasn't sure what it was.

We sat down and Ron stared at us for an awkward moment, and then asked, "So, how long have you two been friends?"

"Ever since Tiffany moved to Natchez a few years ago."

"That's good. She's going to need a good friend one day."

"What do you mean by that?"

"She's going to be famous. You see Victoria; actresses need good friends before they're in the business."

"You think I'm going to be famous?"

"Yes, and rich too," he said, taking a book from the bookshelf.

"Well if you're rich I'm rich," Victoria said.

"Here Tiffany, read this paragraph for me," Ron said, handing me the book.

It felt strange but I stood up and read the words aloud. "It was a cold and miserable day as I sat on the dock searching the horizon for approaching ships. Every time I got a chance, I came here looking for any sign of Christopher's return. I could never be certain that he truly loved me because his journey had taken him so far away from home. And all the women in our village knew all too well that not every man comes back from the sea."

I closed the book with my finger still holding the page saying, "That's the end. Do you want me to read some more?"

"No, just the third line again. And look at me this time when you say it."

I felt silly but I thought if this guy wants me to read with emotion, that's exactly what I'm going to do. So I read it again silently, and then looked into his eyes before saying, "I could never be certain that he truly loved me because his journey had taken him so far away from home."

"Bravo!" Ron yelled while clapping.

"Thanks," I said, sitting down.

Ron stared at me for a moment before asking, "How long will you be staying in Florida?"

"Three more glorious days and then back to hickville we go," Victoria said, pouting.

"Look, why don't you two stay with me for the next three days? I can teach Tiffany some things about acting."

"Only if you will take us out on this boat," Victoria said, sitting down beside him.

"Let's go check you out of your hotel and we'll sail tonight."

Ron stood up quickly, walking toward the stairs. Victoria got up to follow him and I sat there staring into space. I knew I was supposed to say no but as I sat there, I thought, why not?

Chapter 13

As the plane landed, a glimmer of hope that Tiffany would be waiting at the gate passed through my mind. Of course, she didn't know when I'd be arriving, but still I dreamed of seeing her waiting there for me.

It was Mom and Dad who were there at the gate. They both hugged me at the same time and seemed genuinely happy to see me. We rode home as I gazed out the window answering their questions and it was hard not to ask about Tiffany. Mom had this way of pretending that she wasn't a part of my life and we all had a way of going along with her little game. But I think dad could tell Tiffany was the only thing on my mind.

After lunch, Dad and I went outside while Mom cleaned the kitchen. He wanted to know how my classes were going and about my life in New York. The small talk only made me nervous, besides, what could I tell him? I was barely making it? No. That my life sucked more every day I had to live there? No. I couldn't tell him the truth.

Going to look for my girl was the only thing on my mind but Dad continued with his interrogation. After more avoided questions and blank stares, Dad abruptly got up and went inside. Then he came back and sat down, not saying a word he opened his hand. With a smile, I took the keys and picked a few of Mom's flowers before I left.

My stomach felt like it was tied in knots as I pulled into her driveway. Before I got out, I checked my face in the mirror. Other than looking a little tired, I was ready to see her. As I knocked, I hoped she'd be the one to answer the door.

"Hello, Mr. Crenshaw."

"Hello, Steven. Come on in, son, have a seat."

"I came by to see if Tiffany was here."

He turned sharply, with a strange look on his face and asked, "She didn't tell you where she was going?"

"No sir, I haven't talked to her lately."

"I'm sorry. I just assumed she'd write you about her plans."

"No, she didn't."

"She and Victoria went to Panama City, Florida, for spring break. Can I get you something to drink?"

"No, sir. I won't take up any more of your time," I said, abruptly standing up. Then I asked, "Will you tell her I came by?"

"Sure, but there's no need in rushing off," he said, standing up.

"I'm in my mother's car and she told me not to be gone too long," I lied, walking to the door.

"Maybe next time you can join me for lunch."

"That sounds good," I said sincerely, but I could tell he was upset.

"You take care, son. I'll tell her you came by," he said, shaking my hand.

I turned to walk away, than turned to ask, "Will you tell her one more thing?"

"Sure, what is it?"

"On the day she graduates, will you tell her that I'm proud of her and I wish I could've been here?"

"Yes, I will."

"Thanks, Mr. Crenshaw. I'll see you later."

"Come back and see us anytime."

As I backed out of the driveway I waved goodbye. I could hardly believe I was here and she was in Florida. I had the biggest urge to forget about all responsibility and just keep driving. My mind was racing, thinking of ways I could get to Florida before my vacation was over. I didn't care about spending time with my family. I didn't care about seeing my old friends. All I wanted to do was get to Panama City as soon as I could.

****

"Steven, I can't believe you talked me into this," Blake said, turning onto the highway.

"Don't worry about it. Everything will be okay."

"Mom and Dad are going to kill us," he said, gripping the steering wheel with both hands.

"They're going to kill me, not you," I said, trying to calm him down.

"How are we even going to find Tiffany? Do you know what hotel she's staying at?"

"We'll find her. And if nothing else, we'll get to go to the beach."

When we finally arrived in Panama City, we went from hotel to hotel before I found where she had been staying. The clerk said she'd checked out earlier that morning. I just knew in my heart she'd decided to come home early to see me. I cursed myself over and over for being so foolish. It was hard to believe we drove all the way down here and she had left. As I walked back toward the truck, I saw Shane Patterson talking to Blake.

"What's up, Shane?"

"Just heading to the beach when I saw your brother standing here," he replied like he was ready to fight.

"Shane told me Victoria and Tiffany left last night with some old guy," Blake said.

"Yeah, they split with some old rich dude."

"Where were they going?" I asked, completely baffled.

"Out on his boat. At least that's what Victoria told Melissa. She saw them putting their suitcases in a limousine last night."

"Does anybody know who this guy is?" I asked, blown away that she'd leave with a stranger.

"Don't you think I would've told you if I knew?" he asked, obviously upset.

"Thanks for the info, man," Blake said, slapping Shane's hand. He was trying to keep the peace and who could blame him?

"See you, man," Shane replied, walking toward the beach.

"Do you feel any better now, Steven?" Blake asked as we got in the truck.

"No, I don't. Before I just wanted to see her and now I'm worried. What in the world is Victoria thinking?"

"I don't think that chick is capable of thinking," Blake said, laughing.

"This is not funny, bro. They could be with some crazy guy on a boat in the middle of nowhere. Anything could happen to them."

"Yeah, but I doubt some rich guy is going to kill them. Now he might want to sleep with them, but other than that I don't think you have anything to worry about. Where to now?"

"I guess we better head back home. There's no way I can find her now."

"First we're going to the beach and then we'll head back home," he said, waving to a blonde in a pink bikini.

We went and sat on the beach all afternoon. Boats were slowly moving through the water as the sun browned our skin. I wanted to get up and swim across the Gulf of Mexico until I reached one of them. Then I would just hitch a ride from boat to boat until I found Tiffany. Of course, I had to be realistic. My return flight to New York was in just a few days. Not to mention, Mom and Dad were probably worried sick about us. Besides, I couldn't swim that far even if I tried.

My parents lectured us for several hours and even though I was to blame, Blake took the blunt of their anger. It was his truck and they felt he should have been more responsible. My mom yelled and screamed until she started crying. I sat quietly as Blake answered, yes, ma'am. No, ma'am. Then he kneeled in front of her, begging for forgiveness. She looked into his eyes and finally smiled. Then she told him she was thankful that he was still alive as she stared at me. They hugged and I walked to my room to pack.

My parents treated me like a stranger after our trip. I know asking your little brother to go to Florida to look for a girl is the wrong thing to do but Tiffany was not just a girl. So I decided to spend the next few days alone just to think.

****

The plane took off and I felt so strange inside. I had wanted to see Tiffany so badly but now I only felt numb. Every cell in my body wanted to scream and the thought of punching the back of the chair in front of me crossed my mind. How she could do this to me again, do this to us again? It seemed like she didn't care about anything except having a good time.

I arrived in New York safe and sound but couldn't stop myself from thinking about her. My anger was slowly subsiding and now all I wanted was to know why. As soon as I got to the apartment, I excused myself to my room. I had to call to see if she was all right and find out the answer.

"Hello, Mr. Crenshaw, this is Steven."

"Hi, Steven."

"Has Tiffany made it home from Florida yet?"

"Yes she did. Do you want to speak to her?"

"Yes, please."

"Hold on, I'll get her."

"Hi, Steven!"

"Hi," I said happily, caught off guard by her excitement.

"My dad told me that you came by to see me. I'm sorry I missed you."

"Did you have a good time in Florida?"

"We had the best time and you're not going to believe what happened to me!"

"What?"

"Me and Victoria were dancing on this platform at a bar. Then this guy comes up and starts tugging on my pants. His name is Ron Taylor. Anyway, we took a ride in his limo to his boat and ended up spending the next three days on it. He teaches acting out in L.A. and he thinks that I'm going to be rich and famous. He says I have the look! Can you believe that?"

"Wow. What else did he say?" I asked with as much enthusiasm as I could muster.

"He said that when I graduate, I could go to his school for free. Can you believe that, f r e e! He also said that I could work for him part time when I wasn't going to auditions. And he offered me a place to stay until I could get a place of my own. Did you hear that? My own place."

"Have you talked this over with your dad?" I asked, wondering what in the world she could be thinking.

"No, you know how my dad is. He thinks I'm going to college twenty miles from the house."

"Going to school is not a bad thing, Tiffany. At least when you finish you'll always have a degree to fall back on."

"I know, but if I don't go for this, I'll regret it for the rest of my life. And you know it's what I've always wanted."

"I'm not against you pursuing your dreams but I'm worried about this guy. I mean, you don't even know who he is."

"He told me I was good, Steven. I read all kinds of scripts for him. I really want to do it. Ron says I've got what it takes. He came up with my new name. Wanna hear it?"

"Yes, I'll need to know how to get in touch with you when you're a big movie star."

"That's it, Tiffany Starr, with two r's. What do you think?"

"Tiffany Starr, Tiffany Crenshaw, Tiffany Starr, well, it definitely has a ring to it."

"Well, it might end up being something else, we haven't totally decided yet," she answered quietly.

There was a change in her voice that almost made me feel bad for being pessimistic. "I just wonder if you've really thought about this. I mean do you really want that kind of lifestyle?"

"I would love it. Just think of all the clothes and money. I could have a house right on the beach. All my friends could live there. I'm sure they need engineers in Los Angeles."

"You're right I'll be able to get a job anywhere after I get my degree."

"I'm just so excited. Last week I didn't know where I was going to acting school. Of course, I was going to L.A. but I really didn't know what I was going to do when I got there. And now everything is just falling in place for me. It's like it was meant to be."

"So, when are you thinking about going to Hollywood?"

"As soon as I'm out of school, Ron can't wait for me to get there."

"It seems like you've got your mind made up. If there's no way I can talk you out of this then please listen to me. Be careful, remember, not every person in this world is as nice as you."

"You know me, I'll be okay. If you weren't living in New York, you could come with me and be my bodyguard."

"I'd like to be guarding your body right now, Ms. Starr."

"You can guard my body any time," she said in a sexy voice.

"I really hate that I didn't get to see you."

She took a deep breath before saying, "I tried to tell Victoria I wouldn't go. I didn't even pack anything until an hour before we left."

"Well, I don't know when we'll have a chance to see each other."

"Maybe we can figure out something during the summer."

My voice lowered and my heart clinched as I said, "If not, I'll see you at Christmas. You will be home for Christmas?"

"Of course I'll be here for Christmas. Just because I go to L.A. doesn't mean I won't be home for Christmas."

I didn't want to ask but I had to. I was so afraid of what her answer would be. "How will I know where to send your letters?"

"When I get there I'll send you a postcard."

"I'll be looking forward to it."

"I guess I should let you go. This is long distance. I'm sorry I've just gone on and on."

"Yeah, it was good to talk to you."

"Thanks for calling. Hopefully I'll see you sometime this summer."

"Yes, hopefully. Take care and I'll talk to you soon."

"You too, bye."

"Bye."

As I hung up the phone, I wanted to hear her voice again. So many questions swam in my head that only she could answer. And I had so many things I wanted to explain. The thought of calling her back consumed me. I could use some excuse but every one I came up with was lame. I was mad at myself for not telling her that I loved her. The fact that those words were getting harder to say filled me with despair.

I sat down to write Tiffany a letter and tore up at least thirty pieces of paper. Of course there was nothing I could write that would change reality. Why I couldn't tell her about my trip to Florida, I guess I'll never know. Perhaps part of it was pride and the other part anger. I wanted to be happy for Tiffany but what I felt was complete madness. She was slipping away from me, so very far away and there was nothing I could do. A butterfly has wings for a reason.

14
Chapter

Living with Ron Taylor was not exactly what I imagined. On board his boat, he appeared much younger and stronger. Now, his dark tan had faded and his shorts were exchanged for a business suit.

As I took the tour of his enormous house his true personality began to show. It was the way he explained where he had bought all of his precious knick-knacks. He'd quote the place and approximate date he'd bought this one and that one. To my surprise, he'd been traveling all over the world before I was ever born.

The dream of becoming an actress was still alive even though sometimes I felt like an intruder in his home. It was huge and everything in it was polished and shiny. Nothing was out of place, however, there always seemed to be someone cleaning.

When I was at the Studio, learning my acting skills, I knew I was doing the right thing. Everyone said I was a natural but if they knew a little about my life, they would understand why. It seemed like I had to pretend that I was happy for as long as I could remember.

The months passed by so quickly but the seasons hardly changed. It didn't even feel like Thanksgiving as we sat down to eat turkey with a group of Ron's fifty closest friends. And to think that Christmas is just around the corner is completely crazy.

It had been a very long and tiring day but I still put on my bathing suit when Ron asked me to join him in the hot tub. He wanted to talk but all I could think about was going home. I had to break the news to him and it had to be tonight. Finally, he leaned back and closed his eyes.

"Ron?"

"Yes."

"I want to go home in a few weeks."

"What's wrong, babe? Haven't I done everything I told you I would?" Ron asked, taking my hand.

"Yes, but I want to go home for Christmas."

"I know you want to see your dad but now is not a good time to leave."

"I'm going whether you like it or not."

"You can go home. In fact, you can do whatever you want. But if you lose the part of Catherine because you're running home to Daddy, don't come crying to me," he said, turning away.

"I can't believe you're mad at me because I want to go home for a few days."

"I want to remind you of something, Tiffany. There has been a lot of time and money spent on you."

"I know you've helped me and I appreciate everything you've done."

"All I want you to do is listen to me. If you're smart, you'll wait for a better time to go home."

"I know you're right. But my heart…"

"So you miss your dad. Look, why don't we fly him out here?"

I turned to face him, immediately saying, "No, I don't want to do that. I want to go home. You know, sleep in my own bed and see some old friends."

"Well flying your dad out is the best I can do for you. I can't bring your whole damn town here."

"I'll only be gone for a few days. What will I miss, two or three parties at the most? It hasn't helped me get any parts yet."

"I tell you what," he said, looking me in the eye. "If you go home, make sure you pack all your things before you go."

"If you want me to leave, I'll go right now. I don't have to wait until Christmas," I said, getting out of the hot tub.

He completely ignored me, turning away when I looked back. I went to my bedroom to change clothes and within moments Ron stormed into my room.

"What are you doing?"

"Get out of here, I'm not dressed!" I yelled, grabbing my robe.

"I just have to ask you one question. Are you even thinking about what you're throwing away?" He asked, with his face inches away from my face.

"I won't go if it's that important to you," I said quietly, putting on my robe.

"It's not important to me, it's important for you."

"I just wanted to see my dad. It's not like I wasn't coming right back. And how I am going to explain this to everyone who's expecting me to come home?" I asked, sitting down on the bed.

"We'll figure out something," he said, sitting beside me.

"Ron, you know if you want me to leave, I will."

"I don't want you to leave, sweetheart. We're so close to making you a star. Trust me, the sacrifices you make today will be worth it tomorrow," he said, patting my hand.

He walked out of the room and I picked up the phone to call my dad. How was I going to tell him? If he knew Ron was the reason I wasn't coming home, he would demand I leave right now. I told Steven I'd be home, no matter what. Keeping my word to him was very important. Then I thought about the applause I received at the studio. I just had to stay a little while longer, to see if I could make my dream come true. Steven and Dad would just have to understand.

In the long run, one missed Christmas would never measure up against the possibility of being a movie star. My heart was racing as I dialed the number and said hello.

"I was just thinking about you," dad said.

"How are you?"

"Good. How's everything in Hollywood?"

"Great! I'm up for a very important role and that's why I'm calling you. I'm not going to be able to make it home for Christmas this year. I hope you understand."

"Are you sure you can't make it, baby? Just for a day or two?"

"I wish I could."

He hesitated before saying, "Well, if you change your mind, let me know. I'll be here."

"If there was anyway I could get out of it, I would," I said as honestly as possible.

"It's just; I haven't seen you in so long. This house is empty without my girls here," he said sadly, like we had both been gone for years and years.

"I miss you too, Dad. I promise I'll come home soon."

"Anytime will be good," he said solemnly.

"I know. Well, I wish I had more time to talk but I got to let you go."

"Call me soon. Don't let it be so long next time."

"I won't. I love you."

"I love you too, baby. Oh, before I let you go, what do you want me to do with Steven's letters?"

"Oh darn! I still haven't sent him this address," I said, laughing nervously.

"I'll just mail them to you with your Christmas present," he replied in a strained voice.

"Thanks, Dad. Take care of yourself."

"I will, and you be careful out there."

"I will, don't worry. I love you."

"I love you too, bye."

"Bye."

I just sat there and listened until there was a dial tone. I couldn't believe my dad hadn't insisted that I come home for Christmas. Reminding myself of the future, I hung up the phone and thought of Steven. I opened my nightstand drawer and found his postcard I never mailed. My heart ached as I thought of him. How would he feel when I didn't come home? I turned it over and was searching the drawer for a pen when Ron opened my door.

"You're not ready yet! Do you realize we're supposed to be having dinner in thirty minutes?"

"Sorry, I didn't know…"

"Get dressed! You don't have time for a shower. Put your hair up and I'll pick something out for you to wear."

"I think I want to wear…"

"Get in there and put some makeup on that face. I'll pick out something for you to wear. Hurry up! The world isn't going to wait for you, Ms. Starr."

****

Hollywood moves faster than the speed of light and leaves very little for normalcy. Between auditions, classes and the parties there's hardly enough time to think. I barely noticed that the holidays were here until I received a package in the mail from dad.

What is it?" Ron asked.

"It's a Christmas present from my dad."

"Need some help?" he asked, taking it out of my hands.

"Sure, why don't you open my present for me," I said sarcastically, plopping down on the couch.

"Let's see," he said, opening the box.

"Well, what is it?"

"He sent you a sweater. Does your dad know you live in Southern California?" He asked insinuating dad was an idiot.

"He was born here, Ron! He didn't migrate here like you did," I said, taking the sweater, holding it up to my body.

"Here's some perfume that can go straight into the trash," he said, holding it between two fingers.

I couldn't believe he was being so nasty and I was beginning to get mad. "Dad always gives me this kind of perfume. My mother use to wear it."

"Please don't put any of that on around me."

"Does making fun of my presents make you feel like a big man?"

"I was only being honest. Now, this must be the real present," he said, handing me a jewelry box.

I tore off the wrapping and opened the box. "It's beautiful. Look, it's a necklace."

"That's real cute, Tiffany, you'll have to wear it sometime."

"You are so unbelievable. My dad could send me a grain of sand and it would mean more to me than you could ever understand."

"Tiffany, I'm…."

"I don't want to hear it," I said, putting my hand up. "Is there anything else?" I asked, trying to take the box.

Ron rustled the tissue paper and with a wicked smile said, "No."

"Hand me the box, Ron!" I yelled, because I could tell he was lying.

"Calm down. Now this must be what you really wanted," he said, holding up a large envelope.

"Give it to me."

"It's really heavy. Your dad must have a lot to say."

"Just give me the envelope," I said, leaning up, trying to grab it.

"Why are you being so defensive?"

"What do you mean? Those are my gifts, not yours."

"Here," Ron said, throwing it at me, walking out of the room.

I put everything back in the box and went to my room. Who does he think he is? My boyfriend? My father? The more I learn about Ron Taylor, the more I know I won't be living here much longer.

I picked up the envelope and it was heavy and thick. I knew Steven's letters were inside as I held it in my hands. I stuffed it in my purse and went into the bathroom, sitting it beside the tub. I took my clothes off and piled them beside the door. I sat in the cold empty tub and turned the water on slow so it would take a long time to fill up. There were too many letters to read at one time so I started with the last three.

My darling,
The leaves are orange and red and I wonder where you are.
This emptiness fills my soul as I long to see you once again. I wait
for your written words, but they never come. I still can see glimpses
of you whenever I am not feeling too cold. I see your rosy cheeks in
wintertime; I feel your gloved hand in mine.

Where have you gone my darling? Will I see you in wintertime
again? The story remains to be told and I'm anxious to begin. I can't
stop thinking of you, no matter if you have passed me by. The love I
feel for you has no measurement of time. If I were to die, before I see
you again, I want you to know now and always, I am your biggest fan.

Not knowing where you are is hard to take. I write to you now, so
you won't feel the same. I miss you more than words could ever say. I
pray that you will be safe… and know that I do pray. I want you to be
happy and never feel any fear. I make it alone, waiting for Christmas
time to appear. For then I will hold you in my arms until our moment
in time has passed. I wait to see you my love, at long last.

Love,
Steven

My baby,
The tears Tiffany, they keep falling as I think of the past. My heart
is a desert; do the tears fall in vain? I'm going crazy not knowing of
your path in life. If I could see the sun again with you, then maybe this
sadness would pass. I don't know what I am doing here. How could I
be here without you? Is the universe so cruel as to pass our love by?

Now that I am older, I feel like we didn't even get to try.

If only you could write a few words, maybe you could end this pain. I dream of you at night and it is the only thing that keeps me sane. I saw you sitting outside of my parent's house and I sat beside you. They were staring out of the window at you and I. We were talking about children and things that grown-ups do. We were so happy there, still so very young. I never felt more alive then in my dream when I was talking to you.

I wait to hear the sleigh bells that will bring us home. I want to make new memories with you as soon as possible. Continually I escape with thoughts of you in my head. Constantly looking down memory road, we once shared. I dream of seeing you again, my angel, whenever I am alone.

Love,
Steven

My everything,

The excitement is starting to build. The time draws closer where for a few moments I can live. It is hard to breathe when I never see your face. I wonder if I am a fool, but these feelings I cannot change. I will be home again, in less than two weeks. If you are not there, my heart will certainly bleed. No one will be able to heal my wounds. Only you possess that loving spoon.

I look to the sky in search of what I can't find. The love I feel for you, I am unable to deny. If you now love another, tell me, I will try to be strong. I only want for you happiness. Can that be so wrong? I trust you; I heard you promise that we would see each other again. I hang onto those words to keep my world sane. The hour is drawing close when my love will take flight. I know I will see you this year, at Christmas. Soon I will graduate and the miles will not keep us apart. Until then, my love, remember, you are always in my heart. If I could stop the hands of time, well, you know I would. We could spend eternity, exactly where we should. Tell me the truth, please never lie...

"Tiffany, what are you doing in there?" Ron asked, trying to push the door open.

"Taking a bath. I'll be out in a few seconds," I said, stuffing the letters back into the big envelope.

"Well hurry up! You're going to look like a grape if you don't get out of the water soon," he said, sticking his head around the door.

"Get out of here, Ron!"

"I'll be waiting for you on the terrace, darling."

"Ron!"

"Yes, sweetheart," he answered, peeping back in.

"Can I invite Victoria to come out for a visit?"

"If it'll keep you happy, you can ask her to come live with us," he replied, then walked away laughing.

I was shaking as I got out of the tub. Anyone that saw me would have said it was because I was cold. But it was Steven's words that made me tremble. I could almost feel his touch while reading his letters.

The tears were welling up in my eyes as I fought to remain calm. The thought of running away entered my mind as I sat on the bathroom floor. The worst part is Steven doesn't even know how much I miss him. All I wanted to do was lie in bed and read every one of his letters but the tap on the door reminded me I wasn't alone. So, I slipped my nightgown on and slowly walked out to the terrace where Ron was waiting for me.

Chapter 15

Summer came and went while working endless hours on my grandfather's farm in New York. I asked Blake about Tiffany every time we spoke. Was she still living there? Had he seen her lately? Occasionally, he would give me a vague answer, but most of the time he never had much to say. When fall came around and he moved away for college, my questioning had to end.

Fall passed quickly and the snow of winter lay deep on the ground. As of yet, I have not received the postcard Tiffany promised. The speculation consumes my life daily. I felt like I had been shut out, unintentionally or not, but still shut out. I hung on to the promise Tiffany made that she would be home for Christmas. If she kept her word, it wouldn't be long until I could see her again.

As the plane landed, I wondered if she was home yet. Mom was at the airport to pick me up and of course, I couldn't ask her. After we got home, I made an excuse to go to the store and left before anybody could say anything.

I drove as fast as I could to Tiffany's house, wishing she would answer the door. But when it opened, my heart sank when I saw the look on her dad's face.

"Hello, Mr. Crenshaw."

"Steven, I was hoping you'd come by. Come in, son."

I followed him into the dining room and sat down at the table. "Is Tiffany here?"

"No, she couldn't make it home."

"Did she move?"

"I'm sorry, I thought you already knew. She's in California," he said, sitting down at the dinning room table.

"Is she staying with Ron?"

"Yes. Have you met him?"

"No, but I'd like to."

"Me too," he said, sounding like a protective father.

He got up to go into the kitchen and continued talking. His voice was distant as I thought of how long it had been since I'd seen her. I was trying to keep my emotions under control but it was difficult. Sitting in this house where she and I had shared so many good times was not helping me at all.

"I'm sorry, Mr. Crenshaw, I couldn't hear you. What did you say?"

"Is there anything you want to talk about?"

"I don't know. I think I'm just a little bit confused."

"Well, you know you can talk to me. Whatever we discuss will always be just between us."

"It's about your daughter, sir. I don't want to say anything to upset you."

"You've never said or done anything to upset me, except maybe keeping Tiffany out too late. But that was a long time ago."

"She promised she would be here for Christmas. She also told me she'd send a postcard to let me know how she's doing. I've spent the last seven months wondering if she's okay, waiting to hear something."

"Well, I can tell you she wanted to be here. And I sent your letters when I mailed her Christmas presents."

"Thanks," I said, looking down.

"Here, let me get her new address for you right now," he replied, jumping up out of his seat.

"Wait, I don't know if I want it, Mr. Crenshaw," I said in a low voice, not looking up.

"Steven, I understand that you're upset but please don't be mad at her. She needs you more than you know."

"How much of an influence can I be when I never see or hear from her anymore?"

"Through your letters. You can reach her through your letters."

I hung my head, thinking out loud, I said, "Sometimes I wonder if she even reads them."

He squatted down in front of me and said, "Of course she does. You know she does."

I looked up, staring him in the eye and asked, "Am I suppose to just move on with my life, Mr. Crenshaw?"

"Son, even if I was going to give you my opinion that is all it would be, just an opinion. But I can't answer that one for you. You're the only one who can decide what you want to do with your life."

"I'm sorry, I'm just upset. I've been looking forward to seeing her for a long time."

"Me, too."

"Thanks, Mr. Crenshaw."

"You should know by now that you're always welcomed here, whether Tiffany is home or not," he said, standing up, putting his hand on my shoulder.

I don't think he ever thought of how painful it was for me to be here, in her house, when she wasn't home. I politely made an excuse and quickly walked to the door. All I wanted to do was get in the car and drive. But he wouldn't let me leave before giving me her new address.

Hours passed as I drove around arguing with myself, trying to find some way to explain why she would break a promise. I had felt so much anticipation only to be let down again. When I came to the conclusion I couldn't take it anymore and I was done, I remembered her smile. Then my heart begged for forgiveness because I had decided to quit loving her.

On the way home, I stopped at the park and sat under the old oak tree. I pulled out her new address from my pocket and stared at it. That's when I knew I couldn't stop writing her even if I wanted to. To stop myself from loving her, from needing her, I would have to die.

Closing my eyes to say a prayer for us, raindrops began to fall. All of my memories about us began to flood my mind and I knew it was impossible to forget about her. I sat silently under the tree, thinking about the future, until the rain passed me by.

I left the park that evening as a different man. As I drove home, I felt stronger, much stronger than I'd ever felt before. Looking out my window, I saw the most amazing rainbows. There was one big bright one and another faint one above it. And as I witnessed their beauty, I knew that there was something beautiful about Tiffany and me too. And suddenly, I wasn't worried anymore.

After Christmas, I headed back to New York a day early and Linda came to pick me up from the airport. She hugged and kissed me and I tried my best to hide my true feelings. Despite the way I felt, I didn't want to be alone, so I accepted her offer to cook me dinner.

We sat down to eat but each time she tried to start a conversation I was unable to carry it. It felt so awkward to be here with her but there was a part of me that didn't want to be anywhere else. It wasn't Linda, it was me and deep inside I felt sorry for her. She had done nothing wrong, nothing to feel bad about but I could not pretend that I was okay.

"I'm sorry, I don't mean to be giving you the silent treatment."

"I was worried I had done something to upset you."

"No, you haven't. I guess it was just going home."

"Well, you're back here now so you can just leave all of that stuff behind and forget about it," she said, caressing my hand.

"That was delicious," I said, getting up to take our plates to the kitchen.

"Thanks. It's one of my grandmother's recipes," Linda said, following me.

I turned on the water and she started rubbing my back. I wanted her to stop; but it felt good. She gently began massaging my shoulders and I sat the plates down. I bent over slightly, so she could reach my neck. Her fingers dug deeper into the muscle as I told her how tense I had been feeling. She leaned forward and kissed the back of my neck, pulling my shirt up. I turned around to stop her but when I looked into her eyes, I didn't say a word. I closed my eyes and with all the sorrow I felt, kissed her. Then I kissed her with all the pain I felt. My head was spinning and my heart was hurting but I didn't want to stop kissing her.

"What's wrong, Steven," she asked, pulling away from me.

"Come here. I'll be gentle, I promise," I said, taking her into my arms.

"And what if I don't want you to be gentle?" she asked, kissing me harder.

I moved to lead her into the living room and we stumbled, falling onto the kitchen floor. We only laughed for a moment before starting to kiss again. We rolled over and she lay down on top of me. I closed my eyes trying not to think of Tiffany but knowing I wouldn't see her when I opened them was almost unbearable.

"I missed you, Steven," she said softly, unbuttoning my pants.

"I need you," I said, through lips that didn't feel like my own.

"I want you," she said kissing my stomach, getting up and reaching out her hands.

We walked down the hallway, to her bedroom and I closed the door behind us. We took off the rest of our clothes and got underneath the covers. I turned off the light then put my arms around her. Closing my eyes, for one split second I almost believed this was right. In the next moment, the truth came back and suddenly all I wanted was to go back to Mississippi and never, ever come to New York again.

Chapter 16

"**Y**ou got it, Tiffany!" Ron yelled, hanging up the phone.

"I got it? I got it!"

"You got it," he yelled, hugging me and picking me up off the floor. "I told you a long time ago, you got the look."

"Do I get to play Ruby?"

"You are Ruby. Look at you. You're perfect for that part. Where's the script?"

"It's in my room," I said, sitting down, overwhelmed by the news.

"Don't sit down, go get it," he said, pulling me up off the chair.

"I can't believe it. I'm going to play the lead part in Capturing Rainbows? Me? Tiffany Crenshaw?"

"Believe it, doll! I told you I'd make you a star. You didn't believe me, did you?" He asked, hugging me tightly.

"I believed you; I just didn't know I'd be this scared when it happened."

"We're wasting time. Go get the script so you can start practicing," he said, pushing me toward the hallway.

Everything was moving in slow motion as I walked off in a daze to my room. I couldn't believe I'd be working on my first movie in just a few weeks.

I knelt in front of my bed and thumbed through the pages. The name Ruby seemed to be on almost every page and I had to catch my breath. I held the script close to my heart and turned to look in the mirror. As I looked into my eyes, I could see the future. I wondered what Steven would think about me then. Will he be proud of me when I'm successful? But more importantly, will he think I made the right choice?

Chapter 17

Graduation day began just like any other day. The alarm bolted me out of sleep and onto the edge of the bed. I slowly stood up, went into the bathroom and took off my clothes. In the shower, the water ran down my body, bringing me back to life.

The shaving crème covered my three-day beard and I looked into my eyes. How I wish Tiffany could be here today. I wonder if she even realizes that I'm graduating and soon, I'll be back home.

Rubbing my face with aftershave, all I could think about were her beautiful blue eyes. I hoped that she was happy in California. And then I wished I were leaving New York to go there and be with her forever.

Once I was dressed, I headed over to the football stadium. From a distance, I could see all the caps and gowns, and then for the first time realized how important today is in the roadmap of life. Now, I'd be able to plan for the future and decide exactly what I wanted.

When they called out my name, I walked forward to receive my diploma. But to me, it felt like I was being released from prison. Because now, I was free to do whatever I wanted and go wherever I wanted to go.

The ceremony was over, as the caps flew up in the air. I quickly picked one up and started looking for my parents. There were so many people that I began to wonder if they were here then I saw them standing by the fence.

"We're so proud of you, Steven," Mom said loudly.

"I couldn't have done it without your help. Thanks Mom, thanks, Dad," I said, hugging my Mom and shaking my Dad's hand.

"What about me?" Blake asked.

"Thanks for all your help," I said sarcastically, shaking his hand and patting him on the back.

"Your grandparents are waiting for us over by the fence," Mom said.

"Let's go," I said, leading the way.

"Steven! Steven!"

"What are you doing here, Linda?" I asked, surprised to see her.

"I've been looking for you everywhere. I didn't think I'd find you," she answered, trying to catch her breath.

"I'm right here," I said awkwardly, as we hugged.

"This is my Mom and Dad. This is Tiff, oh my gosh. I'm sorry, Linda. Mom, Dad, this is Linda. And this is my brother, Blake."

"Hello Mr. and Mrs. Cross, it's nice to meet you."

"It's nice to meet you, Linda," Mom replied.

"Hi, Blake. It's nice to meet you, too."

"Hi, Li Li, Linda,"

"Linda would you like to go out to eat with us?" Mom asked quickly, trying to cover up Blake's rudeness.

"Sure, I'd love to," Linda replied politely.

We walked to the fence, with Linda trailing behind. When I looked back at her, she looked away, like she was upset. Then I almost felt angry that she'd come here knowing my family would be here.

"We're so proud of you, son. Come here and give me a hug. Your grandpa has something for you," Grandma whispered, after kissing my cheek.

"Thanks, Grandma."

"There's my engineer, grandson. I sure am going to miss your help on the farm this summer. Here, use this wisely," Grandfather said, shaking my hand and putting an envelope in the other.

"Mom and dad, this is Linda, she's Steven's friend. She's going to eat supper with us tonight," Mom said.

"Hello," Linda said shyly.

"Hello, Linda. Well, aren't you just the sweetest little thing," Grandma said, reaching out for Linda's hand like she'd known her all her life. They started talking and Grandma led her away.

"I guess that means it's time to go," Grandpa said, following Grandma and Linda toward the parking lot.

We sat down at the restaurant and Linda barely had a word to say. When we were almost finished with dinner Blake kicked me on the leg. I was about to say something when he gave me a funny look and moved his eyes. He stood up and I quickly stood up too.

"We'll be right back," I said, following him.

He opened the bathroom door and asked, "So, who's the new redhead?"

"Don't worry about her. Have you heard from Tiffany?"

"No, I haven't heard from Ti Tiff Tiffany," he said, laughing loudly, pointing at me.

"Man, I can't believe I blew it like that."

"I know. I almost busted a gut."

"Well, you didn't have to make it worse by stuttering her name. I don't know what I'm going to say to her tonight."

"Tell her the truth."

"Which is?"

"That you're only going out with her because she has red hair," he replied, giving me a funny look.

"That's not the truth. Linda and I have a lot in common."

"Yeah, like you live in the same apartment complex."

"Don't you ever have anything good to say?" I asked, looking in the mirror.

"I talked to Victoria."

I turned sharply, suddenly serious and asked, "What did she say?"

"She told me she went to California to spend a week with Tiffany. She said Tiffany has finally got some big part in a movie. The way Victoria talked about it; you would think it happened to her."

"What's the name of it?"

"Something about Rainbows, obviously a chick flick," he said, opening the door.

"Wait a minute," I said, taking him by the arm. "Did Victoria say anything else?"

"No, that's it."

"We were wondering what happened to you two," Dad said coming into the bathroom.

"We were just talking," I said, letting go of Blake's arm.

"And now it's my turn to talk you," he said, holding the door open for Blake.

"What is it, Dad?"

"Steven, I want you to know you can come home and stay as long as you like," dad said, putting his hand on my shoulder, looking me in the eyes.

94

"Thanks. I'll be coming home in a few weeks. I just have to pack my things and say goodbye to everybody."

"That's good, son. Your mother will be happy to hear the news," he said, walking out of the bathroom.

I started to follow him but remembered the envelope my Grandfather had given me earlier. I took it out of my coat pocket and opened it. There were two notes inside, one from him and one from my Grandmother. There was also a check for ten thousand dollars. I couldn't believe it, as I looked at all the zeros.

I left the restaurant that evening, with a newfound confidence. The fear of starting my life faded into excitement for the future. Piece by piece, I was putting together the puzzle of my life. Maybe, I'd have to work awhile till I figured out exactly where each piece fit but I finally knew that everything would be all right.

*****

After I moved back in with my family, I had a job a few days later. It was a starter position with pretty good pay and benefits. I had my Dad's connections to thank for it. So, all my efforts were concentrated on saving money for a house.

Linda had refused to speak to me before I left New York but I hardly think about it. When I'm not working, I go to the places where Tiffany and I use to go. The time I spend alone is consumed with thoughts of what she's doing now. Anytime I see someone we knew, I ask if they've heard from her. The only answer I ever receive is no.

So, just to hear about her I got in touch with Tiffany's dad. He told me she's doing fine and her movie, Capturing Rainbows, was the main topic of discussion.

Fall came around, right on time and I began to miss Tiffany even more. I don't know if it's because I thought she might come home for the holidays or just living in Natchez, where we fell in love. But the colder it gets and the longer I stay, my letters are becoming lengthy and my heart hopeful.

My love,
While lying in my old room at night, my thoughts turn to you. Sometimes, in my mind, I can bring you here, next to me. What fate is this, that has played a cruel trick on me? Certainly I wasn't given these feelings for it to end like this. My heart is a puzzle and only you have the missing piece. If I could put my arms around you now, I would never let you go.

95

The Letter

Oftentimes I wonder, what your life is like. Could you perhaps miss my love in the same way? I know the years have flown by and we are changing each day. Can you believe I have finally begun my career? As I begin mine, I know you are doing the same. I pray for your success and to see your name in lights someday.

The fear of living without you and never telling you I love you, is wearing my soul thin. When will I see you again? If passion leads you down the right road, then my soul demands that the words be told. I love you…and as I write these words, know it is in the purest way. I expect nothing from you; I already have what you gave. A feeling that most men will never share, a desire and longing that few would even dare to feel. I regret nothing, not even the pain. I know that all the love I give away, will certainly come back to me someday.

Did I tell you that I still see you here? Sometimes when I'm alone I can feel you near. When I feel that you are too far away, I drive out to the orchard, for a long stay. I go over the memories that you and I share. I know I am the richest man, whenever I'm there.

I hope you feel my heart's true meaning in these words. That no matter what happens, it is you that I cannot desert. I gather strength to carry on, because my love for you is that strong. At this point in my life, I can only live as if our future is almost in sight. I feel it so strongly; it's pointless to deny the truth, that you are where all of my journeys shall end.

Love forever,
Steven

Chapter 18

My suitcases sat by the door as I took a long look in the mirror. Would Steven see me differently now? Could I possibly be worth the risk of leaving everything behind? After all, I wouldn't be a burden to him now because I have enough money that we could go anywhere in the world to live. But as I looked at myself, Tiffany Crenshaw was all I could see. The same girl he left standing in the driveway so very long ago.

Reaching down for my bags, I decided it was time to see him. I had to go home. Only by looking in his eyes could I know the truth. And the truth, no matter what it is, will set me free.

"Hurry up, you're going to be late for your flight," Ron said, as I walked into the living room.

"My flight?"

"I'm not sure I want to go," he said, like he was too good to go to Natchez, Mississippi.

"I stayed here last year, with the promise I could go home for Christmas this year and I'm going with or without you," I said, dropping my bags at his feet.

"What do you have packed in your suitcase, bricks?" he asked, trying to pick them up.

"Just clothes and stuff."

"You're only going to be there for three days," he said, dragging them to the door.

"I guess that means you're not coming with me."

"I think it would be better if you made this trip by yourself."

I picked up my bags and walked out the door. Ron closed the door behind me as I walked toward the limo, never looking back. I wasn't going to let his attitude keep me from going home.

The closer I got to the airport, the more excited I felt. I would be home in just a few more hours. It had been so long since I'd been to Natchez and it would feel so good to be there again.

****

Dad picked me up from the airport and we talked about the movie all the way home. I gave him the complete behind the scenes scoop about my co-workers. He still talked about them like they're movie stars but I knew them differently now. And then I began to realize how much had changed since the last time I was here.

After Dad and I got home, it wasn't long before our conversation turned to the subject of Steven. Dad told me he was doing well and living at home with his parents. Even though I was surprised to hear it, I was so thankful he was still here. I excused myself and walked upstairs to my old room. As I sat down, I hoped the phone number hadn't changed because I still know his parent's number by heart.

"Hello."

"Hello, Steven. This is Tiffany."

"Tiffany."

"I just got here and I wanted to let you know."

"I can't believe it's you. I've been hoping you'd come home for Christmas."

"I'm finally here but only for three days," I said sadly.

"Three is the magic number."

"You always have a way of making everything seem better. That's one of the things I miss most about you."

"I went to see your movie."

"You got to see it!"

"Yes, you did a good job."

"Thanks, it changed my life forever."

"I know. You're a movie star now, Ms. Tiffany Starr."

"You can call me, Tiffany Love. Only my closest groupies get to do that."

"So I've been upgraded to the status of groupie?"

"No, actually I am going to crown you king, since I'm a queen now."

"How can you crown me king, when I'm already the King? Thank ya! Thank ya very much," he said, in his best Elvis impersonation.

"Wella, blessa my soul what's awrong with me. I can't seem to stand on my own two feet," I sang in my best impersonation.

"Does this mean that you'll be cutting your own album next?"

"Yes it does. Tiffany Starr sings Elvis' songs is what it'll be called," I said in a low baritone voice.

"Tell me Ms. Starr, what do you think Elvis would have to say about it if he could talk to you from heaven?" he asked, changing his voice to sound like a reporter.

"Well I believe, being in heaven, Elvis would bless me and be happy that I sang his songs," I said in a sweet Southern voice.

"Did we just regress about five years?"

"Yes, but didn't it feel so good?"

"I always enjoy talking to you Tiffany, and I guess I always will."

"It's a miracle to me that you still talk to me."

"What do you mean by that?"

"I've put a lot of things off because of my career. I feel like I let a lot of people down, but I didn't mean to."

"Are you talking about the postcard?"

"Yes. I'm sorry. You wouldn't believe how busy I've been."

"Don't worry about it. I just wonder sometimes if you want me to stop writing."

"No, I don't want you to stop."

He paused for a moment before saying, "Then I won't."

"When can I see you?"

"Whenever you want," he answered softly.

"Can you come over in an hour?"

"I'll be there."

"I'll be waiting for you." I said, not wanting to hang up.

"Okay, I'll be there."

"Okay, I'll be the redhead with blue eyes at the front door. Don't be late!"

"Are you kidding me?"

"Okay, bye, darling," I said slowly.

"Okay, bye."

I kept the phone to my ear, waiting to hear the click. "I don't want to hang up."

"Well you didn't hear me hanging up, did you?"

"Okay, we'll do it together. One, two, three."

I brushed my teeth, touched up my make-up and went downstairs. Dad had started dinner and was happy that Steven would join us tonight. I made myself a cup of hot chocolate and took a blanket to sit on the front porch. My emotions ran rampant as I thought of our past, remembering the good times and the bad.

And just like always, he was early. I sat my hot chocolate down and ran to his truck. I opened the door and my arms were around him before he could get out.

"I missed you," he said, hugging me tightly.

"Not as much as I missed you." We held each other close for what seemed like eternity, and then I asked, "Do you want to go inside now?"

"Yes, I do."

"Dad is cooking dinner," I said, taking his hand. We walked into the house and Dad was standing in the entryway.

"Steven, I'm so glad you came over. How are you, son?"

"I'm doing great, Mr. Crenshaw," I replied, shaking his hand. "How about you?"

"I couldn't be better, now that Tiffany is home."

"Yes, she does have a way of making everything better," Steven said, looking at me then taking my hand as we walked to the kitchen.

"I feel better just being here with both of you," I said, reaching over to take my Dad's hand.

"Thank you God for blessing us," my Dad said looking up to the ceiling.

"Are you praying, Dad?"

"No baby, just being thankful."

"We have a lot to be thankful for, Mr. Crenshaw."

"I know I am thankful for you," I said kissing Steven's cheek, "And I am thankful for you," I said kissing Dad's cheek.

I sat down, listening to the two of them talk. They got along so well and I wondered why I'd never noticed it before.

Steven's looks had changed since the last time we saw each other. His shoulders are broader and his arms are bigger. I couldn't resist asking, "Where did you get all those muscles?"

"I started lifting weights again. It really helps to relieve stress," he said, turning to look at me.

"Do you remember when we use to lift weights together?"

"Yes. I think about you sometimes when I'm working out," he said, walking over to stand in front of me.

"I need to start doing something like that, I'm not getting any younger," I said, reaching out, touching his arm.

"No, but you are getting more beautiful."

"Thank you, Steven. And may I say that you are becoming more handsome each time I see you."

"I don't believe it, but you can say it anyway."

Dad seemed uneasy with all the compliments so he interrupted, asking Steven and I if we would set the table for dinner.

Chapter 19

After dinner, Tiffany and I drove to the park. We tried to make small talk about the movie but there were long awkward moments of silence.

Finally, I reached out for her hand, looking into her eyes. She only looked at me for a second and turned away, looking out the window. I let go of her hand and rolled down the window, feeling the coldness of winter, I quickly rolled it back up.

A few moments later, I tried to catch her eyes again but she looked right past me, saying, "Hey, there's our old oak tree."

"Sometimes, I come here just to sit under that ole' tree."

"Do you think about me?"

"How could I not think about you?" I asked, leaning closer.

"You did tell me you loved me under that tree."

"Yes, and you told me the same," I said as I was drawn to her lips.

"We can't do this," she said softly, turning away.

"Why?"

"Let's go to my house. Dad will probably be asleep by now."

"Are you sure?"

"Yes, I've waited too long for this. I don't want to wait any longer," she said pulling me close and kissing me passionately.

We drove to her house and walked inside hand in hand. Her dad was asleep in his recliner, so we sneaked past him into Tiffany's old room. It was exactly the way I remembered and it felt strange to be here.

Tiffany excused herself to go to the bathroom, taking off her shirt as she walked away. As I watched her, I realized where I was and what was happening. In a few minutes I would be making love to Tiffany, the girl I've been in love with my whole life. To every other man who had seen her movie, this moment was a fantasy that they could only dream of. Somehow, it made me more excited to know I would be the envy of thousands of men tonight.

Tiffany called me into the bathroom as she stepped into the shower. I pulled my shirt off and threw it on the chair. The steam from the shower was rising as I walked into the bathroom.

Tiffany opened the shower door, peeping out and asked, "Are you going to get in?"

"Let me get undressed."

She closed the door and I unzipped my pants. As they fell to the floor, I could feel the blood rushing through my veins. I took a deep breath and looked at Tiffany's body through the glass. I was visibly shaking as I slid my underwear down my legs. I opened the shower door and stepped in.

Tiffany opened her arms and pulled me close. We turned around together so I was shielding her from the water with my body. I closed my eyes and kissed her like she was mine. She returned my kiss with more passion and desire than I had ever felt. I wanted her so badly that I wished there was a way I could be under her skin. The thought of my body being inside of Tiffany's was the oddest fantasy. But unbelievably even the thought of it thrilled me.

She stopped to look at me, asking, "What are you thinking about?"

"Crazy stuff, like wanting to be under your skin."

"Will you wash my back?" she asked, handing me a washcloth.

"I would do anything you ask."

"That's good to know," she said leaning forward, arching her back.

"You should already know that."

"You'll have to forgive me if everyday life overshadows my memory," she said, suddenly sad.

"That's why we have to keep making new memories."

She turned to rinse off and I watched as the water ran down her body. Tiffany closed her eyes and tilted her head back. Long red hair fell over slender shoulders laying down straight on her chest. At that moment, I think I could've stayed and watched her bathe for the rest of my life.

Tiffany turned the showerhead and handed me a washcloth. I took the soap and lathered the cloth until it was dripping with suds. She took it from my hand and started washing my neck. In a gentle circular motion, she worked her way slowly down my body. No one had ever bathed me before and I must admit I was nervous. Feeling her fingertips on the edges of the washcloth made chills run down my spine. When she had finished with the front of my body she turned me around to wash my back. I closed my eyes and put my hands on the wall in front of me.

We rinsed each other off and quickly got out of the shower. Tiffany handed me a towel and I started to dry her body. She bent over, picked up another towel and started drying my legs. We both got in each other's way and laughed at ourselves. Then she ran to the bed, still very wet and fell back onto it.

"You didn't let me finish what I started," I said, wrapping the towel around my waist.

"Come over here and I'll let you finish."

As I walked to her bed, I felt so excited. But when I kneeled in front of her, I suddenly felt serious. Kissing her toes as she giggled, I moved slowly to her ankles. Working my way up, I stopped at her knees, paying extra attention to the inside. Then I kissed my way up her entire body until my lips were touching hers.

We began to kiss and make love with a fury unknown to man. We were no longer Tiffany and Steven; at that exact moment, we had become one person. As the fire between us grew, she titled her head back and closed her pretty blue eyes.

I stopped immediately and said, "Look at me, Tiffany." She opened her eyes and moved her head to look directly into my eyes.

"I missed you," she said sadly.

"I missed you more than you'll ever know."

"Don't stop," she said, closing her eyes to kiss my lips.

"Don't close your eyes. I want to see them."

We were lost, as if in a trance, as we looked deep into each other's eyes. As we made love, I could see the whole world in blue. I saw my past, I could see the present and I looked for the future. Our children were there and our life together as husband and wife. My heart belonged with her and I knew I would go on loving her, forever. I could even see us with gray hair and Tiffany would still be the most beautiful woman in the world to me.

We fell asleep in each other's arms, talking about all the things we wanted to do while she was here. I felt so close to her and I wondered why couldn't we be together all the time?

*****

"Wake up, Steven. I think my dad is awake," Tiffany whispered, shaking me.

"Oh shit," I whispered, sliding off the bed onto the floor.

"Be quiet," she said, putting her finger over her lips, walking to the door.

She tiptoed back, knelt down beside me and I asked, "Did you see him?"

"No, but I heard him."

"What do you want me to do?"

"I want you to climb out the window and down the drainpipe. Then I want you to put your truck in neutral and push it out of the driveway. Then just roll down the hill a little ways before you start the engine," she said, laughing.

"Shhh, you're going to get us busted," I whispered, trying not to laugh.

"We've already been caught."

"You are so bad, come here," I said pulling her onto my lap.

"I haven't been that bad."

"Tell me what you want for Christmas. It's Christmas Eve and if you want Santa to get you something, you better tell him now."

"I want, I want, I want you."

"You have me. You always have," I said, seriously.

"That's good, because I need you," she said, looking into my eyes as we heard a knock at the door. "Yes?"

"Tiffany?"

"Yes, Dad?"

"Do you and Steven want some breakfast?"

We both started laughing and she said, "Yes, we'll be down in a minute."

After breakfast I went to the mall. Everything I saw, I wanted to buy for her but I had to remember what I'd been working so hard to save for. Instead, I chose to buy a heart shaped ruby ring in honor of her recent success. Then I spotted a big pink teddy bear that I just had to get.

I pulled into the driveway and Tiffany ran outside. She opened my door and was in my arms before I could get out.

"I was getting worried about you."

"I'm sorry, it took longer than I thought," I said, gathering the shopping bags.

"Give me a kiss."

"Come here," I said, dropping the bags, kissing her softly.

"What did you buy?" she asked, bending over to look.

"Some new clothes," I said, pushing the bags away with my foot.

"What else?"

"Don't look!"

"Come on, Dad's cooking dinner," she said as we walked toward the house.

"Well, you made it back alive. You're a brave man to go to the mall on Christmas Eve. Do you need some help with your bags?"

"No thanks, Mr. Crenshaw," I said, walking to the stairs.

"I'll come help you," Tiffany said following me.

She stood in the doorway watching me put the bags in her closet. Looking over my shoulder, I said, "I want to tell you something important, baby. Can we sit down for a minute?"

"Come over here and sit on the bed."

"I know we haven't talked much about you and L.A."

"I work all the time. That's my life in California."

"Do you remember when you told me you wanted to buy a house out there?"

"Yes, I remember."

"Well, my grandparents gave me some money when I graduated from college. I added it to the money I already had and I've been working steadily ever since I moved back home. I've managed to save twenty-one thousand dollars. That's more than enough to make a good down payment on a house."

"I have plenty of money, Steven. I'm still living with Ron because I need him right now. You see, in Hollywood, it's all about who you know and who they know. It's fifty times worse than any clique you could ever imagine in high school. If I leave now, I may lose my career. There is nothing-sexual going on between us. You do know that, don't you?"

"No Tiffany, I didn't know anything," I said, feeling the rain pounding down on my parade.

"He worked really hard to get me the role of Ruby. And I do owe Ron something because he's the reason I'm where I'm at in my career. When I didn't want to go anymore, he pushed me. When I didn't think I could do it, he pushed me harder. When I didn't think it would ever happen, Ron made it happen. Do you know how he did that, Steven?"

"No, I don't."

"He did it by talking to the most influential people in the movie business. He didn't just say it once. He would tell them over and over again. Ron would talk to his friends, his enemies, and anyone who would give him the time of day. Now if he made me a star by talking good about me, what would happen if I walked out on him right now?"

"I guess he would say bad things about you."

"That's right. Then I'd never be able to work in that town again."

I could hear Ron's words coming out of her mouth. It sounded like she was reciting a line out of a bad movie. I was stunned that she truly believed Ron's big bully act. To look at Tiffany, she appeared to be a wise and worldly woman. To know Tiffany, was to know she was a child, in a world where she shouldn't be alone. I wanted to tell her Ron was a liar but I knew she would have to find that out for herself.

When it was time for Tiffany to return to California, my happiness turned to sadness. How could one person bring so much joy and take away even more when they leave? I could tell Mr. Crenshaw had to hide his feelings too. Both of us could see the invisible wings that Tiffany did not know she had. We wanted to tie them down, but she would have certainly died if we did.

As we walked into the airport, I thought of begging her to stay then I realized how selfish that would be. I wanted her to give up everything she'd worked so hard for, for what? I had nothing to offer her, nothing to bargain with. The only good reason I have, is that I love her.

My heart was breaking as she let go of my hand and said, "Steven, I want to thank you for something."

"What's that?"

"For spending Christmas with me. I haven't been this happy in a long, long time."

"It's been my pleasure."

She stopped, turning to face me, saying, "I also want you to know, I'll buy a house soon. Then I want you to come and stay with me. Will you do that?"

"You know I will, Love," I said, kissing her softly.

"Are you ready to walk me to the gate?"

"Not really."

"I know, I can't believe I'm leaving already," she said, taking my hand as we walked down the corridor.

"I know. You just got here, but in another way it feels like we spent a lifetime together."

"It's always been that way with you and me. Every time we see each other we just pick up right where we left off. Like yesterday was the last time we saw each other. Do you know what I mean?"

"Yes I do, but time is passing us by. You are so busy you probably don't feel it like I do. All I know is life is short."

"It is not that short, Steven."

"It's shorter than you think, Tiffany. We're not getting any younger," I said, trying to make her understand how much I needed her.

"This is my gate."

"And it's time for you to go. I'll miss you," I said, pulling her close.

"Whenever you have that feeling of missing me, know that I'm feeling the same way about you. Okay?"

I nodded my head but I could feel tears in my eyes. She stared into my eyes then kissed me gently. We didn't care if anyone was watching. Every person in the airport was invisible to us. In my mind, Tiffany and I were the only ones there. Then a strange man tapped her on the shoulder asking if she was Tiffany Starr.

She turned around, smiling and said, "Yes, yes I am."

"Can I have your autograph?"

"Sure."

She turned around and smiled this strange smile then turned back around. Several other people came over to see what was happening and I stepped back, while she signed autographs. It wasn't but a few minutes and then we heard the final boarding call. She turned her back to the crowd, ignoring everyone and apologized. I just smiled and took her in my arms, turning her back to the wall. We hugged until the last second and kissed one more time before she walked away.

Chapter 20

When I arrived in Los Angeles, Ron was at the airport to pick me up. He had fantastic news, as far as he was concerned. A director named Alan Johnson had talked to him about an upcoming film he was doing and he had already chosen my next role.

When he had spoken his name my heart skipped a beat. Could it be the same Alan Johnson I had known before we moved to Natchez? The boy who gave me my first kiss and I went out on my first date with? It couldn't be, it had to be someone else with the same name.

The name of my character was Sophia and of course, Ron thought I was made for the part. He said that Betrayal In Paradise would be the perfect movie to further my career. Filming would begin in Hawaii in two weeks and that was the only part of his news that sounded good. I wanted to go back to work immediately so I wouldn't have time to think about the last three days in Mississippi.

As we walked out of the airport, I was recognized by a group of men. They started following us, calling out my name and I turned to smile. Ron grabbed me by the arm and started walking very fast.

"Let go, Ron. You're hurting me!"

"I've got to get you in the car before someone hurts you," Ron said, half pulling, half dragging me.

"If you're in that big of a hurry, let's run," I said, extremely upset. Ron ran behind me, out to the limo and the driver opened the door.

"James, go and get Ms. Starr's luggage," he gasped.

"Yes, sir."

Ron reached over, locked the doors and we sat there looking at each other. He could see the anger in my eyes so he smiled, trying to smooth everything over. I didn't return his smile; instead, I turned away.

"Did you have a good time?" he asked, sarcastically.

"Yes," I answered, quietly.

"Then what's wrong?"

"Nothing...and everything."

"This is exactly why I didn't want you to go. If I'd known it was going to make you this upset, I would have demanded that you stay here."

We sat in complete silence during the drive to his house. The second we walked through the door, I wanted to leave. I wanted to go back to Mississippi. I needed nothing, except to be in Steven's arms again.

Instead, I went to my room and read the entire script for Betrayal In Paradise. Even though Sophia wasn't a role I would have picked, I was glad to be leaving soon for Hawaii.

The next day I awoke, still fully dressed, with the script lying beside me. Jumping out of bed, I quickly got ready to go. I was going to see Alan Johnson today, and then I would know if it was my Alan or just a coincidence. Regardless, I had to go sign the paperwork and discuss his plans for the movie.

I arrived at his office early but he asked to see me right away. I walked in and instantly knew it was the boy I had always called my first love. Only he wasn't a boy any longer. Alan had grown into a very handsome man and by the looks of things a very accomplished man. We talked for over an hour about everything. We talked about Natchez, we talked about our childhood home, Santa Maria, and we talked about us.

Then we finally got down to the details of how he wanted the movie to look, the thoughts I had on Sophia and my life with Ron. Before I left, he asked me to go to lunch and I couldn't refuse.

He took me to a famous Italian restaurant named Culina and I couldn't help but feel special. Everyone knew him, from the most famous movie stars, down to the busboys. Alan was so nice, speaking to every person who spoke to him. He was not bothered by their interruptions, and was proud to introduce me. I met more influential people in those couple of hours than through all the parties Ron had dragged me to.

The next two weeks, all I did was practice my lines for Betrayal in Paradise day and night. I looked forward to working with Alan and seeing him again. Ron and I barely spoke to one another during that time. The day before I was leaving for Hawaii he barged into my room without knocking.

"You got a letter today," he said, throwing it down on the bed beside me.

Ron stomped out, slamming the door and I realized my letter was already opened. I went into the bathroom, closing the door. I got into the empty tub and quietly read it aloud to myself.

My other self,

I could feel my heart fly away as I watched you take flight. I am blind once again, for without you; there is no light. Why must I live without you? My Beloved, are we silly fools? I feel your hand as if it were within my soul, and no other hand can I hold. I live without you, through blacken days and endless nights. When will I look in your eyes again?

I had a taste of our happiness, a rare moment in the sun. I was lost in your embrace my darling, as we became one. My only true love, there is no direction without you. And in what new way can I tell you, that we should never be apart? The voices I hear deep within my soul, tell me we cheated the story to be told. I am lost in a cold world without your love. It is a narrow and hideous world that I am imprisoned in. Won't you unlock the door my love and let your beloved come in?

I fear that I will die and you will never truly know me. I wish I could tell you, but it is something that I have to show. If I ever am to go, please know eternally, you are my everything.

Love forever,
Steven

Chapter 21

When Mr. Crenshaw called and asked for help with his yard, I immediately said yes. Any chance I had to find out about Tiffany, I took it. He was raking leaves when I pulled into the driveway. He dropped the rake and waved as I got out of the truck.

"There you are, Steven."

"Hello, Mr. Crenshaw."

"Thanks for coming over," he said, shaking my hand.

"No problem. What do you want me to do?"

"Let's go inside so I can get something to drink and talk for a minute," he said, walking toward the house. "I can't believe how fast spring got here this year. Look at how tall that grass is already."

"I know, time flies when you work as much as I do."

"How many hours are you working?" he asked, opening the door.

"At least fifty, sometimes up to seventy or eighty."

"What are you planning on doing with all of that money?"

"I plan on buying a house."

"Where are you planning on buying?" he asked, pouring a glass of tea.

"A long time ago, Tiffany and I talked about buying one in California. But I've been looking around here."

"Have you found any you like?" he asked, sitting down at the table.

"Yes, I've seen a few. One of them is over on Third Street."

"Well that would be nice. Then you'd be closer to me."

"Mr. Crenshaw, have you talked to Tiffany lately?"

"Yes, she's still in Hawaii working."

I waited a moment, feeling nervous then asked, "Does she seem to be happy?"

"She seems to be fine, son. Don't worry so much. She actually seems a lot happier since she isn't living with Ron."

"Yes, but she'll be back there soon."

"No, Steven. She isn't going back to his house," he said, seriously.

"Where is she going to live?"

He took a deep breath before saying, "She and the director of this movie have grown really close. Tiffany told me she's going to stay with him when they finish filming."

"What's his name?"

"It's nothing to get upset about, son. She said it's just a business relationship. She just doesn't want to live with Ron anymore, that's all. "

"What's his name, Mr. Crenshaw?"

"Alan, Alan Johnson. He's a director, oh yeah, I already told you that."

I stood up, asking, "How could she just decide to move in with somebody else? Wait a minute. Did you say his name is Alan Johnson?"

"Yes, I did. Just try to understand that Tiffany is doing the best she can. It's not easy to do what she's doing."

"But there are things we talked about that you don't know," I replied, looking down at him.

He stood up and said, "Ron read one of your letters, he won't even speak to her anymore. I think she's going to stay at Alan's just until she buys her own house."

"Did Ron do anything to hurt her?" I asked, suddenly struck with guilt.

"No, nothing like that happened. I don't think he even knows she's not coming back to live with him. Tiffany just took everything she could before she left for Hawaii," he said sadly, sitting back down, hanging his head.

"How do you feel about it?"

He looked up, saying, "I'd rather she come home but I feel a lot better knowing she is staying with someone we know."

"What do you think I should do?"

"About the house?"

"Yes, about the house," I lied.

"Why don't we ride over there and take a look at it."

"Sure, let's go. It's just around the block," I said, pulling the keys out of my pocket.

I tried to act normal but he could tell I was upset over the news. We looked at the wooden frame house, situated in an old subdivision. There were two bedrooms, one bath and an office. It needed a lot of repairs but nothing I couldn't handle. The front porch was the main reason it had caught my eye in the first place. I envisioned Tiffany, sitting beside me in a swing, drinking ice tea on a hot summer's day.

Mr. Crenshaw told me I should buy it because it was perfect for my needs and the price was right. Regardless of his opinion, I wasn't going to make a decision until I knew what Tiffany was going to do. Besides, how could I buy a house here when she lived clear across the country?

****

It was the middle of summer before I went to see her dad again. I could have never expected the news he would give me on that hot day in July. Tiffany was engaged to her old boyfriend, Alan Johnson. I could hardly believe what he had just told me as my emotions ran wild.

Mr. Crenshaw was visibly shocked and upset by the news too so I kept most of my thoughts to myself. Before I left, I had to ask him if he thought I should continue to send Tiffany letters. Mr. Crenshaw didn't say a word. He just got up and wrote down the new address.

I drove down the road toward home, feeling like I was falling apart. I almost started to scream, but instead turned the truck around and went over to Third Street. The little house Mr. Crenshaw and I went to look at, surprisingly, was still for sale. I got out, pulled the For Sale sign out of the ground and put it in the back of my truck.

Chapter 22

The butler summoned me to the white room and I followed him, reluctantly, through the enormous house and stepped aside as he opened both doors. The white marble floors shined brightly under the artificial light.

Alan loved this room but it always made me feel uncomfortable. When I walked in, he waited a moment before turning to watch me walk toward him. His frown slowly changed to a smile and I smiled back. He sat down on a white leather sofa and beckoned me to sit beside him with the pat of his hand. He poured a glass of champagne and handed it to me.

Our conversation started out with the normal questions. How was your day? What are your plans for tomorrow? Nothing too important just small talk. Then the mood changed and our conversation turned to marriage again.

"I just want a definite date from you, Tiffany. Is that too much to ask?" Alan demanded.

"No, it's not."

"August and September have come and gone. Now it's October and we still don't have our wedding date set."

"It's just that we don't want the same things."

"I've had all the fuss before. Believe me, it's not all it's cracked up to be," he said sarcastically.

"You've had your perfect wedding, so why shouldn't I have mine?"

"Is it the fact that I've been married before that's bothering you?" he asked, completely ignoring my question.

"No. I think you're not listening to what I'm saying."

"Okay, maybe you're right. Let's compromise on this deal. I get Vegas and you get the white dress. You get your dad and I choose not to have a huge crowd. We both get the reception, and I get the first dance with the bride."

"I guess that kind of sounds fair. Can I decide where to go on our honeymoon?"

"Yes Love, we can go anywhere you want. You name the place and we're there," he offered, kneeling before me.

"I want to go to Italy."

"That's such a long flight. Why don't you pick some place closer, darling?" he asked, standing up and walking over to fix another drink.

"I have picked it, Alan! Were you even listening to a word I said?"

"Italy it is. But I still have to have a date for my assistant, Sarah, to book the flight," he said, rhythmically.

I dug through a side table drawer pulling out a small calendar. I looked at November, but it was just too soon. I flipped over to December and felt so weak inside that I had to sit down.

He looked over my shoulder and asked, "December the seventh?"

"The seventh sounds good to me," I whispered.

"That will give us plenty of time to get everything prepared. When do you want to go shopping for a dress?"

"Tomorrow," I said solemnly.

"I tell you what. I'll have Sarah call a few shops and let them bring the dresses to you. Can you be at home tomorrow at two?" he asked with enthusiasm.

"Yes, I can be here at two."

"What else do we need? Let's see, we need invitations, and flowers, and.... "

"I don't know, Alan."

"Sarah can tell me what we need. Don't you worry about a thing, beautiful. I have complete confidence in her, she won't let us down," he said, kissing me on the forehead.

"I'm not worried."

"Then tell me, why the long face?"

"I don't feel very well. I think I'll go upstairs to my room and lay down."

"Okay, Love, I'll start on the wedding plans and you can look them over later. December seventh?"

"December seventh," I said over my shoulder, walking out of the room.

116

As I walked up the stairs, my heart felt a sickness I had never experienced. Trying to push the thought out of my mind that I was making a big mistake was almost impossible. But I tried to think of what the future would hold for me if I became Mrs. Alan Johnson.

As soon as my head hit the pillow all I wanted to do was fall asleep. But no matter how I tried, sleep would not come. I finally got out of bed at three-thirty in the morning and opened the wooden box Victoria had given me. I took out Steven's last letter and reread it by candlelight.

My sweetheart,

I can only think the days have been kind to you since I saw you last. Now that summer is gone, I prepare myself for winter. My house, which is your house, is coming along just fine. If you ever need a place to go, then you have mine.

I know you will exchange your wedding vows all too soon. I long to be there with you on your special day. I ask God, but get no answer. I guess he wanted it that way.

I wish for you happiness and a love like you never knew. I demand this man give you kindness and devotion that is true. I never, no never, will forget your beautiful face. I may slip behind, but I will surely pick up the pace.

I saw that the role of Sophia won you an award. When I found out about it, I felt immense joy. Me? Well, I'm just fine. I go out more often, and I work all the time.

No, not a day passes that you are not in my heart. I see you clearly as we slowly drift apart. But Tiffany, I want you to know, no matter what, I am here to stay. You will never have to worry about me going away.

Take good care of yourself, Love; no one else can do it like you. If upon a chance, you ever need me, know that I am never too far away from you.

Forever,
Steven

Chapter 23

Everyday blended into the next but they all felt the same. Tiffany was too far away from me, engaged to a man I didn't even know. My thoughts were consumed with questions. Is she happy? Does she love him? Could I stop this from happening? Does she even think about me anymore?

These days, work was the only distraction from reality. On my day off, I usually sat on the porch, just thinking. And it never failed, somebody always showed up, uninvited. Deep down inside, I knew it was because they cared but all I wanted was to be alone.

"Hey, Steven. When are you going to clean up your yard?" Brad asked sarcastically, kicking a pinecone across the grass.

"Whenever I feel like it."

"Come on, man. I can't believe you're still hung up on that girl. It's past time for you to start thinking of reality."

"I am thinking of reality."

"I don't think you are, buddy. Now, here's the scenario. Guy meets girl, girl likes guy, they like each other. Guy moves to college, girl becomes a party queen, but they still have the hots for each other. Girl gets big movie deal. Guy gets a degree in engineering. Do you see where the paths took different directions?"

"You just have this all figured out, don't you, wise guy?" I asked, standing up.

"Yes, I do. Do you want me to tell you how their story ends?"

"No. I want you to tell me how the guy gets the girl not to marry her old boyfriend?" I asked, not wanting to hear Brad's ending to our story.

"Here again the picture isn't good. Let's see, rich director, middle class engineer. On one hand you have Hollywood, and the other nowhereville. Let me see, money and power or surviving and love. Most girls I know would choose the rich guy."

"So you're telling me to give up?"

"I'm telling you that you should've already given up!" He exclaimed, right in my face.

"Just for the record, Brad. How many long term relationships have you been in?" I asked seriously, staring at him.

"None," he said, looking away.

"Then I move, your honor, to strike the witness's testimony as uneducated and inexperienced," I turned and said, trying to lesson the tension.

"Well as inexperienced and uneducated as it is, it's the truth your honor and I therefore request that it not be stricken from the record," he said to the invisible judge.

"The truth hurts, Brad."

"That's what they make beer for, man. Are you ready for another one?" he asked, opening the ice chest, trying to lighten the atmosphere.

"Hand it to me. What are you going to do tonight?" I asked, hoping he had other plans.

"There's a party at Susie's house. Now that's one hot babe I'd love to go out with."

"She's too cold-hearted for me."

"Hey, what about her friend Angela? I saw a little something going on between the two of you the other night," he said, in a strange voice.

"What you saw were two drunken people holding each other up."

"What about your ex, Amber? She's still looking good."

"After the way she treated Tiffany, I can barely stand to talk to that girl."

"Well, what about Cindy? She always had a crush on you."

"I know, but I just can't do it, man. I'm still hoping Tiffany will come to her senses before she marries Alan."

"Even if you sleep with all of them, she'd never know."

"But I would."

"If I had your conscience, I could keep myself out of trouble."

"It's not hard to have a conscience when you're in love, Brad. Just wait till it happens to you," I said, looking over at him.

"I don't ever want to fall in love if it means going through what you've been through. Hell, totaling my truck would be less painful," he said, laughing.

"Yeah, but wrecking the truck is only half of it. Think about when you buy the truck, it's all brand new and shiny. Let's not forget about what a thrill it is to go for your first ride. Tell me you're not driving down the street with a big ole' smile on your face. Now over the years, there might be a need for some repairs but you wouldn't just let some old geezer walk up and drive your truck away. Would you?"

"Now you do have a point, sir. Me? I'd just let that old truck go. Then I'd call my truck dealer and ask him to deliver a brand new one."

"Every man has a different solution for every problem."

"What kind of solution do you have? Just wait around forever for her to come back to this town? She's been outta here since the first chance she got and she's never coming back, man. Do you really think she'd be marrying this guy if she didn't want to?" Brad asked, suddenly upset.

"I don't know what to do. I do know she lived with Ron when she really didn't want to. Maybe she's doing the same thing with Alan. I wish I knew more about the man and I could give you an honest answer."

"Is she coming home for Christmas this year?" he asked, sitting down.

"I don't know, I doubt it."

"All I know is whether she's here or not, we're going to party like its nineteen-ninety-nine," he said, snapping his fingers and smiling. "Hey, why don't we have a party here, at your house?"

"Why not? I probably won't be doing anything else."

"Cool! I'll start spreading the word. We'll have the biggest blow out this little town has ever seen. I bet Jimmy and his band would come over and play for free…"

Brad went on and on about the party but I could barely hear him because I was consumed by my own thoughts. I think he thought if I started dating someone else I'd forget about Tiffany. But if that were the solution it would have happened when I was with Linda.

All I wanted was to see her, not have a party. I didn't want to hear a band. I wanted to hear her voice. I didn't want to be here. I wanted to be wherever she was at.

Chapter 24

"Ruby! Look Momma, it's Ruby."

The little girl pulled on my dress, looking up at me. I looked down, saying, "Hello, sweetheart."

"I can't believe it's you. It is you?" her mother asked.

"Yes," I said, pulling down my sunglasses.

"I love your movies."

"Thank you. Come here, sweetheart. My, you are such a big girl," I said, picking her up.

"I love you, Ruby."

The little girl kissed my cheek and looked at me with big brown eyes. I was disconnected from reality, when the child spoke those words to me. It wasn't because she had my name wrong. It had just been so long time since I'd heard those words from another person, who meant what they said.

"Are you okay?"

"What?"

"I'll take her now," her mother said.

The woman must have seen the pain in my eyes as she reached for her daughter. I hesitated before letting her go, not knowing why. In those moments, I longed for the family I could have had, if my choices had been different.

"It was nice to meet you, Ms. Starr."

"Nice to meet you too."

I could hear the little girl calling out my character name as they walked away. At first she was saying it loudly and then she was screaming it as loud as she could.

I turned around and even though they were far away I could still see her. She had her arms stretched out over her mother's shoulder in my direction. I stood there and watched, until I couldn't hear the child anymore. Then I walked out to my limo and got in for the long ride home.

"Why are you late?" Alan asked as I walked inside the house.

"I didn't know I was late," I said, taking off my coat and shoes.

"Why do you do that? You know I can't stand it when you're a slob."

"Please don't start on me the minute I walk through the door."

"Well, if you would grow up and act your age, then I wouldn't have to."

"I have a father, Alan. I don't need you to tell me what to do?"

"I'm just trying to help you become a better person," he said, opening the closet door.

"We have servants to do that kind of stuff."

"Since I married you, I've become the servant," he said, under his breath.

"I heard that," I said, walking across the room.

"Well, since we got married it's almost like you haven't learned a damn thing."

"How can you say that? I've worked my butt off since the day I said I do to you. If I can't leave my shoes and coat at my own front door, then maybe I need to find a new place to live," I said, walking up the stairs.

"If you leave me, I'll ruin your name in this town. You won't be able to get a part in a commercial!" he yelled, running up the stairs, grabbing me.

"Don't touch me, you bastard!"

"I'll touch you whenever I want to. You are my wife, aren't you?"

"Unfortunately."

"You should be thanking your lucky stars that I married you. You would be nothing, if it wasn't for me."

I turned to face him and couldn't resist saying, "I have made you more money in the last year than you've made in your entire miserable life."

"You ungrateful, bitch!" Alan yelled, slapping me across the face.

I fell down on the step, hanging on to the rail, as I slid down.

"Look at you. You'd be nothing without me."

He walked past me, up the stairs, without another word. The real Alan had just shed his disguise. Now I finally understood why he frightened me sometimes.

As one of the maids came down the stairs, she stopped and looked back to see if he was watching. "Come on, Ms. Tiffany. Come with me," she whispered.

Ms. Hattie took me to her room and I lay down on the bed. She wiped away my tears, telling me everything would be okay. I cried for a long time as she hummed Amazing Grace and stroked my hair gently.

"Why do you think Alan hates me so much?"

"Child, I don't think he likes himself very much. When you don't like yourself, it's hard to like anybody else."

"You've known Alan for a while now, Ms. Hattie. Was he this mean to his first wife or is it just me?"

"No honey, things were real bad between them two. Worse than anything he's ever done to you. Whenever he would try to lay his hands on her, she would give it right back to him. Some nights, I didn't get to sleep at all because of all the fussing and fighting that went on. That woman loved to drink. The more she'd drink the meaner she'd get, but she was never meaner than Mr. Johnson. Then late one night, well actually it was early in the morning, she left him. I haven't heard from her or seen her since."

"I didn't know that. He only told me her name was Jenny and that she left him for another man."

"I doubt that. What's weird is you and her look so much alike that it's strange sometimes. You'll be walking down the hallway and I'll catch just a glimpse of you and I'll think for a second, Ms. Jenny is home. Then I have to remind myself that it's you."

"Does anybody know where she is now?"

"No honey, nobody knows where she is. She didn't even take her clothes or any of her belongings."

"You didn't ask what happened to her?"

"Nooooo, I can't ask questions like that. It's none of my business. I could get fired if I ask one wrong question of that man."

"Thanks for helping me, Ms. Hattie. I really appreciate it."

"Well now you know where my room is, Ms. Tiffany. You can come here any time you need me."

"Thank you. If there's anything you ever need, don't hesitate to ask. Okay?"

"I'll remember that."

From that night forward, I secretly planned my escape. Everything Alan wanted me to do; I did with a smile on my face. And I worked as much as I possibly could to stay away from him. But still, I constantly wondered what happened to Jenny. Of course, I dared not try and investigate. I couldn't even sneeze in this town without him knowing about it.

Chapter 25

The winter was spent mostly alone, trying to get myself together. The party life had made me neglect my work, my house and everyone else, including me so it had to come to an end. So instead of partying I began to read a lot of books and went for very long walks in the park.

Spring came with the bloom of the daffodils, making me long for Tiffany and wishing I had made different choices. Every where I went, I could still see her, no matter the fact she was married or how far away she was. I would see her in other people's faces, when there was some aspect of them that reminded me of her. Sometimes I heard her voice when I was in a crowd, turning to look; I would realize she wasn't there.

When the days started to get hot, Brad started dropping by after work. And now that Blake was home from college, he spent most of his time at my house, too. Before I realized what was happening, we fell into our old routine again. I worked all day and partied all night. I guess the truth was I didn't have anything better to do with my time.

Brad made plans for us to go swimming this weekend and I didn't really care what we did as long as we were in the sunshine.

It was late in the afternoon before we were ready to go. I went out on the porch and Brad joined me to wait on Blake, and then asked, "Have you met your new neighbor yet?"

"Yes, I met her yesterday."

"What's her name?"

"Hanna Smith. She's from North Carolina, she's a school teacher."

"Why didn't any of our teachers look like that?" He asked, carving her hourglass figure in the air with his hands.

125

"I don't know, but she's beautiful."

"What! Did I just hear the word beautiful come out of your mouth?" he asked, punching me in the arm. "Did you ask her out?"

"I just met the lady, Brad."

"Well if you're not going to ask her out, can I?"

"How many women are you going out with right now? Five, Six, Seven?"

"Four, just four. I can't handle no more," he said, laughing.

"Then why don't you leave this one alone?" I asked seriously.

"Okay, man, back off. She's yours. Do you know if she has a friend?"

"I doubt it, she just moved here."

"I thought you only liked redheads," Blake said, joining us on the porch as we watched Hanna working in her yard.

"Gentlemen prefer blondes," Brad said loudly.

"What is she, about five six, and curves in all the right places," Blake said in a strange voice then asked seriously, "what color are her eyes?'

"Green," I replied, deep in thought as she looked over and smiled at us.

"I think we need to have a party this weekend. Go ask Hanna if she'll come," Brad said.

"You want me to go over there right now?"

"No, I want you to go over there next summer. Go!" Brad yelled, forcing me down the stairs.

****

Hanna came to our party, only I don't think she understood what kind of party I'd invited her to. She was completely overdressed and obviously uncomfortable. When she told me she was going home, I insisted that she stay a little while longer. After a few drinks, I persuaded her to take her jacket off and it wasn't long before she loosened up and we started having fun.

After that night we slowly started spending time together. We spent our days off at the lake and we would go walking down to the park in the evenings after work. We talked about Tiffany and the love of her life, Sam. Her experiences with him mirrored a lot of my experiences with Tiffany. It was so nice to finally have someone who was unbiased to talk to.

Hanna started doing nice things for me and I tried to help her out too. She didn't know anyone in Natchez and on a teacher's salary was constantly trying to fix things around the house by herself. I really liked spending time with her but there was something unusual about her that I could never quite put my finger on.

When the seasons started to change and there was a cold chill in the air, her ex-boyfriend showed up unexpectedly. Hanna left him sitting in her living room to come over and ask me what she should do. I told her to talk to him because there might be a way for them to work things out. I thought it was good that Sam was here and she needed to take advantage of the opportunity. She needed to tell him how she truly felt inside her heart.

Hanna just sat on my couch, contentedly listening while I went on and on about what I would do if I could just talk to Tiffany. When I finally stopped, she stood up and looked at me with uncontrollable rage. Hanna mumbled obscenities under her breath walking to my door. When she got there she turned around and glared at me. Needless to say, I was stunned. I had never heard a curse word come out of her mouth before. She gave me a mean look and walked out, slamming the door behind her. I could still hear her cursing as she walked down my driveway toward her house.

Over and over in my mind I reran the moments that had just transpired; then I finally got it. She wasn't in love with Sam anymore and she wanted me to make him leave. I thought about her going on and on about the guy for months, telling me Sam had meant everything to her. That he hurt her so badly she didn't know if she could ever be in another serious relationship. Had Hanna mimicked all of my feelings I shared with her about Tiffany? Were they all lies?

I decided not to do anything about her ex being at her house. Hanna was a grown woman and she could take care of her own problems. Then I decided I wasn't going to be her friend anymore. Everything was just getting too complicated between us. Then this strange feeling came over me. And before I knew what I was doing I walked over to her house and told Sam that it was time for him to go.

Chapter 26

Christmas was only a couple of weeks away and I played my role as loving wife to perfection. Alan never missed a beat either, pretending to be the caring and devoted husband. He believed I wanted to go home for the holidays to visit my dad. But if he'd known my true intentions, he would have never let me go.

Two days before I left, I received a long awaited letter from Steven. It only reaffirmed my decision to ask him to move to Los Angeles and live with me.

My dearest,

The words that I must say to you remain locked within my heart. Therefore you will have to read between the lines. Soon it will be Christmas time again and my only desire is to see you, even if we are just friends.

If you had ever felt only half of my love, you would already be at my side. But I guess fate had another plan for you and I. Forever, I am with you, no matter where you are. You are always here with me, whenever I look up at the stars. Time is passing by us, as if in a race. Oh what desperate longing I feel to see your beautiful face. I make up my mind that you're okay but this nagging in my heart seems here to stay. If it would only stop, I would be free to walk away.

I fill up my days and nights, somehow. I search endlessly for the moment when I get to see your smile. Even if I could just touch you as a friend, my heart would be comforted then.

I want you to know that I dreamed the other night. I awoke on the couch from a scene of fright. You ignored me; you walked right past me and didn't speak. I consoled myself for days on end. Then I had another dream, and again we were friends.

The reason I tell you this is because I hope you hold no anger for me in your soul. I am just a boy who fell in love with you, when you were fifteen years old.

Forever,
Steven

Chapter 27

The day was slipping into night as I put the key into the doorknob. Everything was a mess but I overlooked it and walked into the kitchen. Opening the refrigerator, I picked out my frozen dinner and popped it into the microwave. As I walked toward the bathroom, I stopped long enough to turn on the television. Over twelve hours had passed since the last time I'd looked into the mirror. My eyes told the story well and I couldn't wait to get off of my feet.

As I walked back to the kitchen the bell rang on the microwave. I took my dinner to the living room, sitting down on the couch and somebody knocked on the door. The last thing I wanted was company but I figured it was Hanna, so I yelled, "Come in, the door's open."

"Hi, it's me."

"Tiffany," I said, jumping up as my dinner hit the floor.

"I didn't mean to startle you."

"It's okay. I just wasn't expecting it to be you," I said, kneeling down to pick my dinner up off the floor.

"I was in town and my dad told me where you lived. I wanted to surprise you."

"Well, you definitely surprised me. I'm sorry the place is such a mess."

"I didn't come here to see your house, Steven," she said, opening her arms.

"I can't believe you're here," I said, hugging her tightly.

"I'm finally here," she said softly, with a sigh of relief.

I stepped back and asked, "Can I get you something to drink?"

"What do you have?"

"Tea, orange juice, and water, unless you would like a beer. I also have a bottle of tequila."

"I think I'll have a beer, and a shot of tequila. If I can have both?"

"Of course you can."

"I like your house," she said, following me to the kitchen.

"Thanks," I said opening the cabinet.

"Can I help?" Tiffany asked, walking up behind me.

When I felt her so close to me, my heart raced and my knees went weak. "No, I've got it. Here's the salt and I might have a lemon."

"That's okay, I'll drink it straight."

"So how's married life?" I asked, leaning back against the counter.

"Not what I expected. How are you?" she asked, drinking the shot.

"You look good," I said, ignoring her question while pouring her another shot.

"It's your turn."

With the shot glass empty, I reached out for her hand and said, "Come in the living room so we can sit down."

"It's good to see you. It's been too long," she said, stepping in front of me to sit on the couch.

"Way too long."

"You can't imagine how busy I've been, Steven."

"I can't tell it by looking at you," I lied.

"I'm surprised you can't see it."

My feeble lie held no truth as Tiffany stared deep into my eyes. There was something missing in her eyes that worried me. I stared back, only because I couldn't help myself. My heart felt weak in her presence and I longed to kiss her lips.

She must have felt the same because she reached out for my hand. I watched as she softly kissed the back of my hand and raised it to her cheek. I had the overwhelming urge to pick her up and carry her to my truck. Once we were inside we could leave this place and drive to wherever we could be together. It seemed so ironic that now I was the one who wanted to beg her to run away.

Time had flown by since the last time we saw each other but the same feelings were obviously still alive. I could not deny it, nor did I want to as long as she was here with me. I took her hand within my hands and turned it over. Raising it to my lips, I gently kissed the palm of her hand. I could feel Tiffany trembling so I let go and sat back. I closed my eyes and took a deep breath. She instantly moved closer and put her head on my chest. I put my arm around her shoulder then leaned back and closed my eyes again. We sat there in silence, just holding one another and I wished this moment would never end.

"I miss you," she said, almost whispering.

"I missed you more."

"I feel so safe right now."

I pulled her even closer; desperately wanting to kiss her lips but safe wasn't what I was feeling at all. Time would take her away from me again, for some reason or another. It made me want to break every clock in my house, like that would somehow stop the inevitable.

"I need to tell you something very important, Steven. Well, actually, I need to ask you something."

"Are you okay?" I asked as her crystal blue eyes filled with tears.

"It's my husband, Alan, he worries me sometimes."

"Does he hurt you?"

"No, it's nothing like that. There are just some things that don't add up about him."

"You know whatever we talk about is just between us?"

"Yes, I do."

Tiffany stared at me and I leaned forward, drawn to her lips. Just when we were about to kiss, I heard someone walking up the front steps.

"Steven," Hanna called out, opening the front door and walking in.

I stood up quickly, saying, "Hanna, this is Tiffany. Tiffany, this is Hanna, she's my neighbor."

"Hello, Hanna. It's nice to meet you."

"Tiffany, I never thought I would have the pleasure," she said, walking over to shake her hand, and then sat down on the couch beside her.

"I know, I heard a knock and thought it was you but it was Tiffany," I explained.

"Well, isn't that wonderful. It's not everyday that Steven has such a special guest drop by."

"I just flew in and had to come see him," she said sweetly, looking at me.

"I bet you did, Tiffany," Hanna said, with a condescending attitude.

"So, Hanna, how long have you known Steven?"

"Oh we've been going out for a while now. He didn't tell you?"

"No, I've only been here a few minutes."

Getting up to walk to the kitchen, Hanna said under her breath, "You move fast, don't you."

I leaned over and whispered into Tiffany's ear, "Don't listen to a word she says," which made both of us laugh.

"What is it with you two?" Hanna asked, peering around the corner.

"Oh nothing," Tiffany said casually. "Will you be a doll and bring me a shot of tequila?"

"Yes, I'll be a doll and do that for you."

Hanna's voice sounded almost evil and Tiffany gave me a strange look. I shrugged my shoulders wishing Hanna would just disappear.

"Is that your girlfriend?" Tiffany whispered, while pointing toward the kitchen.

I shook my head as Hanna came into the living room and stood beside me. She leaned over me to hand Tiffany her shot, then sat down on the floor at my feet and looked up at us.

"I want to make a toast," Tiffany said, raising her glass, completely ignoring Hanna, "to true happiness."

"To true happiness," I repeated. We drank to happiness and then began to reminisce about the past. Hanna was getting madder by the second, but I didn't care. It was like Tiffany and I belonged to a private club and she didn't have a membership.

Hanna interrupted and asked, "So, how long are you planning on staying?"

"I don't know, a few days, maybe a week. Who knows? I guess until I finish what I came here to do," Tiffany said sarcastically.

"What could Tiffany Starr possibly have to do in this two cent town?"

"Well, I guess that's where we have a difference of opinion, Hanna. Natchez is my favorite town in the whole world. Why, the two people I love most live here."

I could feel the pressure building between the two women, so I excused myself to the bathroom. I could hear their conversation through the door as it began to get louder. Frantically, I thought about what I could say to calm both of them down.

When I went back into the living room I knew it was too late. They were in a heated debate about one of the roles Tiffany had portrayed in a film. So, I sat on the other side of Tiffany, as far away from Hanna as I could and said, "Why don't we change the subject."

"Yes, why don't we," Tiffany agreed.

"Hey, I know a good one to talk about. I know Steven would like for us to discuss it. Tiffany, since you are finally here, why don't you tell us the truth. Do they sell pen and paper out in Hollywood?"

"Hanna!" I yelled, jumping up.

"No Steven, it's okay, I can answer my own questions. I've dealt with much more ruthless critics than this girl. To be perfectly honest with you Hanna, Steven and I have a private and personal relationship and it's none of your business."

"I'm sorry *doll* but he's made it my business."

"Hanna, that is enough! I think it's time for you to go," I said, walking to the door.

"Excuse me! You want me to go?" Hanna asked in disbelief, pointing at herself as she stood up.

"Yes, I think it would be best if you'd leave right now."

"Just give me a minute," she said quietly, turning to open the end table drawer.

"What are you doing, Hanna?"

"I'm leaving! Can't you see I am getting my things and leaving?"

"I didn't come here to cause trouble. Maybe I should go," Tiffany said, obviously uncomfortable.

"No, please don't go. You just got here. We get to see each other all the time."

"I told you! I told you! How could we spend so much time together if we aren't dating?"

"Hanna you know damn well that we are not dating. Why are you doing this to me?"

"Why would you want her to stay and ask me to leave?" She screamed, throwing a book across the room.

"Okay, I've had enough. I'm out of here," Tiffany said, walking to the door.

She had the saddest look on her face that almost brought me to my knees. I leaned forward, almost whispering and asked, "Can I go with you?"

"I think you have something a little more important to do right now, like protect your property."

"I don't care about this house," I said desperately.

"You don't care! Then why don't you leave? Go ahead, Steven. Leave!" Hanna yelled.

Tiffany looked over at Hanna and walked right past me, out the door. Hanna started laughing and I slammed the door behind me, running after Tiffany.

"Wait."

She looked over her shoulder and said, "I didn't come here to cause any problems."

"I know you didn't," I said, catching up with her.

"It's so weird how you and I experience the same things in life, at almost the same time," she said in a dreamlike state.

"What do you mean by that?"

"I'll tell you about it, when we have the chance to sit down and talk."

"When?"

"What about tomorrow?"

"Well, I have to go to work, but I could call in sick."

"No, I don't want you to miss work because of me. Just come over to Dad's house when you get off. I'll be there waiting for you."

"Okay, I'll see you around six."

"I can hardly wait," she said, leaning up to kiss my cheek.

I closed her door and couldn't help but feel excited as I waved goodbye. Turning to go back in the house, my excitement quickly turned to anger.

"Why did you do that to me, Hanna?"

"How could you treat me like that in front of her, after all I've done for you?"

"Why would you treat us like that when you know how we feel about each other?"

"That shit is all in your head, Steven. I have listened to you moan and cry about that girl since the day I met you. She doesn't love you. I'm the one who cares about you."

"Did you think I was moaning about her? I was confiding in you about how broke my heart was and you think I was complaining?"

"All I want to know is if she broke your heart why do you want her in your house?"

"Because I still love her."

"She doesn't love you. Look at her, and then take a good look at yourself. Are you blind?"

"Nobody knows the way we feel about each other. And you'll never know how it feels to love somebody like that," I said, opening my front door.

"I already know what it feels like."

"I don't think you know what you're talking about, Hanna."

"And I don't think you know what you're saying right now. That girl has you confused."

"I'm not confused. I know exactly what I'm saying."

"She'll go away again, she always does. Then I will be the one here to clean up the mess she'll make of you."

She walked past me, out the door with her arms crossed. Closing the door, I sat down on the couch and put my head down in my hands. I went over the events that had just unfolded in my mind again. The only part I couldn't understand was why Tiffany was not still here, in my arms.

****

Last night I could barely sleep because of the adrenalin pumping through my veins. I contemplated what Tiffany's question could be, over and over again in my mind. Whatever she wanted, whatever she asked for, if I could give it to her then my answer would be yes.

It was hard to make it through the day. Work could not hold my attention when I knew she was waiting to see me tonight. I left a few minutes early and sped all the way to her house. As I knocked on the door, my heart anticipated holding her in my arms once again.

"Hello, Steven. Merry Christmas."

"Merry Christmas, Mr. Crenshaw."

"Come on in, I've been expecting you."

"How are you doing?"

"Not so good," he said, sitting down.

"What's the problem?"

"Well, there's been an accident."

"Is Tiffany okay?"

"Yes son, she's fine. She didn't have an accident. Her husband wrecked his car. It didn't sound too major, but Alan demanded she fly home immediately."

"She's not here?" I asked, standing up, looking around.

"No, she left this afternoon."

"Is he in the hospital?" I asked, sitting back down.

"No. I know I shouldn't tell you this, but when she hung up the phone, it was not a look of concern on her face, it was fear."

"I got the same feeling from her last night. She told me she wanted to discuss something about Alan but we didn't get the chance."

"Well, you know what I think? I think he had that little accident on purpose, if he even had one."

"But why wouldn't he just ask her to come home instead of lying?"

"I don't know son, but something isn't right about this whole thing."

"What can we do about it?"

"I don't know. I think I'll try to schedule a trip to California soon. Just to check things out for myself. I know something you can do for me," he said, changing his tone of voice.

"What is that, Mr. Crenshaw?"

"You could come over and eat Christmas dinner. I could use the company, if you're not busy."

When he offered me the invitation, I had to swallow hard. I was so caught up in my own world that I forgot how upset he must be right now. "I'd love to."

"Thank you, Steven."

"Well, since we're asking, can I ask something of you?"

"Sure."

"Can I come and help you cook?"

"Of course, I'd love to have your help," he said nodding.

I could see the emotions he was holding back but still had to ask the question. "Tiffany told me last night that she had something to ask me. Do you know what it was?"

"No, I don't."

"Will you ask her the next time you talk to her?"

"Yes, that doesn't mean she'll tell me but I'll ask," he said, winking.

Mr. Crenshaw had already cooked dinner, so I stuck around to eat. We talked late into the night and he invited me to stay over. I wanted to for his sake but it was too hard for me to be here without Tiffany.

As I drove away, I became very angry with Hanna. She had stolen precious moments I could have spent with Tiffany away from me. Moments I had waited so long for that I could never have back again. And the closer I got to home I didn't know if I would ever be able to forgive her.

137

Chapter 28

The little bump on Alan's head was hardly noticeable. And it didn't take long to realize his true intentions for my untimely return. It was about a stupid party that he felt he had to have me on his arm to make an appearance. And even though I couldn't change the way I felt, I put on the silver gown he'd bought and went to the party.

Alan was drinking, as usual, and I was fighting back tears all night. Steven never left my mind even though I mingled from crowd to crowd trying to keep a smile on my face. The midnight hour was approaching and I could hear Alan calling out my name. I started to turn and walk into another room but he caught my eyes. The look on his face made me turn and walk toward him. He put his arm around me, squeezing me tightly. All I could smell was whiskey and suddenly felt nauseous.

"Happy New Year, darling."

"Happy New Year, Alan," I said, before closing my eyes to give him a kiss.

"Give your husband a real kiss, baby," he said loudly.

"I can hardly wait," I replied sarcastically.

"You don't want to make a scene, do you, Tiffany?" he asked, warning me with an intense glare.

"No. But I'm ready to go home," I said, turning away.

"Then walk your skinny little ass to the car and go home. I'll deal with you when I get there," he said, through his gritted smile, so no one could tell he was talking.

"Please don't Alan…"

Alan turned me around and we walked to the door with smiles on our faces. I hoped it didn't appear that I was being dragged to the door but I don't know how it couldn't. Halfway there, my long dress caused me to twist my ankle. I fell to the floor and everyone turned to stare.

"Stop Alan, you're hurting me!"

"Oh darling, are you okay?"

Alan sounded concerned but by the look on his face I could tell that I was in trouble. Then several of the men around us kneeled down to help.

"I've got her!" Alan yelled, pushing the other men out of his way as he pulled me up.

He walked me out to the car and I got in the limo without another word. He turned to go back to the party and I told the driver to take me home.

My mind was racing, because I knew I had to make my move soon. I didn't want to end up like Jenny and I didn't want to live in fear anymore. Every thing was almost in place; I just had to wait a little while longer.

Chapter 29

Winter passed without a word from Tiffany, while I mailed hundreds of them. I drove myself crazy thinking about her. I wanted to stop, but it was out of my control.

Hanna and I were still talking, but I never spoke to her about Tiffany anymore. It was nice to have her around sometimes, as long as I didn't do anything to upset her.

After a long day of working in the yard, I invited Hanna over for supper. I opened a bottle of wine as she helped me finish cooking. The sundress she wore was blue and she had a white ribbon in her hair. I wondered why she'd wear something so dressy to come to my house. Then I remembered what she had worn the first night she came over to the party Brad and I threw and I had to laugh.

"What are you laughing about," she asked, smiling.

"Oh nothing."

"Come on. What is it?"

"You look nice tonight."

"Thank you," she replied, taking my hand.

I held on for a moment, looking into her eyes. They seemed to shine brighter than I had ever seen them before. She laughed innocently, turning back toward the stove and I walked over to the sink to wash my hands.

We finished cooking, made our plates and sat down at the table. After we finished eating, I looked at the clock, noticing it was getting late. But I was enjoying her company so I asked if she wanted to stay for another drink. She insisted that I come over to her house, telling me she wanted to change clothes.

Her house was immaculate and smelled like wild flowers. Before she walked into her room, she stopped and lit a few candles. I poured us a drink, picking mine up and sat back on the couch. She came over and sat beside me, asking how she looked now.

"You look comfortable," I said, looking at her pink cotton halter and shorts and watching how fast she drank her drink.

"I think I need one more," she said, handing me the empty glass.

"Don't you think you've had enough?" I asked, realizing she had started slurring her words.

"One more and then I'm going to bed."

"Okay. One for the road."

She drank this one slower and I followed suit. The glow of the candlelight softened her skin and her eyes seemed to dance with the flicker of the flames.

She stood up so I finished my drink and said, "I guess it's time for me to go home."

She stumbled over the coffee table catching herself on the arm of the chair, saying, "Let me walk you to the door."

I laughed, walking over to help her and said, "Why don't you let me help you get in bed."

We walked to her room and I turned on the lamp as she sat on the edge of the bed. I pulled back the covers and helped her lay down. She pulled me closer, kissing me hard, trying to pull me in the bed with her.

"Hanna. I think you've had too much to drink."

"I think, I need you," she said softly, kissing me again.

I closed my eyes and kissed her back this time. She pulled me on top of her and it felt so good that I couldn't even tell her we needed to stop.

"Hanna…"

"Shhhh," she whispered, leaning up to kiss me again.

In the darkness, everything I wanted in this moment was here. Right now, there were no thoughts of yesterday or tomorrow. I simply wanted to feel her skin against mine.

"Please don't stop, please…" she whispered in between kisses.

"We can't do this, Hanna."

"Yes we can. Nobody will ever have to know."

"It's not that. I don't have a condom."

"It's okay. I'm on the pill," she said, kissing my neck.

141

****

A few weeks later Hanna came over and said we needed to sit down and talk. She seemed very serious and anxious so I invited her inside and sat down on the couch beside her. For a few moments she looked down studying her hands that were tightly folded in her lap. After a long sigh she looked up and smiled.

"I'm pregnant."

I was shocked, uncertain what to say, but then doubt began to fill my mind. "You're pregnant? How? You said you were on the pill."

"It didn't work."

"What do you mean it didn't work? Are you trying to say it's mine?"

"You are the only one I slept with, so what do you think?"

"I don't know what to think. We were only together one time."

"Obviously it only takes one time."

"How do I know how many guys you've been seeing?"

"Steven, you know me. I go to work and come home. I haven't slept with any one since Sam, except for you."

"I just can't believe you're pregnant," I said standing up and backing away from her.

She got up and ran out the door toward her house. A few minutes later she was back, handing me a pregnancy test. It read positive, but I still couldn't believe it was true. But what could I do, make her do the test again in front of me?

She'd already told several ladies she worked with at the school the good news. In fact, a lot of people knew she was pregnant before I did. It wasn't long before the whole town knew and I felt trapped.

My mother and dad made a special trip to my house to persuade me to do the right thing. They would not entertain my doubts, only the concern of their standing in this town. Their son was not going to get a school teacher pregnant and abandon her in her time of need.

So, Hanna and mom began to spend a lot of time together, planning our wedding. And even though she wasn't Amber, my mother did her best to accept the newest member of our family.

They started going shopping on a regular basis, buying things for our wedding and the baby and bringing them over to my house. It was if my decisions had been made for me. No one asked what I intended to do. They just assumed I would do as I was told.

Those days, I spent as much time as I could by myself. One minute I was happy with thoughts of a newborn child. The next minute I was sad, as thoughts of Tiffany would enter my mind. This was not the way my life was supposed to go. I never wanted to have a child with anyone else and I certainly never wanted to be married to another girl. Something seemed terribly wrong about the whole situation but what could I do to change the future?

Chapter 30

The party had lasted for two days but the drugs and alcohol had not completely dulled my senses. I still felt shocked about what Alan was asking me to do. In my heart, I didn't want to give in this time because I knew it was the wrong.

Alan walked into the room and kneeled down in front of me. I could tell by the look in his eyes that he wanted an answer but I didn't have one.

"Why do you want me to do this?"

"Everybody does it, baby. People just don't talk about it."

"I don't want to."

"What about what I want?" he asked, sitting down, putting his arm around me.

"I just don't know," I replied, lying back on the bed.

"Just one time, Love. That's all. You can't tell me you haven't ever thought about it," he whispered in my ear, touching my neck.

"I just can't do it," I said, closing my eyes.

"Here, take another one of these. It'll help feel better."

"Will you fix me another drink?" I asked as Alan walked over to the bar.

"Will you do what I want you to do?"

"I think you're making a big mistake," I said, closing my eyes again.

"Just do what I ask you to do, Tiffany. Now, take your pill and this drink and go get in the tub. I'll come get you in a little while," he said firmly.

I took off my clothes and sank back into the water. My head was spinning as I tried to wash my body. A few minutes later I heard voices in the bedroom. Then somebody turned on the music and I laid back and closed my eyes.

Hands reached down into the water, pulling me out. I tried to open my eyes but it made me dizzy. They were holding me up and drying my body at the same time. Then I was picked up and carried into my bedroom by Clay, Alan's best friend. I really don't remember a lot about the rest of that night but Alan got what he so desperately wanted.

"Wake up, Tiffany," Alan said.

"What time is it?" I asked, sitting up in the bed, startled by his voice.

"It's time for you to get up. I have to fly to Atlantic City today, for a meeting."

"How long will you be gone?"

"I'll be home tomorrow evening. What happened last night is just between you and me, alright?" he asked, holding my chin in his hand.

"I understand," I said, lying back down.

"I'm going to be late for my flight, sweetheart. I'll see you tomorrow," Alan said, kissing my cheek.

As soon as he was gone, I got out of bed, washed my face and brushed my teeth. I put on my robe, trying to push last night out of my thoughts and went downstairs.

There were still a lot of people around but that was nothing unusual. I sat down at the dinning table and Clay walked into the room. He acted as though nothing had happened and sat down beside me.

Clay and I sat around and talked until after noon. Finally, I insisted on going upstairs to get dressed. But the only way he would let me go is if he could come with me and choose what I would wear.

He went in my closet to pick out a few dresses, demanding that I model each one. As he poured us a glass of champagne, I changed into the first dress. He shook his head no and I headed back into the bathroom to try on the next one.

After several more wardrobe changes, he finally decided that I should wear the first one I tried on. I picked up a pillow and smacked him on the head, complaining we had wasted over an hour. With the first dress back on, we walked downstairs and joined the rest of the party.

When Alan didn't come home the next day I tried every possible way to contact him but he was nowhere to be found. It wasn't like him to be out of touch for too long and I became frantic with worry.

After a few days of searching without finding him, a messenger arrived. Ms. Hattie called for me to come to the door and I was scared about what he had to say. The man asked if my name is Tiffany Starr. I answered yes and he handed me some papers and quickly walked away. I stepped back, closed the door and opened the envelope.

There was a post-it note on top of another envelope in Alan's handwriting that read, 'You should have been faithful'. And all I could think was isn't that what he wanted. Then it hit me, the day that he left, Clay and I had been alone in my room with plenty of eyes watching. Alan Johnson had left me, and filed for divorce, without even saying goodbye.

****

"Hello."

"Hi."

"Are you okay, sweetheart?"

I took a deep breath and sat down. "Dad, Alan filed for divorce."

"I'm sorry to hear that, baby. Is there anything I can do?"

"I don't think so," I choked out. "It's really for the best. I was planning on leaving him soon anyway," I said, wiping away the tears.

"Well, then this is good news you're giving me instead of bad?"

"It's good, and bad."

"What happened?"

"It's something I'd rather not talk about right now," I replied, knowing I could never tell him the truth.

"Just know that I'm here Tiffany, if you ever need to talk," he said sincerely.

"I know."

"So, what are your plans now?"

"I don't know. Right now I'm still living in his house. He has most of my money tied up so I may just rent an apartment until I figure out where I'm at financially."

"That's a lot of money you're talking about," dad said, suddenly angry.

"It's not like he has all of it but of course he'll probably end up with most of it, knowing him."

"You know you can always come home."

"Thanks, dad. Have you heard from Steven lately?"

"No, I haven't seen him in awhile. I do have some news for you though."

"Is he okay?"

"I don't know, like I said, I haven't talked to him. I heard he got married to someone named Hanna. Do you know her?" he asked in a strained voice.

"I've met her," I replied slowly, shocked by the news.

"I heard she's pregnant. They were married last week. I happened to be driving by the church when they walked out. I almost stopped to congratulate him, but then I figured, if he didn't invite me, I shouldn't stop. Tiffany. Are you there?"

"Dad, are you sure it was him?" I asked slowly.

"Yes, baby. It was him."

"Dad."

"What is it?"

"Nothing. It's not important anymore. I love you."

"I love you too, sweetheart."

Chapter 31

At the beginning of fall, Hanna took an unexpected vacation from work to go visit her family. Her mother wanted to take her shopping for baby clothes and even though I didn't want her to travel, she left anyway.

She'd been in North Carolina for three days when she called me crying hysterically. She had taken a nap that afternoon and woke up severely in pain. Her parents rushed her to the hospital but it was too late to save the baby.

As she told me the story I felt no sense of loss in my heart. If it was the truth, there was only one thing I couldn't understand. How could it happen so quickly? She was too far along for it to be that uncomplicated. I tried to be sympathetic toward Hanna but it was one of the hardest things I've ever had to do.

Not long after that, I saw Mr. Crenshaw and he told me Tiffany was getting a divorce from Alan. After losing the baby and hearing the news about Tiffany, I fell into deep despair. My boss was understanding and gave me a leave of absence but when it was over, and I was still unable to return to work, I was fired.

After the New Year began, I finally found a job but I had to travel. Hanna didn't seem to mind, as long as I went back to work. It was ironic, but I found peace of mind, being in strange towns, far away from home.

I spent the spring in Kansas City and the summer in Chicago just to catch up on the bills. I would only go home for a few days about every month or so. Sometimes, I was away from home even longer. Hanna and I didn't have financial problems anymore. But she felt scared about being alone so I asked my old friend, Brad, if he would come by to check on her occasionally.

****

Work kept me away from home for two months and I was ready to go home. My plan was to take the next two weeks off because I really needed the rest.

The night I arrived, Hanna wasn't at home. She finally showed up a few hours later, stumbling through the door. I could smell the alcohol on her breath when she hugged me. Her eyes were bloodshot and puffy, as though she'd been crying for a long time.

The next day Brad came over and the two of them were acting rather strange. It was nothing I could put my finger on; it was just a gut feeling. I continued to watch the way they acted toward each other and then I knew something was going on between them.

When Hanna left for work on Monday, I called my boss. I told him it was time for me to get back to work. He told me there was a one-man job I could do in Houston, Texas so I packed my bags and left, without even saying goodbye.

When I got there, I hardly had time to think about Hanna, except at night. Then I would go over everything I knew in my mind again. If she and Brad had an affair I felt like it was their business. But I knew I wasn't supposed to feel that way.

Eventually, she found out where I was staying and called every night. I tried to listen to her explanations but I really didn't care. Most of the time it was hard for me to even speak.

It was my last Saturday afternoon in Houston and I didn't have to work so I decided to go for a walk in the park. I noticed a large group of people watching what looked like a movie set. As I walked by, I decided to try and see what was going on.

That's when I saw her. Tiffany was far away, but I could still see her beautiful red hair. She was talking to some man and there were several other people standing around them. I tried to walk over to say hello but the security guards wouldn't let me by. I explained to them that we were old friends and some jerk beside me starting telling them the same thing. I kept calling out her name but she couldn't hear me over the crowd. One of the guards told me that if I didn't stop yelling, I would have to leave. So I walked to the other side of the crowd to watch her.

"Quiet on the set everyone! Quiet on the set!"

The crowd began to whisper and the actors got ready to act out the scene. Tiffany walked in my direction and I thought for a second she saw me. Then the guy yelled once again, "Quiet on the set!"

"Action!"

She was in a scene with a black-headed girl and a guy I had seen in some movie, but couldn't remember his name. Everyone was quiet so I yelled out as loud as I could, "Tiffany!"

She turned to look in my direction and immediately ran toward me. The director yelled cut and everyone around me moved back as Tiffany jumped into my arms. The bodyguards surrounded us as I spun her round and round.

"Steven! I can't believe it's you. What are you doing here?" she asked, hugging me tightly, kissing my cheek.

"I'm here working," I said, pulling back to look in her eyes.

"What's more important Ms. Starr is we are trying to make a movie," the director said.

"Yes sir, I'm sorry. This is a friend of mine from high school, Steven Cross," Tiffany said innocently. She was beaming with happiness and almost breathless but this only seemed to make the man more upset.

"Well isn't that special," he said in a mocking voice then turned around abruptly, yelling commands to the crew.

Turning to one of the bodyguards, Tiffany asked, "Will you take Mr. Cross, to my trailer?"

"Certainly, Ms. Starr. Come with me, Mr. Cross," he answered with authority.

"I'll be there as soon as I'm done," Tiffany said, walking in the other direction.

"I'll be waiting," I said, and then looked back over my shoulder at the crowd. Everyone was staring right at me and I waved goodbye to the jerk who had said he knew her too, then I walked away.

When I sat down in her trailer, I was dying with anticipation, knowing she would walk through the door any second. After an hour passed, I was a little calmer but beginning to get impatient. About thirty minutes later, she finally walked in and it startled me so badly; I jumped up out my chair.

"Sorry, I should have knocked first."

"That's okay," I said, taking her into my arms, giving her a big hug.

"That mean ole director knew I wanted to be back here with you. He made us do the scene over and over. What are you doing in Houston?" she asked, sitting down.

"I got a new job. I travel all over the country fixing things."

"That sounds interesting," she replied, leaning back and putting her chin on her shoulder to look at me. "So, how are you?"

"I'm happy to see you," I said, reaching over to take her hand.

She looked down at my hand, saying, "I see you're still married."

"Yes, I am."

"Happily?"

"No," I said, looking down.

"I always thought you would marry Amber."

"No, I didn't marry Amber. Your dad told me that you're divorced."

"Yes, I am, happily. Come in," she said as someone knocked on the door.

The tall black-headed girl I'd seen earlier walked in and said, "Hi, my name is Pamela."

"Hi Pamela, I'm Steven," I said, standing up to shake her hand.

"I know who you are. Tiffany has told me all about you," she said, staring at me with piercing green eyes.

"I haven't told you everything about him," Tiffany said, pulling me back down as Pamela sat down beside me.

"You know what I mean," Pamela said, reaching over to touch my knee, slinging her shiny black hair over her shoulder.

"Are they ready for us yet?" Tiffany asked, suddenly anxious.

"We just got back here. There's still plenty of time for us to talk," she replied coolly, leaning back, crossing her long slender legs.

"Pamela, I hope you don't mind, but could you give us a few minutes alone."

"Oh sure, sweetie," she replied, quickly walking to the door.

"It was nice to meet you, Pamela," I said as Tiffany stood up.

"Nice to meet you too, Steven. I'll come back and let you know when they're ready for us."

"Thanks," Tiffany said, closing the door and locking it.

"Is she a friend of yours?"

"Actually, she's my roommate. We met last year while I was working in New York. So, Mr. Cross," she said slowly, smiling. "What are you doing tonight?"

"Nothing important, I'll probably go out to eat, maybe catch a movie or something. Don't you have one out right now?" I replied slowly, teasing her with every word.

"You know I do."

Her smile was so big and I looked into her eyes remembering how much they sparkle when she's happy. "What are you doing tonight, Ms. Starr?"

"Hopefully, I'll be having dinner with an old friend."

"I'd love to have dinner with you," I said softly, looking in her eyes.

She smiled and said, "That sounds great. I'm staying at the Hilton, the one that's downtown. I'm registered under the name Betty Barker and the password at my door is cinnamon."

"Code names and passwords. Are you sure you're not an F.B.I. agent?"

"Actually, I'm a spy," she whispered.

"Who do you work for?" I asked, playing the game.

"If I tell you, I would have to kill you."

I started laughing and said, "I'm not ready to die, yet."

"No, your dreams haven't come true yet. Have they?" she asked with a serious look.

"No, they haven't."

Silence hung thick in the air as I searched her beautiful face. Whatever I was looking for in my life could only be found in her eyes. If only I had the strength to say the right words, I wouldn't feel this way.

Tiffany hugged my arm, putting her head on my shoulder and said, "There's still time Steven, don't worry."

It was hard for me to understand how she felt there was enough time to wait. Everyday I spent away from her seemed like another wasted twenty-four hours.

"It's time to go, Tiff!" Pamela yelled, trying to open the door.

"Just a minute!" she yelled then asked,"How about eight o'clock?"

"You got it. Can I bring anything?"

"No, but you can walk me out," she said, opening the door.

"I'm so glad that I saw you. I almost didn't come over here to see what was going on," I explained as we walked back to the set.

"Thank God you came over," she said as the make-up girl stopped her. She automatically tilted her head back and closed her eyes.

"Yes, thank God," I said quietly, feeling out of place. "Well, I'm going to get out of here. I know you're busy," I said, squeezing her hand.

"Wait just a second," she said, not letting go. As soon as the make-up girl finished, she said, "Give me hug."

I hugged Tiffany for a long time then whispered, "I'll be with you soon."

The crowd had grown larger and everyone was watching as I walked toward them. I knew what was on their minds because I could see it in their eyes. I turned around and Tiffany was watching me too. I waved goodbye as she blew me a kiss and I looked back at the crowd with a big happy smile.

Chapter 32

Steven arrived a few minutes early, just like I thought he would. My suggestion was we stay in my suite and have dinner delivered. He said I looked far too beautiful to be sitting in a hotel room. However, he understood that going out is difficult, so I offered him a stack of menus from the best restaurants in town. We ordered dinner then we walked out to the balcony, gazing up at the stars.

Steven talked about what had been going on in his life, and I told him some about mine. Then the subject changed to us, as it always seemed to do. We talked about the good times and we talked about the bad times. I began to realize how much I loved him. I loved him for who he was. I loved him for how he treated me. But most of all, I loved him because he was my friend.

Dinner was delivered around ten p.m. and we took our time, savoring each course. Right before dessert, Pamela interrupted us and asked if we wanted to go out dancing. Against my will, we agreed to go with her for one hour.

We danced for an hour and a half before I realized what time it was. Pamela didn't want to leave but she refused to stay there alone. On the ride back to the hotel, she just couldn't resist flirting with Steven. He was polite, a perfect gentlemen and strangely it made me admire him more.

We walked Pamela to her room and said goodnight. She walked backwards through the door, pulling a security guard in her room. Pamela was laughing and the guard looked like he was in shock. I couldn't understand why she had to make a scene, especially in front of Steven.

I took his hand, pulling him away and said, "You know she's just messing around."

"She reminds me of Victoria."

"Come on, I'll race you."

"That's not fair! You got a head start," he yelled, running after me.

The security guard opened my door as we ran toward it. I ran straight to the bathroom with Steven right on my heels, yelling, "I win!"

"It was definitely a tie," he said bending over to catch his breath.

"I need a hug."

"I need one too," he said, picking me up off the floor in a strong embrace.

"I'm so happy you're here."

He sat down on the edge of the tub, saying, "I wish my life was like this everyday."

I kneeled down in front of him and said, "Don't think about it."

"I don't write the script, Tiffany. I just play my part."

"Nobody gets to write their own script, Steven. We all just do the best we can."

"But it's so hard."

"What are you talking about?"

"Catching these five minutes in the spotlight with you," he replied with a strange look in his eyes.

"You are a light."

"But there has to be more to life than this."

"You always have me."

"Right here," he said pointing at his heart.

"Steven," I said softly, looking up at him.

"Yes."

"I want to go look at the stars."

"Do you want to race?" he asked playfully, standing up.

"No. I want you to carry me," I said seriously.

His marriage seemed like a lie while he carried me to the balcony. In his arms, was the only place I felt safe. In his eyes were all the words he couldn't speak. What could be the point of forcing the issue? Nothing in my life or his mattered, when I was this close to him.

Steven set me down gently then stood close behind me. We looked up into the clear night sky together, once again. I don't know if a moment passed or an hour before Steven touched me. My heart dropped as I leaned back against him. There were no questions in my mind. I never thought of yes or no. Steven kissed my neck and it just felt natural. Was there anyone else in the world that should kiss me there? Then he kissed me again and reality melted away. Pressing harder against him, I slowly tilted my head to the side.

Breathing heavily, soft moans began to escape my lips. Steven knew exactly how and where to touch me. My desire grew as I turned to face him then he looked at me and I had to close my eyes. With trembling lips and frail hands I embraced him. If only this moment could last forever, then maybe, my life would have true meaning.

Steven stepped back and for a moment I thought he was going to walk away. But he just stared at me, never saying a word. I started to speak and he touched my lips. Then he hugged me. He hugged me so hard that I could barely breathe. After several minutes, I began to wonder if he was ever going to let me go.

My desire to kiss his lips overtook my entire body and mind. Our first kiss was soft but with each passing moment they grew with passion. As I lifted my arms, Steven took my dress off. While kissing his body, I took his shirt off. The world was watching as I leaned back on the railing and closed my eyes. He kneeled down in front of me, hugging my waist and kissed my belly. I giggled and looked down as he stared up into my eyes.

"I've really missed you, Tiffany."

"Not as much as I've missed you."

"No, I've definitely missed you more," he said, taking my shoes off.

"Do you want to fight about it? Come on, put up your dukes," I said with my fists held up.

"There's no need for violence when you know you're right," he said, putting his hands over my fists.

"I'd rather make love, not war," I said seriously.

"Making love to you is the only thing I want."

"Then make love to me, Steven. Make love to me."

We struggled to kiss while removing the rest of our clothes. The stars were shining brightly as he took me in his arms again. Steven laid me down on a chase lounge and leaned over me. I lay perfectly still and closed my eyes. He touched my face and gently moved his hands down my body. He stopped at my knees, kissing each one. Every movement of his hands and lips gave me the most wonderful sensations.

Natural reactions took over my body as he began to kiss my neck. I pulled him to me, hungrily kissing his lips. My body began to tremble as he said my name softly. Lost in ecstasy, I moaned as our bodies became intertwined. Looking up, I saw all the lights of downtown Houston as we began to make love.

Within moments, Steven looked at me with tears in his eyes. All I could feel were the tears I had to hide. I wanted to look at him but I had to look away.

"I love you, Tiffany. I, love you…I love you."

"I love you, too," I whispered.

Steven made love to me like never before. The boy I once knew was a man now. Every touch, every move of his body brought pleasure to mine. His actions were totally in control as the night lingered on. Then he held me in his safe strong arms, right where I belonged.

A few minutes later Steven got up and I reached out for him, saying, "Where are you going? Please don't leave."

"Do you want to go to the bedroom?"

I asked softly, "Will you carry me?"

"Yes Love, I'll carry you. Come here."

Before we ever left the balcony we were kissing again. Steven carried me to the bedroom and we lay down on the bed. With renewed energy, we let our passion guide our every movement. By the look in his eyes I knew he felt the same unique chemistry. Hours passed by as we took each other to greater heights of ecstasy. Completely exhausted, we fell asleep in each other's arms.

We woke up around noon and took a long hot bath together. Then we made love again, pretending we didn't have a care in the world. We spent the afternoon feeding each other room service and talking about the places we'd like to visit in the world, while lying in bed.

Steven and I finally got dressed when the sun was setting. Then we went for a drive, just for a change of scenery.

He was flying to Chicago in the morning so we spent the rest of the night, both happy and sad. I gave him my new address, asking him to come see me in California and he promised me he would.

Steven didn't wake me up in the morning before he left. He left a tearstained letter on the pillow beside me. I think he was just trying to make it easier on me. In a way it did but in another way it didn't.

My love,

The memories that we just made, have filled my heart with joy again. It's as if God could read my heart, and let me see you once more. You are my bread, my cool water, that lets me know I am still alive. After just one taste of your wine, I feel I will live forever. I can close my eyes, anytime I want, and see your beautiful face. But can I walk through this life with my eyes closed?

My search to live honestly is there in your eyes. Smile sweetly my love, we still have the time. If I should die before we both discover the obvious truth, know there will still be someone waiting for you.

I want you to know, when I left, I kissed you goodbye. You were peacefully asleep, and I didn't want you to see me cry. I will spend Christmas time without experiencing your grace. You'll be here in my heart, that's something that no one can erase. I can hear your voice still and feel your soft skin. Whenever I close my eyes, it all happens again.

I pray for you Love, that God will keep you safe. I think of your love, every single day. Most of the time, it's the only thing that pulls me through. I am lost in a cruel world, without someone like you. I search for the door, hoping you will be there. My love, I often wonder if we will ever get the chance to begin. For my heart is worthless to anyone else here on earth.

As you close your eyes tonight, please darling, come to me in my dreams. I will beg you, to forgive me, because my love for you is too strong. Oh what deep hatred I hold for these days without you. You, only you, will complete my soul.

Love forever and a day,
Steven

Chapter 33

Hanna rolled over and looked at me. She sighed deeply, asking, "What's wrong with you?"

"Nothing. I just don't have anything to say," I said, sitting up on the edge of the bed.

"You never have anything to say."

"Just because I get out of bed doesn't mean you have to follow me."

"Why are you being so mean to me, Steven? I missed you."

"You need to get some sleep. You have to go to work in the morning," I said, putting on my jeans.

She put her arms around me and looked up into my eyes. "I can't go to sleep without you."

"You do it all the time."

"Why don't you love me anymore?"

"You're upsetting yourself over nothing. I can't sleep, that's all," I said, breaking free from her embrace, walking to the living room.

"Do you realize that it's the end of February and you left at the end of December? Two months! Two months you've been gone and then you get here and treat me like I don't exist. Why did you even come home?"

"Because I live here."

"Could have fooled me."

"Does my check come to this address every week?"

"Yes."

"Does the mailbox have my name on it?"

"Yes."

"Was I living here when I met you?"

"Yes, you were," she said softly, lowering her head.

"Look, I don't want to argue. I've had a long trip and I really don't feel like having this conversation."

"All I want is to make love to you."

"Like I said Hanna, I had a long trip. I'm tired."

"Traveling man with a girl in every town. I've heard about men who travel for a living," she said, accusing me with her eyes, as her voice got louder with each word.

"Are you sure you're not just feeling guilty yourself?" I asked, not giving her time to respond, turning to walk to the kitchen.

"What would I have to feel guilty about?"

I turned around sharply and said, "Only you know that."

"Where are you going?" she asked, grabbing my arm.

"For a drive," I said, opening the door.

"At two o'clock in the morning?"

"Yes, at two o'clock in the morning," I said, walking out the door.

She didn't have a hold on me any longer. Her fake charms and dry love were as welcomed as a trip to the artic circle. She was use to telling me what to do but those days were long gone.

Without even thinking, I drove down to the bog and started a fire. I turned up the music loud then I sat on my tailgate, watching the flames flicker. There was something special about being here by myself. Suddenly, thoughts of Tiffany filled my mind and I felt at the same moment, she was thinking about me.

On the drive home, I decided to completely change my life. I had to ask Hanna for a divorce. All the way there I practiced the lines over and over again in my mind. In my heart, I believed she was already going on with her life. Besides, I wasn't in love with Hanna anyway.

I opened the door quietly and sat down at the kitchen table. She would be awake soon and I felt good about my decision because it's the right thing for both of us. But I knew all too well the way she could react sometimes so I was determined to break the news gently.

When I went to the bathroom, I could barely open the door because Hanna was lying on the floor. Taking her hand, I said her name softly. When she didn't wake up, I shook her gently. I grabbed her wrist checking for a pulse. She was barely breathing, cold and not responding so I started screaming her name.

Picking up her limp body, I ran to the car. We rushed to the hospital and I carried her inside.

About forty-five minutes later the doctor came out to talk to me. He asked if she'd ever tried to commit suicide. He told me Hanna had taken a lethal dose of Valium. He said if I had waited another ten minutes before going to the bathroom, my wife would be dead.

The entire month of March was spent taking care of Hanna. The thoughts of divorce I buried deep in my mind because I knew right now she couldn't handle it. Eventually, our relationship would end because she wasn't in love with me either. But no matter how I felt about our marriage, I didn't want anything bad to happen to her.

When it was time for me to leave for work, Hanna became very distraught. One of the last things she said was she knew I was going to leave her. I told her not to worry; it wasn't good for her health. Even though I tried to console her, we both knew she was right.

Chapter 34

My cell phone had been ringing all day and I was tired of answering it. After the fifth ring I grabbed it, saying, "Hello."

"Hi," Pamela said, innocently.

"I'm glad you finally called. How's Mexico?"

"It's great! I wish you were here."

"When are you coming home?"

"That's why I called. I need an answer about the script I sent you, Familiar Friends."

"Oh yeah. When does shooting begin?"

"May twenty-fifth, in New Orleans. Then we have to go to Miami. We could have so much fun, Tiffany. Please say yes."

"May twenty-fifth is only a few weeks away. Do you know how many things I'd have to cancel to do this?"

"Whatever it is, it'll be worth it. This movie is going to put us over the top, girl."

"I haven't had time to read the script yet."

"I have," she said with reassurance.

"I need to read it before I can give you a yes or no. When do you have to have an answer?"

"Look, they're kind of waiting for me to call them."

"Well, I have a meeting in thirty minutes. Can I call you back later?"

"Do you trust me, Tiffany?"

I paused a moment before giving her my answer. "Yes, I trust you. But that has nothing to do with making a business decision."

"I just hope you know that I'd never lie to you. I've read the script and it's really good. Kathy is the perfect role for you plus we would get to work together for the next few months. I miss you, girlfriend."

I answered reluctantly, "Okay. Call them back and tell them yes."

"You won't regret it," she said happily.

"When will you be back from Mexico?"

"I won't make it back to California so I'll just meet you in New Orleans. I can't wait! They're going to rename Bourbon Street, Tiffany and Pamela Street."

"Okay, I'll see you soon, love ya."

"Love you too, bye."

"Bye."

I lied to Pamela. I had looked over the script. The story line wasn't too bad but some of the writing lacked maturity and I didn't even like the title. But the fact that I would see Pamela soon made me happy and I knew we'd have a good time in New Orleans.

****

Filming Familiar Friends was more difficult than any other movie I'd been in. It wasn't because of stunts or subject content but because of the director. He seemed more like a dictator and our personalities totally clashed. His working hours were extremely long and his attitude caused many arguments on the set. And the heat of the New Orleans summer only made things worse.

Pamela and I still managed to have fun but most days we were too tired to go out. The nights that we did, we really paid for it the next day. The director could always tell when we had been out partying and he made sure those days were the hardest ones by being completely overbearing.

We arrived in Miami on July twenty-first and I was happy to be near the beach. We were only there for two days before Pamela found a local bar where we could go after work. It was mainly an older crowd so we could go without causing too much commotion.

Every person in the bar told us the story of his or her life. We heard about the sailors lost at sea and the women left behind with broken hearts. They told us about sunken treasures and devastating hurricanes. There were also stories of miracles and of course, local heroes.

They all began to feel like family after going there for a couple of weeks. When it was time to go back to California, it was hard to leave them behind. I promised the bartender that I'd be back to visit someday. I told him I would bring my friend, Steven, when I came back. I knew he would love this place and the people, with all their stories. When my thoughts turned to him, it wasn't so hard to leave and suddenly, I became curious to know how many letters might be waiting for me at home.

****

As I went through the stack of mail, I was shocked to only find one letter. I dropped the rest of the mail on the table and ripped the envelope open. They were beautiful words, that only Steven could write but it was what the words didn't say that left me feeling empty. In fact, all it accomplished was raising my concern about his state-of-mind. If Hanna wasn't in the picture, I'd know exactly what to do. The next flight to Natchez would have seat with my name on it.

After we got home, Pamela didn't have any work lined up so she lay around the condo sulking everyday. She seemed to be bothered by my presence and I almost began to feel like an intruder in our home.

After looking over my offers, I accepted a role that would take me to Australia for the next few months. Maybe distance would give me the chance to sort everything out. I needed to keep my mind occupied and besides, I just wanted to be alone.

The day before I left, Pamela told me she'd decided to go and stay in New York for a few months. It was too late for me to back out of my commitment so I left for Australia filled with animosity. Pamela knew I was tired and needed some peace and quiet but she just had to wait until the last second to tell me she would be gone. It made me want to run away. But where was I going to run?

****

The Australian lifestyle was ideal for me. Nobody seemed to be too uptight or judgmental and there was always some kind of party or event to attend. I made a lot of new friends while I was working down-under. It was weird, but I rarely thought about home until we wrapped up the movie.

Before Christmas, Pamela and I were back at home and we decided to throw a party for the opening of Familiar Friends. The party ended up being a huge success but the movie was a total flop. I knew it had to happen eventually, yet I couldn't help but be mad at myself.

The day after Christmas, Pamela left me a note on the kitchen table. She decided to go to New York for New Year's Eve. Everyone was talking about Y2K this and Y2K that and she used it as her excuse.

But I couldn't believe she didn't even have the decency to tell me in person. Especially since we had plans to go to a party together.

When New Year's Eve arrived, I decided to skip the party and spend it alone. So, I opened a bottle of champagne and watched television, just to make sure everything was going to be okay. I spent the hours before the New Year began, reading some of Steven's poetry from his high school journals. After all this time, he was still the only person in the world that I knew absolutely loved me for me. Right before midnight, I made a promise to myself that the year two thousand would be the best year of my life.

Chapter 35

One day at work, I received an emergency phone call from the hospital. Hanna had been drinking and took one too many pills again. How she could care so little for her own life is beyond my understanding. But there was nothing I could do, except leave my job and head to the nearest airport.

When I got home, she was a total wreck. Hanna told me she was sorry about getting sick. She had only wanted to go to sleep and didn't mean to cause any problems. I did everything I could and never left her side, until she was better.

Hanna finally went back to work and I was just hanging around for a few days before going back to Louisiana. I had played the model husband but I was so tired of her attention getting schemes. She knew, deep down inside, I wanted out and she was trying to make me look like bad to anyone who would listen. Most of the rumors I heard around town were just lies and it wouldn't have bothered me too much except for some of the looks I received. But I knew what they couldn't know. No one can see behind closed doors.

Before I left town, I ran into Brad's younger sister, Kim at the grocery store. She told me we needed to talk and asked me to meet her outside. By the tone of her voice, I knew it wasn't something I wanted to hear.

Kim told me about what happened the night Hanna overdosed. She said Brad was having a party and Hanna and Brad walked into the woods together. When they returned, they were fighting and she could tell Hanna had been crying. I asked Kim what it was about and she told me she wasn't sure. But whatever it was, it must have been bad because Brad left town in the middle of the night and Hanna tried to commit suicide.

As I drove home, I realized there was no way for me to know for sure what had happened between them. But then, I started feeling like I didn't want to know. Besides, what difference would the details really make?

My fury raged again when I thought about the fact that she'd tried to make me out to be the worst husband in the world. Only to a few people did she show her true colors. In the meanwhile, I was getting a bad reputation in my own hometown. The saddest part about the whole thing is the day I told Brad I wanted to ask her out I'd lied. I just felt a twinge of competition between the two of us and blindly went for it. I really won that competition didn't I?

I was so mad when I got home; I left the groceries on the kitchen floor and packed my bags. Within twenty minutes I was gone, not leaving Hanna the decency of a note. I drove away faster than the law allows, even though I didn't know where I was going. But the farther away from home I got, the better I felt.

With nowhere to go, I called my boss to see if he had any work. He said he could use me in a couple of days on a job in Arizona. Since I didn't have any thing better to do and needed some time to think, I declined to fly and told him I'd drive instead.

Work kept me busy and it was several weeks before I finally called Hanna. She wasn't at home so I left a message on the machine that I was in Arizona and wouldn't be home until May. I figured this would give us both some time to think and I really wasn't ready to see her again.

When I finally came home, Hanna seemed to be a completely different person. She was acting like a perfect devoted wife and was even dressing differently. She had also cleaned out the entire house of any knick-knacks or clutter and had bought new furniture. It was as if everything here had changed, except for me.

I spent the next few weeks at home and she never said a word about Brad or the way I left. She didn't even ask why I hadn't called her for so long. I didn't feel like talking either so I joined in on Hanna's way of avoiding the truth.

My next job assignment had me heading for California and I was excited. It would be my first trip out there and I wondered if it was fate. I would be going to San Francisco and couldn't help but think about going to see Tiffany.

I took some time off from work to go to L.A., knowing there was a chance she wouldn't be home, but I had to take it. It had been so long since we'd seen each other and I couldn't wait any longer. All I kept wondering is if everything between us would be the same.

I flew down to Los Angeles, rented a car and began my search. I bought a map and in no time had found Tiffany's condo building. I needed a code to park in the parking lot, so I had to park down the street. On my walk back to her building, I noticed a florist shop and went inside to buy her some white daises.

When I walked into her building my heart was racing as if I were running a marathon. A guy stopped to ask me who I was there to see. Then a lady at a desk spoke up and said Tiffany Starr doesn't live here. I explained that I was certain she lived here because we were old friends. The lady shook her head no and told me I must be mistaken. I understood why she was doing this but I was going to see Tiffany with or without her permission. But as I tried to walk toward the elevator, security guards grabbed my arms on both sides. They escorted me outside and ordered me not to return.

I walked behind them, explaining who I was but they never looked back at me. They walked back through the door and turned to face me, standing shoulder-to-shoulder, blocking the entryway. I had come all this way and now wasn't even allowed to knock on Tiffany's door.

As I stood there, trying to think about what I was going to do, Pamela drove by and saw me. I ran over and she told me to wait there while she parked her car. When I walked back in with Pamela everyone in the office apologized. I told them not to worry, that I understood they were just doing their job.

Pamela explained that Tiffany was out of town but I was welcome to stay. She gave me the grand tour and then we sat down out on the balcony to talk.

Pamela was definitely trying to give me the impression that Tiffany wasn't as innocent as I thought. She told me about the men in her life, risqué situations and things she'd said about me. I felt angry. I felt sick. Then I looked at Pamela, and I knew all that she was saying couldn't be true.

She offered me a drink as we were watching the sun go down. She fixed us a Long Island ice tea and I drank the whole thing within a few minutes. Pamela quickly got up to fix us another as the stories she told me were swimming in my head. I wanted to leave and I wanted to stay.

I didn't think anyone else in the world could understand how I felt. But just being where Tiffany lived, even though she wasn't home, made me feel closer to her.

Pamela was being overly flirtatious, so I had to be careful about what I chose to say. She was making me nervous but I still didn't want to leave yet. Some of her friends showed up and we continued to drink and talk on the balcony. Before long, my head started spinning and I had to lie down so she told me to go and lay on Tiffany's bed.

I made my way down the hall to her room and fell back on the bed. There was something pink in the corner and I tried to focus on it. Then I realized it was the big teddy bear I'd bought her for Christmas. Sliding down the side of her bed, I crawled over to get the bear. I lay back down, with the teddy bear in my arms and fell asleep.

Opening my eyes the next morning, it took me a few moments to remember where I was. I rolled over and Pamela was lying right beside me. Accidentally, I pulled the sheet down and realized she didn't have a nightgown on. Then I realized I didn't have any clothes on either.

"Pamela, Pamela! Wake up."

"Stop it," she said, pushing my hand away.

"What are you doing in bed with me? And what happened to my clothes?"

She turned toward me, barely opening her eyes and stretched. "I always sleep in the nude, I thought you did too," she said in a sexy voice.

"But why are we sleeping in the same bed?"

"Because I hate sleeping alone."

Pamela rolled over exposing herself and I turned my head, pulling the sheet up. "Please go get dressed."

"You go get dressed, Steven! I'm still sleepy."

"Where are my clothes?"

"Right over there."

I jumped out of bed and grabbed my pants, holding them in front of me. "What the hell happened last night?"

"You got really drunk," she said, watching me get dressed.

"No, I mean between you and me? Who took my clothes off?"

"I took your clothes off," Pamela said, getting up to go to the bathroom.

"Wait a minute. So we didn't do anything?" I asked through a closed door. "I don't even know why I'm asking you that question because I know we didn't. I would remember that, no matter how much I drank," I said aloud to myself.

She walked out of the bathroom, crawled back into bed and asked, "So you don't remember, do you?"

"Look, this is nothing to smile about. Why didn't you just leave me alone last night?"

She had a wicked grin, staring at me with piercing green eyes and said, "Tiffany would be so upset if I let one of our guests sleep alone. We always make sure every man that stays here wants to come back and see us again."

"Why did you do this, Pamela?" I walked into the bathroom and closed the door behind me because I didn't even want to hear the answer. I used the bathroom and washed my face and walked back into the bedroom. She was still nude, sitting up in bed, smoking a cigarette.

I sat down on the edge of the bed and said, "I'm sorry, I know you were just taking care of me and I appreciate it. I shouldn't have gotten so upset, but when I woke up and you were in the bed with me, it freaked me out."

"I'll take care of you anytime, sweetie."

"I don't suppose it would do any good to ask you not to mention this to Tiffany? I know it would just upset her, plus she doesn't need to know what happened," I said, walking to the door.

"I won't whisper a word of it to her, darling. Don't you worry about a thing; it'll be our little secret."

I was scared of Pamela before, but when I walked out of the room, I was terrified. Terrified that Tiffany would find out about what happened and never speak to me again.

Chapter 36

For Dad's birthday, I decided to surprise him and flew to Natchez unannounced. He was walking outside as I pulled up to the house. He ran to the street, opening my door before the driver could get out.

"Tiffany, you're home! Why didn't you call me and let me know you were coming?"

"I wanted to surprise you!" We hugged tightly and he softly kissed my cheek.

"I'm so glad you're here. Do I need to get your things?" he asked, walking to the trunk.

"No, he'll get them," I said, walking toward the house. Dad put his arm around me and I asked, "How are you doing?"

"I'm fine. And how's my girl?"

"Glad to be home," I said walking in the house, looking around. It seemed like nothing had changed since the last time I was here.

"Can I get you something to drink?"

"No, I'm fine," I said as the driver came in. "You can leave them by the door."

Dad walked over, taking my suitcases and said, "I'll take them upstairs for you right now."

"We can do that later, Dad. Where were you going when I pulled up?"

He sat down beside me and sighed, saying, "They're having a fund raiser tonight at the school. The playground equipment is run down, so they're raising money to repair it."

"That's nice," I said, thinking about the old school. It held so many special memories for me and suddenly I got lost in them.

Dad touched my arm, repeating his question. "Would you like to go with me?"

"Sure, that would be great," I said, standing up.

"Do you need to change or anything?"

"Am I overdressed?"

"No baby, you look fine," he said.

"Let's go in the limo, it'll give us a chance to talk."

"We can go in my car," he said, pulling out his keys.

"Come on, Dad. Let somebody else drive for a change."

As we approached the car, the driver opened the door and we got in. We caught up on each other's lives as we drove to the school and my dad seemed to be happy. But the closer we got, I couldn't help but wonder if Steven might be there.

When we pulled up to the gym, I felt nervous. There were so many people and I didn't have any security guards with me. It's just the kind of thing you get used to in my line of work. That is, if you're successful at it.

We walked inside and all eyes turned to look as Dad and I moved through the crowd. We both tried to pretend that it wasn't happening but then the younger children started asking me for autographs. The crowd grew larger and I began to feel anxious so dad put his arm around me. He announced that I could only sign ten more. I signed the last one and looked around the room, searching for Steven but couldn't see him anywhere.

"We would like to thank Buck Sellers for his donation of seventy-five dollars," a lady said, speaking into the microphone. "Please hold your applause until the end," she told the crowd when they started to clap. "We would also like to thank Doctor Slade and his wife for their generous donation of one hundred dollars!" she exclaimed as the crowd ignored her admonition and started clapping again. "We are now at twenty-four thousand, seventy-nine dollars and twenty-two cents. To reach our goal of fifty thousand dollars we need another," she said looking for the right piece of paper, "another, twenty-five thousand, and nine hundred twenty dollars and seventy eight cents. Please think of the children and open your hearts and your wallets tonight."

Dad and I walked over to the donation table so he could give them a check. I took one of the envelopes and started filling it out. The little girl at the table said, "Ms. Starr, I know you just came to visit, but I have to tell you I love your movies! I've seen every one you've ever been in. I can't believe you went to school here."

"I did. It was only for a few years but it feels like I went here most of my life. A lot happened to me here," I said, looking around the old gym.

I wrote out the check and handed her the envelope. She touched my hand as I gave it to her. I just smiled and turned away.

We walked over to get something to drink and everyone moved out of our way. I put my arm under my dad's and searched the crowd for Steven's face. I was having flashbacks of different things that happened between us here and it only made me want to see him more.

The lady got back up on stage, to make another announcement so Dad and I walked closer. She had a whole stack of notes and my dad seemed impatient to hear his name. When there were just two cards left in her hand, I knew which ones she had.

"We would like to especially thank Henry Crenshaw for his donation of one hundred fifty dollars!"

Dad smiled and hugged me as the crowd yelled and clapped loudly. He was so proud. It was the biggest donation yet and I almost felt bad about what I'd done.

"I would now like to announce that our fundraiser is officially over because Ms. Tiffany Starr has generously donated fifty-thousand dollars!"

The crowd went wild and dad picked me up off the floor, hugging me. By everyone's reaction, you would think I had just won the Miss America contest.

"Come on up here."

I deferred but my refusal was useless. Dad helped me to the stairs and I walked onto the stage, looking out into the audience.

"Please say something to our students," she said, handing me the microphone.

"Good evening ladies and gentlemen. Let me just take this opportunity to speak to the children who attend this school. I use to be a student here, back in the eighties. I know that was a long time ago, but it doesn't seem very long to me. I want you to know that any one of you can be successful. As long as you know what you want and you're determined. Determination is the key to success, no matter what you choose to do with your life. I hope that the new playground will not only be a source of entertainment but also a tool for imaginations, for many generations to come. Thank you, and good night."

As the crowd applauded, Dad reached out to help me offstage and said, "You didn't have to do that just because I brought you here."

"I wanted to, Dad. This old school holds a lot of memories for me."

"Are you ready to go home?"

"Whenever you are."

"Let's stay just a little while longer. If that's okay with you?"

I nodded and as he turned around, I saw Steven walking in our direction. I wanted to run to him, but I kept the same pace as dad.

"Tiffany, what are you doing here?" Steven asked, hugging me tightly then turned to shake my dad's hand. "Hello, Mr. Crenshaw."

"She came home to see me, Steven," he replied.

"I'm here to see both of you," I said, looking over at dad.

"I heard about your donation. That was really nice of you," Steven said, taking my hand.

"Thanks. So, how are you doing?" I asked, looking in his eyes.

"Here you are, Steven," Hanna said loudly, as she walked up.

We immediately stopped holding hands when we saw her, but it was too late. "Hello Hanna, it's nice to see you."

"Hi, I'm Henry, Tiffany's father," my dad said reaching out for Hanna's hand.

"How did you end up here, Tiffany?" she asked with a condescending tone.

"I came home to surprise dad and he was on his way over, so I joined him," I replied, hardly believing she'd ignored my dad.

"We need you to go get some more ice, Steven. Here's the money and the car keys. Just go over to Shelby's and get few bags," Hanna commanded, completely ignoring Dad and me.

"I'll go get it," he replied softly, taking the keys and money.

"Well, hurry up. We need that ice tonight."

"Will you be here when I get back?"

"Actually, we were just about to leave. Why don't you walk out with us?" Dad asked.

"I'd love to," Steven said, turning to walk away, without saying another word to Hanna.

"Bye, Hanna," I said, taking my dad's arm.

Everyone was watching as we walked to the door. Some of the kids were waving and saying goodbye to me. I smiled proudly, with my dad on one side and Steven on the other.

When we got to the limo, I asked Steven to sit and talk for a minute. We got in and the driver closed the door.

"Are you upset with me, Steven?" I asked, taking his hand.

"No. Why would you think that?"

"The last letter you sent me."

"I wasn't talking about you," he said quietly.

My dad was staring out the window and I leaned closer to Steven. "Are you sure?"

"You've never made me mad," he said, almost whispering.

I knew he was being sincere, but I could think of many things I'd done for him to be upset with me. "I'm just glad you're okay."

"Everything's fine," he said in a normal tone of voice.

I smiled, letting go of his hand and asked, "When can you come see me?"

"I should be finished here in a little while. I'll be there in about an hour."

"Okay, give me a hug."

He hugged me tightly then said, "See you later. Bye, Mr. Crenshaw."

"Bye."

I could tell by the look on dad's face he wasn't too happy about our conversation. He reminded me that Steven was married and I needed to remember that. I told him no matter what was going on in our lives; Steven and I would always be friends. He said that Hanna had given him the creeps and he just didn't want anything bad to happen to me. I told him not to worry, I wasn't afraid of her.

Chapter 37

We drove home in utter silence and I felt lost, deep in thought. How was I going to tell Hanna that I was going to see Tiffany?

We went inside and she changed into her nightgown. I sat down on the edge of the couch and decided to tell her the truth. I wasn't doing anything wrong, just going to visit an old friend and her father. I'd only be gone for an hour and she would just have to understand. She came in and sat down beside me on the couch pulling me back. She put her head on my chest and sighed deeply.

"Hanna, I'm going to see Mr. Crenshaw and Tiffany. I shouldn't be gone longer than an hour."

"If you feel like you have to go see her Steven, then go," she said, scooting away.

"I want to go see both of them but you're taking it the wrong way," I said, pulling her back.

"Please, don't touch me."

"Okay, I won't touch you," I said, standing up and walking to the door. "I'll be back soon."

I expected Hanna to run out of the house, cursing me or throwing things at the truck but there wasn't a sound as I backed out of the driveway. When I was pulling away, I felt a tinge of guilt. At the stop sign, I paused, debating whether I should go back home. Then I put Hanna in my shoes. She wouldn't hesitate to go see an old friend and I wouldn't expect her to.

On the way, I wondered why Tiffany thought I was talking about her in my letter. Her crazy roommate, Pamela, was also on my mind. Could Tiffany be upset because Pamela told her about my visit?

I pulled up in the driveway, taking a deep breath. I thought of how the day had begun just like any other day and how blessed I felt that it was ending this way. I got out of the truck, walking to the door and took another deep breath before knocking.

"Come on in," Mr. Crenshaw said, opening the door.

"Thank you."

"I'm in here, Steven," Tiffany yelled from the kitchen.

The smell of food filled my nose and I had to say, "Every time I come to this house, somebody is cooking."

"I know but isn't it wonderful," Tiffany said smiling, reaching out her hand.

It felt like coming home, being here with the two of them. Tiffany had changed a lot since the last time I saw her. She had a new haircut and was wearing clothes that didn't seem like her taste. She said that going to Australia had really changed her outlook on life. Everyone in America was too uptight and took everything way too seriously. Her dad and I could barely get a word in the conversation because she had so much to say. But neither of us seemed to mind, we were content to hear about her life and adventures.

Before I knew it, a couple of hours had flown by and it was time for me to go. They insisted I stay and I had to refuse several times before they understood I had to go home. I didn't want to go, but I was worried about Hanna. She had been so calm when I left and that wasn't a good sign from her.

I promised Tiffany I would come back and see her tomorrow afternoon. When I left, I felt happy that we got the chance to spend a little time together and could hardly wait to see her again.

When I pulled into the driveway, I noticed Hanna's car was gone. I went into the house and started looking around. Walking into our bedroom, I looked in the closet. Most of Hanna's clothes were gone. I looked down just to see that her shoes were missing too. I turned to look around in our bedroom to see what else Hanna had taken. That's when the writing on the mirror caught my eye. It was written in red marker. I slowly walked over to the dresser so I could read it.

LOVE-

1. A profoundly tender, passionate affection.

2. A feeling of warm personal attachment.

3. Sexual desire or its gratification.

4. A beloved person.

5. A strong predilection or liking for something.

YOU NEVER LOVED ME!!!!!!!

Chapter 38

When Steven didn't show up the next afternoon, I began to worry about him. Dad and I drove over to his house and when we didn't see Hanna's car, we stopped. Steven was sitting outside in the freezing cold, alone. I could tell he'd been crying and I took him in my arms. As my cheek touched his cheek, he felt almost like ice and I insisted we go inside.

Steven's house was cold and dark. We sat down at the kitchen table and I asked him what happened. He told us Hanna was gone. He explained while he was at our house last night, she left. Dad asked why she would leave just because he came over to visit. Steven was silent, looking into my eyes. Then he turned to my dad and told him to go look at the mirror in the bedroom.

Dad and I walked into the room and read what Hanna had written. Only then did we understand the look on Steven's face.

I helped him get some clothes because there was no way I could leave him here alone. We took him home and dad left us alone to talk. Everything I should have said would have been a lie so I kept my opinions to myself. Sometimes, the best thing you can do for someone you love is listen. So I listened about his anger and feelings of betrayal. I could hear the pain and anguish in each word he spoke. And even though I had to bite my tongue, I never said a bad word about his wife.

The next morning over breakfast, neither Dad nor I brought Hanna up in the conversation. I think Steven could tell we were avoiding the subject but I guess he still needed to talk about it.

He stared into his coffee, ignoring my question then said, "I called Hanna's mother this morning. She said she isn't there."

"Do you have any idea where she might have gone?" Dad asked.

"I think she and Brad had an affair," he replied, matter-of-factly, never looking up. "Who knows, she might be with him."

"Do you know where he lives?"

"He's in New Orleans somewhere," he replied solemnly.

"You know if you need anything, or just need to talk, don't hesitate to ask," Dad said firmly, putting his hand on Steven's shoulder.

"Do you think I should go to North Carolina?"

"I think that would be a good idea," Dad said, nodding.

"What do you think, Tiffany?"

I sat silently, looking into Steven's eyes, wondering what I should say. I felt like Hanna had hurt him enough and I wished he could just be happy that she was finally gone. "I think you should do what your heart tells you to do."

"I wish everything in life was that simple," he said, closing his eyes, putting his head down.

After several moments of silence, Steven excused himself from the table and went to the bathroom. I had never seen him this upset before and didn't know what to do. I wanted to take care of him, like so many times he had taken care of me.

Steven must have read my mind because he stayed with us, not even going back home for more clothes. He needed to be with friends right now and honestly, I needed him here too. I loved him and no matter what happened in his life or mine, nothing would ever change that.

I thought of bringing up the situation with Pamela but in my heart, I didn't believe what she'd said. The only reason I thought of asking was because I wanted to hear his side of the story. I knew Pamela pretty well, but I knew Steven better. So I kept my questions to myself and tried not to think about it.

We didn't talk much about Hanna either but I must admit that I had my share of guilt for what happened. My heart made me feel that he was better off without her. The few times he mentioned her I had to bite my tongue. I knew deep down inside that that was just his way. He defended everyone.

I felt torn when it was time for me to go. Dad and Steven begged me to stay a few more days and I could tell they had to lie every time they said they understood. But I had to return for a New Year's Eve party that I couldn't miss.

To make my departure easier on them, I refused a ride to the airport and called for a Limo. They helped me get my things in the car and we had just enough time for a last goodbye. They both acted happy, smiling and waving as I left. Of course, it was a different story but what could I do? I sank back in my seat and quietly cried all the way to the airport.

The minute I got home, Pamela started asking questions about Steven. I blew her off but she continued to follow me around, prodding for answers. I explained that we would have to talk about it later because I had to get ready. I went into my bedroom, shutting the door and she left for the party without me.

Later when I arrived, Pamela was already highly intoxicated. I tried to avoid her but she kept pursuing me. When I ignored her, she began harassing me with nasty insults. I tried to calm her down, which only made her speak louder.

"Don't tell me to be quiet!"

"Please, don't do this, Pamela. Do you want to go home?" I asked in a low whisper with a fake smile.

"Do I want you to take me home? I'll tell you what I want, Tiffany!" she yelled, pointing at herself.

Pamela threw her drink down on the marble floor and it shattered into a hundred pieces around my feet. "Please Pamela, calm down," I begged.

"I want everybody's attention!" she yelled as people began to crowd around us. "I want to tell you the truth about Tiffany Starr! Look at her…you all love her, don't you?"

Everyone smiled and clapped, nodding their heads. I smiled trying to pretend like everything was okay. I was hoping and wishing she wasn't going to say anything bad.

"Well, you're all stupid idiots!"

"It's time for us to go," I said, taking her by the arm.

"Get your hands off of me! Everything is all about her, her life, her career, and her dreams. I bet everyone here would love to know what happened when the love of her life came to our house. He ended up in bed with me. Did you hear that? IN BED WITH ME!"

Pamela was kicking and screaming as two men escorted her from the room. I stood there in shock, unable to move a muscle. I was speechless. I had trusted her with everything, only to be stabbed in the back. I felt so foolish, so unbelievable naïve. How could I have been so stupid? I thought Pamela was my friend.

Everyone at the party tried to console me, but I could barely hear what they were saying. I kept playing the scene over and over in my mind and each time it seemed to get a little worse. And the question I kept asking myself was what had I ever done for Pamela to hate me?

New Year's Day found me sitting in a hotel room, all alone. The events of last night were still swimming in my head with no way of stopping them. If Pamela wanted to treat her best friend that way, she'd have to find a new one. I'd had enough of her outrageous lifestyle and crazy schemes. It seemed as though she was putting my livelihood in jeopardy and our relationship had to end. There was no need for explanations. Last night her actions spoke louder than any words she could ever say.

Sometimes, I looked out the window looking down on the busy streets of Los Angeles and longed to be back in Natchez. It made me wonder why I'd insisted on coming here at all. To get my mind off of my problems, I asked for the newspaper so I could start looking for a new place to live.

The next day, I went by the condo to get some of my things. I knocked on the door and when Pamela didn't answer, I dug in my purse for the key. At first, I thought it was the wrong key but finally it dawned on me that she'd changed the lock. Anger rushed through my body as I knocked on the door one more time. After all I had done to help her; I couldn't believe she would treat me this way. I left, determined more than ever, to start a new life without her in it.

The next few days I tried in vain to get in touch with Pamela but it seemed she'd fallen off the face of the earth. The thought of calling the police, to make her give me back my things, crossed my mind. Not to mention the fact that I own half the condo. But I knew they were only things and I didn't need another scandal that would end up in the tabloids.

A couple of weeks later, I bought a beautiful house on the beach and before long I was moving in. The first night in my new house, the pain of what Pamela had done, subsided. A sudden realization, that everything usually works out for the best put my mind at ease.

After keeping me in the dark for so long, Pamela did the strangest thing. She showed up at my house with a basket of fruit and a box of my stuff. I almost didn't open the door, for fear of her going psycho but instead; I cracked the door open and said hello.

"Surprise!"

"What are you doing here?"

"I just wanted to come by and give you a house warming gift," she said sweetly, holding up the basket.

"Here, let me help you," I said, taking the basket, stepping backwards and opening the door.

"This is a beautiful place," she said smiling, looking around.

"Thanks, Pamela. Forgive me if I don't give you the tour."

"That's okay, I can only stay for a second," she said, nervously.

"You can sit that box right there."

She sat it down, and then began digging in her purse. "I changed the lock at the condo so I brought you a new key."

"Thanks," I said, taking it out of her hand.

"You can take whatever you want."

"I'll only take what's mine. I'll leave the key on the kitchen counter when I'm done."

"I hope you're still not upset with me, I just had a little too much to drink that night," she explained, hanging her head. Then she looked up and said, "I really need a friend right now."

"Don't worry about it. You'll always have a friend in me," I lied, just to keep the peace, then turned and opened the front door.

We didn't waste much time on goodbyes then I shut the door behind her, completely confused by her actions. How she thought that everything would be okay was completely beyond me. But still, I was glad that this final confrontation had come to pass without an argument.

I had everything moved from the condo to the new house the next day. I left the key and a legal document giving Pamela my half of the condo on the kitchen table. She had ruined our friendship in one night and I just wanted it all to be over. There was no telling what she might do at this point and I didn't want to split hairs with her.

****

Springtime filled the hills with flowers and as usual, my thoughts turned to Steven. I hadn't received a letter from him yet so I called dad to see if he had given him my new address. Dad told me he had but explained Steven had received divorce papers on Valentine's Day. He said that Hanna must have paid extra to be that heartless. I didn't know what to say, so I changed the subject.

183

I filled him in about the new movie I was working on and about my new friend I'd met recently at work, Diane. I told him, she's a screenwriter and he asked me what she's like. She's tall with brown wavy hair and big brown eyes. Then I elaborated, the only way I can describe her is extremely intelligent and kind. After spending a few hours in her presence, I feel so alive. She is childlike with an innocence that I rarely see in anyone anymore. There is a way she laughs, throwing her head back, like she doesn't have a care in the world. He said he looked forward to meeting her someday and I told him that would be great.

It was the middle of summer before the movie I was working on wrapped up. I finally received a letter from Steven and it lifted my spirits. Hanna still hadn't contacted him and I couldn't understand how she could be so cold but I was glad for his sake that she was gone for good.

Since the movie was a wrap, I decided to take the next few weeks off and asked Diane if she would like to come and stay with me. When she accepted, I was completely surprised. Diane said the time off would do her good because her best ideas only came during quiet moments. I told her that I had a few movie ideas myself, which seemed to amuse her.

Diane arrived early in the morning and we went straight to the beach. We played in the surf, wetting our bodies then lay in the sun to let them dry and then we'd do it all over again. We talked about our childhoods, families and the great loves of our lives. It was during these moments that I wished I had a closer relationship with my sister, Cheryl.

When we were drenched with sun and our bellies were empty, we went back to the house for lunch. She prepared the salad and I made the sandwiches. We took them out on the terrace and sat down to eat.

"How did you become a screenwriter?"

"My dad, I was born into the profession. When I was a teenager and he had writer's block he would ask me to help him."

"So your dad…"

"He was a playwright. He only worked on two films but it's almost the same thing."

"Like father, like daughter," I said, acknowledging the pride on her face.

"He said one of us had to follow in his footsteps and I was the poet of the family so it was only natural for me to do it."

"Why did you become an actress?"

"You know, I really don't have a unique story to tell you. I felt like I had to do it a lot when I was a child so I thought I'd be good at it."

"Well you are good at it."

"And you do a good job of making a salad. Thanks for helping me make lunch."

"It was my pleasure," she said, picking up her plate and following me to the kitchen.

"So what do you want to do this afternoon?"

She turned to face me, with a funny look and asked, "Do you feel like reading?"

"Sure, I have some magazines."

"No, I meant read to each other," she said shyly, touching my arm.

"That would be nice."

"Great. I brought a book of poetry."

She walked to her room to get the book and I was dumbfounded. I'd agreed but still, the request seemed odd. I guess it was only because no one had ever asked me to read with them before. But when we began to read, the idea seemed perfect. As I listened to her voice, I closed my eyes and wished Steven was reading his poetry to me.

As each day passed, Diane and I grew closer and closer. She felt like a long lost sister and I was so thankful for her company. We did everything together and never once had an awkward moment.

To my surprise, she loved one of my movie ideas and started taking notes. As we decided the setting and the character's names, I couldn't help but get excited. And it was so interesting to hear my story come to life through her words.

Two days before Diane had to leave for Arizona, I received a letter from Steven. I asked if she wanted to come and listen and she said yes. I explained that I usually read his letters in the bedroom, lying on my bed.

It felt just like I was sixteen and Victoria was following me to my room. Diane giggled with excitement as we sat on the bed together. I turned and looked at her seriously, before opening Steven's letter to read it aloud.

My darling,

These eyes can still see you in the summers light, even though you are not here. I look into the night and search through each day to find a way. How could it be, that there may not be one? I just wanted another day in the sun. To see your hair, to watch you smile, your light would shine around me. I would feel better I think, than I have felt in days, or perhaps in years.

My friend, my beloved, cherished angel from above. Am I worthy of seeing you once again? The days pass by, in the blink of an eye and I am alone. Don't worry; I have plenty of friends, but only one you.

Please know that I ask nothing of you, except to think of me. When the rain drops, when the ground is wet, please let me be in your thoughts. When the stars are out at night, I can feel you here with me. Know forever, this is the only way it could be.

This roller coaster ride that always costs the same. I just wonder why, it was blessed with your name. If you ever need me, I'll be there by your side. I will look for you my darling, in my dreams tonight.

Love,
Steven

"Oh my gosh, Tiffany!"

"I know."

She sat up and asked, "Is he a writer?"

"No, he's an engineer, remember?"

"When you write him back, give him my number. If he hasn't written a book yet, he needs to."

"Here," I said, handing her the envelope, "You write him. Tell him I said hello."

"Okay, I'll do that," she said getting up and going to her room.

Diane never asked anything about why I was so short on the subject of writing Steven. If she was even curious, it never showed. She didn't pry into my past to be my friend and it was one of the things I liked most about her.

****

When Diane returned from Arizona in October, she called. She told me all about her trip and I listened contentedly to every word. Her description of Arizona made me long to have been there with her.

I could almost see the sunrise and feel the dry air as I listened to her voice. It seemed like so much had happened while she was there but I had to ask the question that invaded my every thought.

"Have you written Steven yet?"

"Yes I have and he told me to tell you hello."

I paused for a moment, hoping she would elaborate, and then asked, "Was he interested in writing a book?"

"Girl, you're not going to believe this. He had already started a book."

"That's wonderful," I said, shocked by her answer.

"It gets better, Tiffany," she said, enticing me.

"Tell me."

"I read the first three chapters and it was excellent. So, I called a friend of mine in the publishing business and they're going to publish it."

"I can't believe it," I said, taking a deep breath and slowly exhaled. "You've changed his life forever."

"He would have figured it out for himself, sooner or later. But don't get me wrong, I'm happy I could help," she replied, nonchalantly.

"When will it be published?"

"Hopefully, before Christmas."

"How does he feel about it?"

She laughed loudly and I could envision her throwing her head back. "He told me he wasn't going to quit his day job."

"Sounds just like him. He won't believe it until he sees it."

"Can you blame him for that?"

"No, I can't," I said, having a strange feeling she was talking about more than his book.

When we got off the phone I couldn't believe I hadn't asked what the title of his book is. I didn't even ask what it was about. Calling her back crossed my mind but I decided it would be better just to wait and read it myself. But then I began to contemplate so many things it could be about that it almost drove me crazy.

As the days dragged by, I could see everything moving in slow motion as Steven moved even farther away from me. All I knew, was he wrote a book while my letters from him were becoming less and less frequent.

To console myself, I accepted a role in a movie that would take me to Jamaica. The thought of being on an island, surrounded by the ocean sounded perfect to me. If I was far enough away, maybe I could stop thinking about Steven and his book.

I would be in Jamaica for Christmas so I called my mom to ask if she would join me. It was a shock when she accepted so I made arrangements for her flight before she could change her mind. We hadn't seen each other in two years and I wondered if it would feel strange to be with her again.

Mom arrived a week before Christmas, looking exactly the same, like she hadn't aged a day. With her head held high and shoulders back, we walked through the airport without a word. Everyone stared and moved out of the way as we walked briskly. She still had the same air about her, which kept everyone at arms length. I don't think Mom really meant to do it. It was just her way.

On the third day of her visit, we were getting ready to go out to dinner. I tried to push the question out of my mind but was unable to do it anymore. As we stood together in the bathroom, I couldn't stop myself from asking.

"Mom, what happened when you left Dad?"

"I don't understand why you have to bring up the past, Tiffany. I thought you'd be over it by now."

I looked in the mirror at her and said, "I just need to know why you left us like that."

She looked back at me, as though she was uncomfortable and said, "I really don't feel like it was a mistake for me. The way I did it was wrong and I'm sorry if I hurt you."

I turned to face her and she looked back into the mirror, putting on her lipstick. "I need to know why you left and never said good-bye. Do you understand that?"

She turned to face me and said, "I did say goodbye to you, Tiffany. You were sleeping. I came into your room and sat on your bed and told you everything. I kissed your little cheek and you smiled in your sleep," she replied, suddenly full of emotion.

"I was asleep when you told me goodbye?" I asked in disbelief.

"I wouldn't have been able to leave if you were awake."

"You told me goodbye in my sleep! And all these years, I thought you never said goodbye to me. I want to know why you left."

My anger seemed to fuel hers as she threw her lipstick in the bag and yelled, "I left because I couldn't take it anymore!"

"Take what? You had it made! You had a good husband, a beautiful house and two healthy children. What more could you have wanted?"

"I wanted to dance! I wanted to make my own decisions. Do you know that your father controlled every aspect of my life? He wouldn't let me have anything to do with dancing! Except for Cheryl's classes, that's all he would let me have. Just a taste, just a little crumb was all. I didn't want to just watch her dance. Everyday was slipping away, so fast, right in front of my own eyes. Then one day, I just couldn't take it anymore. I left, and I'm sorry if it hurt you, but it saved my life."

As tears rushed down my face, I asked, "Why haven't you ever told me this before?"

"Because baby, I never wanted you to look down on your father. He loves you so much. You mean everything to him."

I had not heard my mother call me baby in a long time and it made me cry even harder. "He means a lot to me too but I still needed you, Mom."

"Come here," she said, opening her arms. "Baby, sometimes, people get together and they're happy for a few years and then life becomes a struggle. Some of the lucky ones find someone to love for a lifetime. It's not that I don't love your father, because I still do. It was just too much of a struggle for us to stay together. Henry would never agree to let the three of us leave," she explained with tears rolling down her cheeks.

"I've missed you," I said softly, looking deep into her eyes.

"And I've missed you, more than you will ever know. You just wait until you have a baby, you'll see," she said, turning to get us a tissue.

We ate dinner almost in silence that evening because neither one of us had much left to say. I knew I had to forgive Mom for my own sake. I searched her beautiful face, lit by candlelight and remembered all the dinners she cooked for our family. She always had a beautiful glow in the candlelight and tonight was no different. I realized I'd been mad at her because she wasn't there to help me grow up. I needed her more back then, than she could ever realize now and I felt sad for her. Mom really didn't know what she missed by leaving her family behind. I knew that whatever pain I'd felt, she had felt more.

Sitting across the table from her, I made a promise to myself. If I ever have children, I'd never leave them, no matter what. Mom had her own conscience to deal with and I didn't want to make anything worse. I forgave my mother completely before we got up to leave and suddenly, I felt light as a feather. I had done nothing wrong and finally I was freed from all my guilt. My whole body felt like it was floating, as if a huge weight was lifted off my shoulders. And with newfound hope, I decided my New Year's resolution was to totally let go of the past and look toward a bright new future.

Chapter 39

Sales for my book, The Cleansing Rain steadily increased as the New Year began. It had spread in popularity solely by word of mouth. There were no book signings, no promotions, just people talking to people.

The people in Natchez started to treat me differently. They greeted me with bigger smiles and stopped to talk when normally they were too busy. But I kept the same job and tried to carry on as though everything was normal.

The strangest part about it was the book started as a letter but it was one I could never send. There was way too much truth and honesty and it was easier to keep on writing than to send Tiffany another letter without receiving a reply. So I kept writing, holding nothing back and all the dreams I wanted to come true, came true on paper.

When the Cleansing Rain hit the Best Seller's List, my publisher offered me an advance for my next book. And by March, Diane convinced me to quit my job and write full time. What she didn't know was that I'd already started my second book months before. I finally found my purpose in life, a way to expend my emotions and I would never stop writing for as long as I lived.

Chapter 40

When I left Jamaica for Los Angeles the movie I had made the previous year was becoming a huge success. So I decided to go right back to work. Italy would be the next destination on my itinerary and I was thrilled because it would give me the chance to see more of the world.

Before I left for Italy, I called Diane to ask her to come spend a week with me but she was too busy finishing the screenplay we started. Diane wouldn't elaborate, but she promised I'd be the first to read it. I asked about Steven and she was surprised I didn't already know.

When I got off the phone, I called a local bookstore and reserved a copy of The Cleansing Rain. I sent my driver to pick it up while I took a hot bath. My stomach was full of butterflies at the thought of reading Steven's words. I spread a blanket in the middle of the living room then gathered every pillow in the house and put them on top of the blanket. It was hard to believe that he'd written a book, much less the fact that I would have it in my hands in a few minutes.

The driver returned with the book and I sat it down in the middle of the pallet. I started lighting candles and decided to cancel my meetings for tomorrow. Once I was on the phone, I went ahead and canceled my appointments for the next day too. That would give me almost three days to read Steven's book and I was filled with anticipation.

It was a life story…love, hate, and all emotions in between. And as I turned each page, I felt closer to Steven than ever before. Somewhere in those pages I could feel him. It's the way he twisted and weaved the story that compelled me to laughter and to tears. I tried to find myself somewhere in his words. Sometimes I would grasp a small piece here and there, but Steven's imagination seemed to be pulling from all aspects of life.

After reading The Cleansing Rain, the strangest thing was that I wanted to read it again. Of course, that would have to wait because I had to get back to work.

The next day, even though I was extremely busy, my mind would wander away with Steven's words. The characters he created lived within the boundaries of my mind. I would think of their trials and tribulations and compare them to my life. And the way he ended his book, left my heart longing for the kind of love he had written about.
****

When I arrived in Italy, the location seemed so familiar to me. I knew I'd never been there before and wondered if I had seen the little town in pictures or something. I brought three copies of Steven's book to the set because I needed other people to read it. I never told them that the author was a friend of mine because I didn't want to cloud their judgment. No one seemed too excited about reading it but once they started, they couldn't put it down.

By the end of April, we wrapped up shooting and nearly everyone on the set had read his book. It was amazing how much closer we became after reading Steven's book. I had never experienced such closeness with any other movie crew. We all left each other with hugs, kisses and promises to see each other again.

On the flight back to Los Angeles, my one and only plan was to sleep all the way home. I snuggled back into the seat, trying to get comfortable but the guy beside me kept digging through his bag. When he zipped it back up, I opened one eye to see what he had. It was a copy of The Cleansing Rain and there was no way I could fall asleep.

We started talking about the book and I told him I was a friend of the author. He began to ask me questions and I wasn't even thinking about my safety. I accidentally took off my dark sunglasses and even though I had a wig on, he recognized me. I put my finger in front of my mouth to keep him quiet.

He leaned over and whispered, "It's nice to meet you. I'm a big fan of yours."

"Thank you. And you are?"

"Jared Evans."

"Nice to meet you, Jared," I said, reaching out my hand.

"The pleasure is all mine," he replied, raising my hand to his lips.

"Are you flying to Los Angeles?"

"Yes, I live there."

"So do I," I said, smiling, letting go of his hand.

"See, we already have something in common, Tiffany. May I call you Tiffany?"

"Yes, you can call me Tiffany."

He leaned closer and whispered, "I've seen all of your movies. Some of them twice."

With Jared so close to me, I could smell the scent of his cologne. That's when I leaned back and took a long look at him. He was very handsome. Dark hair and dark brown eyes with a California tan. He was dressed in a business suit, but I could still see the definition of muscles.

We talked and talked and before I knew it, we were back in Los Angeles. When we were leaving the plane, Jared asked for my phone number. And I felt so close to him, like I'd known him for years that I didn't even hesitate before writing it down.

Jared told me he would call me on Saturday and I was impatiently waiting for the phone to ring. We talked for a long time and made plans to see each other in three days. It had been so long since I'd gone out on a date that I looked forward to it.

The same day that Jared and I were to go out on our first date, I finally received a letter from Steven. I walked into my room, lay down on the bed and opened his letter.

My dearest Tiffany,

I must begin by saying you are the most beautiful creature that has ever graced the silver screen. You took my breath away as I watched your new movie. Is it possible that you became more beautiful with age? Always in my mind, you will remain the same.

I hope by now, you have heard of my good news too. It certainly surprised me and I wonder what it did to you. I haven't changed a thing, except I don't punch a clock anymore. And I must tell you I'm happier now, I feel more alive. I pray that your spirit is soaring high too. I pray for you Love, you know I do.

It's been too long since I've seen your beautiful face. But there is a picture in my mind, which no one can erase. I am writing day and night now, yes it's true. Yet I always have the time to think about you.

Oh darling please, be careful out there and know there is darkness and light. Remember it's hard to figure out which one is there sometimes.

I hope the days will bring us together soon. I need to see you to believe all that's happened to me is true. It is only when I see your face, that I will truly understand. My heart is aching, my soul is insane, and my head changes its mind time and again. Whatever does it matter, my beloved, my only friend? The truth is it doesn't, because there is no way I can win. I love you, and it is so pure, that it doesn't matter where you are. Still, I can look up at the stars and you are here with me.

Love,
Steven

His words brought tears to my eyes and pain to my heart. Then I literately began to feel like my heart wouldn't beat if Steven were to die. After all of these years, we were still so closely sewn together, that if something happened to him, it would still affect me. And I wondered why he couldn't see it in my eyes. Is there a way he could be blind to the truth?

I took a tissue and dried the tears from my face. I walked into the bathroom and looked at the reflection in the mirror. As I studied the person looking back at me, I still couldn't see a woman good enough for a man like Steven.

I resolved to stop longing for him or someone like him, because there wasn't anybody. His life was better off without me in it anyway. My life was too complicated and painful for someone as wonderful as him. I got dressed for my date, hoping Jared wouldn't be able to tell that I had been crying.

****

After our first date, Jared and I started spending a lot of time together. We had many of the same interest and he seemed to understand me. He knew exactly what to say and what to do to make me feel comfortable. He was so kind and gentle yet strong and intelligent and it felt like I had known him my whole life. This was not a beginning feeling, it was like we had been together for years.

It wasn't long before we planned a trip to Hawaii together. We wanted to show each other some of our favorite places, and besides I wanted to escape from reality.

We left the first week of June and the weather in Hawaii was perfect. We rented a secluded beach house and with each passing hour became more intimately entangled. Everywhere we went on the island people liked him. He was the kind of guy who made everyone feel right at ease. I had never known a man like Jared before in my life and I was completely mesmerized.

Our last night in Hawaii, he chartered a boat to take us offshore for dinner. The sun was setting as we moved toward the horizon. Jared poured us a glass of champagne as dinner was served. Our meal was exquisite and I was surprised Jared had gone to so much trouble. We finished eating and then he shocked me when he stood up and kneeled down in front of me.

"I have something to ask you."

"You're making me nervous, Jared. What is it?"

He pulled a tiny box from his coat pocket and said, "Tiffany, I'm in love with you and I want us to spend the rest of our lives together. Will you marry me?"

I looked in his eyes, caught up in the moment and whispered, "Yes."

Jared picked me up out of my chair, squeezing me tightly as he turned round and round. I thought Jared would never stop as my world began to spin. When he sat me back down, I had to grab the railing so I wouldn't fall. I hoped I hadn't made the wrong decision by accepting Jared's proposal but he completely swept me off my feet.

Chapter 41

It had been raining for three days. All the windows were fogged up but it didn't matter to me. I embraced the solitude like an old friend, like someone I knew very well. And when I felt lonely, I took my favorite pen in hand. Then I would write about a world I wished was reality.

Hours would pass by like minutes as I wrote about love. True love with all its highs and lows but true all the same. And when the pen wasn't in my hand, I dreamed of a girl I once knew, the prettiest red head in the whole world.

The phone rang, bringing me out of my daydream as I said, "Hello."

"Hi, Steven, I hope I'm not interrupting you," Diane said.

"No, not at all. What's up?"

"I have wonderful news!"

"Lay it on me."

"I have an offer that you can't refuse."

"Are you going to tell me or do I have to guess?"

"They want to make your book into a movie!"

"What?" I asked, completely blown away by the news.

"It's true. I was just calling to make sure it's okay to give Dean Broderick your number."

"Of course you can give it to him. I can't believe it! You're not just messing with my head, are you?" I asked, sitting down.

"No, I'd never do that to you."

"Thank you so much, Diane. None of this would've happened without you."

"No actually, none of this would have happened if you hadn't been writing to Tiffany all those years."

"That's strange you would say that. So many times I wanted to stop. Sometimes, I would promise myself that the letter I was mailing would be the last one."

"Every road we take leads somewhere, I'm just glad that yours led you here."

"Me too." My voice trailed off, as I truly realized this had happened because of Tiffany. It was my love for her that caused me to write the book in the first place.

Diane brought me back to reality, as she replied, almost in a whisper, "Yes, we're kindred spirits," then she paused before saying, "I'll give Dean your number. Listen; don't sign anything until we talk. They know you're green in the business and there's no telling what they'll try to put in your contract."

"Alright, I'll call you. Hey, before I let you go, have you talked to Tiffany lately?"

"No, but I need to call her. If you come out to see Dean, maybe the three of us can get together."

"That sounds great."

"Okay, bye."

"Bye."

I sat down in my chair and leaned back, putting my feet on the desk. Closing my eyes, I went back through the memories of writing Tiffany. From high school, through college until now and I couldn't believe how many years had passed.

The telephone rang again which ended my reminiscing. Mr. Broderick and I agreed that I'd fly out to Los Angeles in three days. That would give me just enough time to finish editing my new book, Saying Goodbye, before I left. And even though I was going for business, I knew when the plane landed; my only desire would be to see Tiffany.

Chapter 42

Within hours of getting home from Hawaii, I was catching a flight to New York. My sister had called and left a message that mom was in the hospital. Of course, she didn't say what hospital or what was wrong and there was no answer at Mom's apartment or Cheryl's, so I worried all the way, wondering what had happened.

By the time I arrived at mom's apartment, I was frantic. Cheryl opened the door and seemed surprised to see me. When I opened my arms to hug her, she stepped back but I hugged her anyway.

"What are you doing here?" she asked.

"I got your message."

"You could have just called," she said, sounding irritated.

"I tried but nobody answered."

"Tiffany, I left that message over a week ago," she said angrily.

"I was in Hawaii," I answered softly, hoping she would calm down.

"That's just like you. Off having fun while I'm taking Mom from doctor to doctor."

"I got here as soon as I could. Please don't give me a hard time."

"You don't even know what hard is."

"Look, you don't know anything about my life, Cheryl."

Her face began to turn red as she picked up her drink, saying, "I know that you would be a nobody, except you slept with all those men."

"Look, I didn't come here to argue. Where's Mom?"

"I don't see why she's so important now. She never has been before."

"She's my mother too and don't you forget it."

"All these years, you've pushed her aside and now that she's on her death bed you come running. I guess since you're an actress, you'll act like you care," she replied nonchalantly, fixing another drink.

"I do care."

"Well you could have fooled me," she said loudly, slamming her drink down. "All the years she's been in New York, have you ever once asked her if she needs anything, Tiffany?"

I ran the question through my mind but no was the only answer I had. Then I thought, certainly she knew if she needed anything I would give it to her. And instead of answering her question I asked her one. "And when's the last time you've seen your father's face?"

My question shocked her and she paused before saying, "Why don't you just go back to Hollywood? That's exactly where you belong with all the other freaks and whores."

I walked right up to her, saying, "I'm going to pretend you didn't just say that, Cheryl. And I'm going to overlook your rudeness because I know you're just a bitch."

She picked up her drink, like she wanted to throw it on me but I stood my ground. All the years of her mental abuse had finally taken their toll and I wasn't going to take it for another second. She turned and threw the glass at the wall but it didn't even break. Ice cubes slid across the floor and I giggled for just a second.

Cheryl grabbed her purse and for a moment I thought she was going to hit me with it. I crossed my arms in front of me and gave her a look that could kill. She tried to stare me down but I never looked away and finally she turned and walked out the door, slamming it behind her.

I took a deep breath, trying to calm down then walked toward the hallway. My mother lay on the bed and she didn't look well but right on cue, she sat up and tried to look better.

"What's wrong, Mom?" I asked, leaning over to kiss her cheek.

She sighed heavily, staring off into space. "Nobody knows. The doctors have run all kinds of tests and still don't have a clue."

"Everything will be okay," I said, looking into her eyes.

She slowly responded, "I hope so."

I had never seen Mom like this and didn't know what to say. "You probably just need to go on a shopping spree. I'd love to take you."

She rolled her eyes, saying, "Well, if we do any shopping it'll have to be from a catalog."

I sat on the edge of the bed and said, "Actually, that would be fun. I was planning on staying with you for a while, if you don't mind."

"I would like that," she said, taking my hand, finally giving me a smile.

****

I spent the next two weeks in New York until Mom was feeling better. During the day, when she was napping, I would think about the future. I imagined my wedding and what the following years would be like married to Jared. But somehow my thoughts would always drift back to Steven. Even after all this time, his named was still etched across my heart.

When it was time to fly back to California, there was another destination on my mind. Despite all that had happened in my life, Natchez still felt like home. When I got to L.A., I listened to my messages and Diane had called. She said Steven was in town and wanted to see me. It made me wonder if that was the reason he had been on my mind so much. I called her immediately to find out if he was still here.

"Hey girl, I just got your message."

"Where have you been?" Diane asked, sounding upset.

"I had to go to New York. My mom was in the hospital."

"Is she okay?'

"Yes, she's feeling better now."

"You just missed Steven. He left this morning."

My heart sank as I asked, "How is he doing?"

"He's doing great. A friend of mine wants to make a movie based on The Cleansing Rain and he just sent his second book to the publishers."

"Wow. How is he handling it?"

"He's the happiest man in the world," she replied, like I was a stranger.

My mind raced with questions about Steven but considering her attitude, I changed the subject. "Well, I guess I need to tell you about Jared Evans."

"Who is Jared Evans? Is he a fan of yours?"

"A man I met when I was flying home from Italy."

"Oh, so is he the reason I couldn't get in touch with you for so long?"

"Actually, before I went to New York, Jared and I went to Hawaii. He proposed the night before we left."

She paused and then slowly said, "I don't know what to say. Congratulations."

"Thanks. Sometimes it's still hard for me to believe," I said softly, unsure if I should have said anything.

"I bet."

By her reaction I decided to change the subject again, asking, "So, what did you and Steven do while he was here?"

"We went to Santa Monica to go sailing and ended up staying at a little beachside hotel for a few days," she explained, her attitude completely changing from shock to excitement.

"I wish I would've known he was coming."

"I wish you could've been here. We had so much fun," she said, laughing.

"Yeah, he has a way of making you feel good."

"You never told me he was such a good dancer, girl. The night we went dancing I thought I'd never get him off the dance floor."

"Well, I'm glad you had such a good time. Look, I hate to cut this short but I'm going to be late for a meeting."

"Okay, call me later," she said innocently.

"I will. Bye."

"Bye."

I lied, because I was so upset I'd missed Steven that I didn't want to talk to her anymore. The more I heard about his visit and the fun they had, the angrier I got. I knew Diane and Steven were mere acquaintances but if I ever found out they were together, it would crush me.

Chapter 43

The day after I got home from Los Angeles there was a knock at my door. The hair on the back of my neck stood up and for a moment I thought it was Tiffany. I opened it slowly, only to see my brother's face staring back at me.

At first, I couldn't believe my eyes when I saw Victoria standing behind him. Then I smiled and stepped forward, shaking Blake's hand and welcomed them into my home.

Victoria hugged me, patting my back saying, "It's so good to see you."

I slowly stepped back and just looked at her. She hardly looked the same. Her hair was short and she'd gained twenty or thirty pounds. The eyes that once sparkled looked tired now and I wondered what had happened.

"I can't believe you still live here," she said, looking around like she had been here before.

I replied, trying not to sound too sarcastic, "Yes, I still live here, believe it or not."

She picked up a copy of my book and said, "I just thought with all the money you're making you'd have a better house."

"There's nothing wrong with this house, Victoria. It serves its purpose."

"You always were the practical one," Blake said, giving me a sideways glance.

"Thanks for the compliment, if it was a compliment."

"Of course it was," he said, sitting down on the couch. "I guess you're wondering why I came by."

"Yes, I am," I replied as Victoria and I joined him.

"I need your help," Blake said seriously.

"Sure. What do you need?"

"I need to borrow ten-thousand dollars."

"Okay. Can I ask what for?"

"I need to make a down-payment on a house," he said, looking nervous.

I leaned back and told him, "That's a lot of money but if you're going to invest it in a house, I'll get it for you in the morning."

"Thanks, Steven. I'll pay you back."

I looked over at Blake and smiled. He seemed worried but I could tell he was trying to hide it. His request was not what I was expecting and it certainly didn't explain why he was with her.

"So, Victoria, what are you up to these days?" I asked, standing back up, looking over at her.

"Nothing much. Have you heard from Tiffany lately?"

"No. Have you?"

"Not lately, but the last time I talked to her she kept asking about you."

"Really?"

"You've still got the hots for her, don't you?" she asked accusingly.

Blake laughed, touching her knee, saying, "You should've known that."

Before I had the chance to respond, Blake stood up and asked, "What time should I come by?"

"Around eleven."

"Thanks, man," he said as we walked to the door.

"No problem."

"It was good to see you. I'm sure we'll see each other again soon," Victoria said, hugging me goodbye.

"It was good to see both of you," I said, turning to shake Blake's hand. He pulled me closer and I hugged him too.

"See you in the morning," he said, walking down the steps with Victoria right behind him.

"Bye, be careful," I said, walking to the edge of the porch to watch them leave.

He opened her door, waiting for her to get in then closed it. It was strange enough that they had shown up at my doorstep together but for my brother to ask for ten thousand dollars was completely odd. I couldn't help but wonder what was going on between the two of them. That is, if anything was going on. From what I could remember, Blake never liked Victoria very much. Of course, that was a long time ago and things can always change.

I sat back down at the desk but my concentration had been broken. The peace I felt ten minutes ago was gone and nothing I could do would bring it back. As I looked around, I decided Victoria was right about the old house. There really was no reason for me to stay in Natchez anymore and I began to think about where I wanted to move. I tried not to think of Tiffany while I was looking at the map but it was something I couldn't help but do.

The rest of the day, my mind would wander endlessly with thoughts of Tiffany. Where was she? How was she doing? I would find myself reliving moments we had shared together. I would fantasize about making love and could almost feel her skin. I always thought when a man reached a certain level of financial success he would be happy. But I found out the hard way, that's not always the truth.

Chapter 44

It was late July and I had to make a decision. Every script I liked, Jared didn't. He didn't want me to leave town because he wanted me home every night. So, I picked a quirky comedy about two women who become bank robbers. Shooting started in late August so that gave me almost another month off.

My fiancé was in love with me and I should have been happy. But our pictures started showing up in magazines and tabloids. The reporters had dug into Jared's past and it concerned me. If some of the articles held any truth, I wondered if I had made the right choice to marry him.

When Dad read about Jared, he called to check on me. I told him not to worry that we would come to visit him soon and he could decide about Jared for himself. He told me if Jared had beaten up his girlfriend that bad, even though he was young, he could do it again. I tried to reassure him that Jared wasn't like that but nothing I said convinced him otherwise.

We went to spend the next weekend in Natchez and I hoped meeting him in person would put Dad's mind at ease. But Dad seemed so uncomfortable and Jared so out of place that I regretted ever coming. I had never seen either one of them act this way and I couldn't help but feel uneasy myself.

At night, Dad and I would stay up late to talk. He wasn't happy about my engagement and advised me to take things slow. He said that if Jared was in love with me, he wouldn't mind waiting.

The moment we left Natchez, Jared quickly put my mind at ease with his charm and charisma. We boarded the plane and I forgot all about our terrible weekend. Looking into Jared's eyes was all I needed and in that moment, I became certain that I didn't want to spend the rest of my life alone.

When I went back to work, Jared was always waiting for me when I came home. He rarely stayed at his apartment anymore but we never talked about it. We had only discussed a date for our wedding once, briefly, and as long as Jared didn't bring it up neither did I. Everything between us was simple, without any worries and we both seemed content not to plan for our future.

The only thing he ever asked me about was the letters I received from Steven. I explained that we were just old friends and it was nothing for him to worry about. When he respected my privacy, I loved him even more. And with each passing day, I began to think Jared was the perfect man for me.

****

We finally wrapped up the movie in November and a week later Steven's second book Spelling Goodbye came out. The title startled me and I had to find a way to be alone so I could read it in peace. I decided to tell Jared that I had to go to New York to see my mother. I would see her but I also had a hotel suite waiting, just in case I needed privacy.

When I went to see my mother she insisted I stay at her apartment. After spending one night, I lied and told her I had to go back to Los Angeles. I felt a tinge of guilt but there was something more important I had to do.

I went across town, to the solitude of my suite and ordered room service. With a glass of wine and the candlelight softly glowing, I opened Steven's book and began to read aloud.

Chapter 45

It was a very cold November and I still hadn't completed my third book. I was busy looking for a house in the western part of the United States and trying to keep up with my movie script. Some would say I had writer's block, but I really didn't.

I put off the decision of where to buy a house for a later date. Then I called Diane and asked if she would be my go between on the movie deal. She knew more about the movie business and I trusted her. She accepted and became my voice to Mr. Broderick.

I flew down to Miami and rented a house, to clear my thoughts and finish the book. I knew Tiffany had spent some time here and every chance I got, I explored Miami to try and see what she'd seen in this town. I remembered her telling me about a bar she wanted to take me to and I didn't stop searching, until I found it.

It didn't take too long to figure out why she wanted to bring me here. I listened to the locals tell their stories and quickly fell into a routine of writing during the day and going to the bar every night. The best part was listening to them talk about her. And of course, when they told me what she said about me, I was on the edge of my seat.

I finished the book in mid December and called Diane before I went home. When she asked me what it was about I just had to laugh. How could a fellow writer expect you to explain the complexities of a book in just a few sentences? She realized what she'd asked and interrupted by telling me some good news. Her latest screenplay had also been picked up and soon she'd be back at work. We both congratulated each other and I said we'd have to go out and celebrate soon. She agreed and told me it would probably be sooner than I thought, because Dean needed to see me about the script. They were finally on the final draft and I would have to give my okay. I told her I'd change flights and see her tomorrow.

I started to say goodbye and she interrupted once again. Then she said that she'd changed her mind and she would just talk to me about it in person. The tone of her voice made me insist that she tell me now. With sadness, she explained that Tiffany was engaged, to a man named Jared Evans.

On the plane, I decided that I was going to get in touch with Tiffany. She had to know my heart was shattered at the thought of her marrying again. Why my love for her would not subside was beyond my understanding but I had to tell her. I needed to see her and look into those blue eyes before I could believe what Diane said was true. But when I got there, I decided to stay just long enough to see Dean Broderick. Then I headed home to Natchez for Christmas.

On Christmas day it began to bother me that I didn't try to get in touch with Tiffany. The news of her engagement completely caught me off guard and foolish pride got in the way. Besides, I didn't know what I would've said if I had seen her. Maybe I would have begged her to marry me instead or perhaps just told her congratulations. Now, I would never know.

My house was empty and too quiet so I went to visit Mr. Crenshaw. He told me Jared and Tiffany had come to visit him recently and I asked what he thought of him. I knew Mr. Crenshaw was just trying to spare my feelings but it was obvious that he was worried. He didn't have to tell me, I could see it in his eyes. I knew Jared was trouble and no one had to tell me that either, I could feel it.

I spent New Year's Eve looking over house listings and paperwork Mr. Broderick sent concerning the movie. I narrowed down my choices to three different houses. One was in Las Vegas, one in San Francisco and another in Los Angeles.

Then I put all of Dean's letters in order by date and opened them one by one. Most were about script changes or legal matters but the last letter was about which actors and actresses were up for the lead roles. I was thrilled when I saw Tiffany's name on the list. I wrote Dean a letter persuading him to cast Tiffany as Gracie. Then I wrote my beloved a long overdue letter.

Dearest Tiffany,

I hope this letter finds you happy and well. I hear you will be a bride soon and I wish you the best. I would never want more for you than your happiness.

I spent some time in Miami recently and listened to their stories each day. Thank you for telling me; it was such a pleasant stay. The writing game is fulfilling in its own unique way. Still I miss you and continue to pray for you everyday. I see your pictures and you appear perfectly well. But there is this voice in my head that's warning me. I don't know what it means and I won't try to explain.

Just to let you know, I'll soon be moving, closer to your vicinity. My work takes me there. How lucky can I be? I know I'll enjoy the golden sunshine, maybe the aqua-blue ocean or perhaps a mountain view. I can't make up my mind exactly where I want to be but I will be closer to you.

I write to tell you about the part in a movie you'll be offered soon. I wanted to be the first to let you know because I didn't want you to find out any other way. I wonder if you've read the first book that I wrote. There's a girl named Gracie who fell in love with a boy named Jake. Their parents didn't want them together because they thought their love was a mistake. I don't want to ruin the story, in case you haven't read it. They'll start filming the movie soon and if you'll accept the role of Gracie, it is waiting for you.

Please know that whatever you decide I will be thankful either way. If you have prior engagements then let me know. I'll continue writing, knowing someday I will see you again. Take good care of yourself my beloved, my cherished friend.

Forever,
Steven

****

I was at the post office early on January the 2nd to mail Tiffany's letter overnight delivery. I wanted her to know about the movie as soon as possible plus it gave me a reason to send her a letter. I hoped that she would be at home and if this New Year's Eve was like any other, she'd be there. Before I mailed it, I bowed my head, saying a silent prayer that her heart would be open to the offer.

I also sent Dean's letter and hoped he would be persuaded to cast Tiffany in the role. Then I made reservations to go to Los Angeles the next week. I needed to talk to Dean, look at the house and if fate was on my side, see Tiffany.

Chapter 46

Jared and I had a New Year's Eve party like Hollywood had never seen. So many people came and they just kept coming and coming. But after a couple days of partying, I insisted that everyone go home. With our days and nights mixed up, we watched the sunrise before finally falling asleep in each other's arms.

The next afternoon we awoke to the sound of the doorbell ringing. Steven sent a letter via express mail so I opened it immediately. Jared was trying to look over my shoulder as I read it and I kept turning away from him. He became angry and demanded to know what it was about. I was putting it in the envelope, trying to explain, when he grabbed it out of my hand.

"Give it back, Jared!"

"If he's just a friend then why can't I see it?" he asked, holding it over my head.

"Because, it's not yours."

He glared down at me and I stepped back as he put the letter behind his back. "I'll give it to you, if you'll tell me what it says."

"I was trying to tell you before you grabbed it. They're making a movie about a book he wrote. That's all. Now, can I have my letter back?" I asked innocently, holding out my hand.

"Here," he said, shoving it into my hand, plopping down on the couch.

Turning around, I walked quietly out the back door and ran down to the beach. I was still in my nightgown and didn't even care. I walked down the beach slowly, reading his letter once again.

My excitement was soon suppressed by a little bit of concern. In the second reading, I saw more than I did in the first. I hoped Steven would move to Los Angeles, at least then we could see each other from time to time. Then I kneeled in the sand and said a prayer that he would move here.

When I walked back into the house, Jared was waiting for me. He was dressed and said he had to fly to Ireland for business. I kept asking how long he'd be gone but he would never answer me.

We stood at the front door and he brushed my cheek with his lips. I just smiled and said goodbye. He looked back and seemed angry when I didn't follow him out to his car. But Jared had disappointed me and this time I couldn't hide my feelings.

Chapter 47

When I went to Dean's office, I was shocked to see Tiffany and Diane there. The second I walked in, Tiffany stood up and I was instantly drawn to her. Dean and Diane became invisible as she looked in my eyes and my arms surrounded her. It felt like a hundred years had passed us by since the last time I saw her. And in that moment, I realized nothing in life really mattered to me until I held her close to my heart.

The four of us had a long discussion about the movie but during the entire meeting, I couldn't stop looking at Tiffany. I wanted to hold her, I wanted to kiss her, but I had to let my eyes tell her what I was feeling.

There was a change in the way she looked at me, but I couldn't put my finger on it. Maybe it was because of Jared. I just didn't know. She might truly be in love with him and just doesn't see me in the same way. But every time Diane brought Jared up she seemed uncomfortable.

My next guess was the obvious. I hadn't been writing to her very much. I wished she knew the reason why I started writing novels in the first place. It was because I couldn't write her letters when I wanted. Besides, I was writing the books for her anyway. If she knew the truth, I wondered if the look in her eyes would change. No matter what the cause, Tiffany had never looked at me this way and I didn't know how to take it.

We went to lunch and then spent the rest of the afternoon going over some final decisions. Shooting would begin in late February and I could hardly believe this was happening.

After lunch, Diane said she'd take me over to look at the house for sale so I asked Tiffany to join us. Diane made an excuse for her but she accepted anyway and we were off to see my perspective new home.

Instantly, when I walked through the entryway, I felt like I belonged. The house looked exactly like the pictures the realtor had sent and I walked through each room admiring the craftsmanship. Tiffany and Diane were trying to convince me to buy it and the realtor wouldn't give me a moment of silence.

"This house is perfect for you," Diane said.

"It's in a good neighborhood, in your price range and I'd love to do business with you, Mr. Cross."

"You couldn't ask for a better location. With all the trees in the yard it looks like you're outside the city. But you're still close the beach," Tiffany said, following close behind me.

I could hear every word but I was still deep in thought. We walked into the backyard and the pool was shimmering as the sunlight hit the water's surface. There was a hot tub over in the corner near a small hut. And as I looked around at so much beauty, I thought of spending time here with Tiffany.

"Just think, you'd only be twenty minutes away from me," she said sweetly, taking my hand.

I turned to look her in the eyes and she smiled that unforgettable smile. "Then you would come over and go swimming with me?"

"Yes. And you could come over to my house and we could go to the beach."

The softness of her voice made me hot inside and it made my heart fill with desire. I was silent as I led her back through the house. Diane and the realtor joined us and their endless comments were filling the air as we walked through the front door. I walked to the street, as they followed, then turned around to look at the house. I asked the realtor to open her trunk for me. I walked over, pulled the for-sale sign up and put it in her trunk.

After we left, the three of us went to a bar to have a celebration drink and when it was time to go, Diane offered me a place to stay. But I insisted on staying at the hotel with the excuse of working on my next book. They both wanted to know what it was about but I only teased them with bits of information.

Diane and Tiffany took me to the hotel and I got out at the front entrance. I touched Tiffany's hand through the passenger window while saying goodbye and she looked up at me. There was too much sorrow and way too much pain in her eyes. I had to look away, so I turned and quickly entered the hotel.

Once in my suite, I let all the events of the day sink in. I tried to figure out what was in Tiffany's eyes or what wasn't there any longer. But regardless of what it was, after seeing the look on her face, I was afraid I had lost her forever.

****

By February, my new house in Los Angeles was ready for me to move in. It was impossible for me to sell my house in Natchez because I always wanted a place to come home. This meant I didn't have to bring much with me when I moved.

With Tiffany and Diane's help, we began to furnish and decorate the house. I let Tiffany decide what the theme for each room would be and she seemed so happy. I didn't care about the expense as long as I could see the smile on her face.

Tiffany and Diane came over almost every day until each room was finished. Being around her, just to be near her, made me feel more alive. I couldn't have been any happier and I started to feel normal again. There was something about Tiffany. She reminded me of who I truly am and I wanted nothing more than to return to my old self.

The time had come to start filming The Cleansing Rain and right on cue, Jared came home from Ireland. Tiffany acted completely different with him around. Every time I saw her, the light that had returned in her eyes seemed to have faded a little more with each passing day. So I tried to avoid seeing her in the state her fiancé put her in. I began to excuse myself from the set whenever they didn't need me with the excuse of writing.

It was impossible for me to write anything good when Tiffany lived only twenty minutes away and I rarely got to see her smile. I would write a page and tear it up, then write another. With Tiffany constantly on my mind, it was hard to write anything worthy of reading. In vain, I tried to push her out of my mind. The thought of going home to Natchez to finish the book sounded great but I knew I had to be here. I didn't have a choice.

My life kept reminding me of that same old roller coaster ride. Just a few days ago, I was on top of the world. Today I felt, there was no bottom but yet I was still falling. I began to think I had done the wrong thing by moving here. But how could it be wrong when I was so close to Tiffany?

I could plainly see how much pain she was enduring. Looking into her eyes made me feel incredibly helpless. Deep pools of crystal clear blue, not reflections but windows showed unspoken words of agony. If only I could rescue her but in order to be rescued, the other person must be willing to receive the hero.

Chapter 48

As I dressed for the party, all I wanted to do was crawl in bed and go to sleep. Jared insisted we make an appearance but I would've done anything to be lying in bed. Instead, I was standing in front of the mirror. I left my hair down and I put on very little make-up.

Jared was downstairs, singing loudly and it was obvious he'd already started drinking. As I was walking out of the bathroom, I caught my refection in the mirror. Tears began to sting my eyes but I held them back and tried to smile.

At the top of the stairs, I debated whether or not to go to the party. Then Jared yelled out my name, complaining that we were already late.

With my head held high, I took a deep breath and slowly walked downstairs. As I walked toward him, Jared looked up at me making obscene gestures. But I just walked right past him, out to the limo and got inside.

He followed me, complaining about how I looked and the way I was treating him. I knew he was only trying to upset me by using verbal weapons but I remained calm and collected until he started demanding I quit working on The Cleansing Rain.

"You better listen to me, Tiffany."

"Look, there's no way I'm pulling out of this movie, short of death."

He grabbed my arm with one hand and my chin with the other, making me look at him. "I don't ever want to catch you anywhere around Steven Cross anymore!"

I turned my head away, looking out the window. "If you cannot conduct yourself like a gentleman, I'm going back home."

"Well if a whore can act like a lady then I can act like a gentleman," he said sarcastically, moving over to fix another drink.

The minute we walked into the party he started drinking even more. It was already obvious I'd made a big mistake by coming here with him but what could I do? His voice was getting louder and it wasn't long before he began insulting everyone at the party.

When he turned his back, I quickly slipped out of the room. Walking down a long hallway, I heard the sound of music. It was a ballroom filled with people dancing but I didn't go in. I needed a moment of silence, to clear my head from his cruel words. There were doors at the end of the hallway that led outside. I stopped a waiter with a tray of champagne and took a glass with me.

Finally, in the cool night air, I was alone. I walked slowly across the terrace and looked out over the gardens. The air felt cool and crisp as a light breeze blew through my hair. I looked up to the sky and the stars were glistening brightly. I remembered how Steven would say, whenever he looked up at the stars I was with him. For the first time in my life, I think I finally understood what he meant. And as beautiful as the stars looked tonight, I closed my eyes and prayed for rain.

49 Chapter

I sat alone on the couch in my new house, deep in thought. There was no way I was going to Dean's party tonight because I couldn't stand being around Jared. The way he treated Tiffany and his obsessive drinking made him the last person I wanted to see. I decided to stay at home and watch a movie or something. Then I decided that seeing Tiffany for a few minutes was better than not at all. It was getting a little late to show up for the party but I had to go.

As I drove up to the door, part of me wanted to drive right by but something compelled me to stop. It was the same ole feeling that I'd had since the first day I'd met her. I still wanted to find Tiffany and take her with me, wherever I might go.

The moment I walked in the room, Jared's voice was the first thing I heard. He was standing at the bar making a toast and Tiffany was nowhere in sight. I quickly walked through the room, hoping he wouldn't see me.

Walking down the hall, I entered the ballroom and found a quiet place to stand. I looked at every person in the room at least twice but Tiffany wasn't there. Her beautiful red hair would have certainly caught my eye. And then I thought of the possibility that she may not be here at all. But somehow I knew she was; I just had to find her.

Walking down the hallway, I looked into the dining room but she wasn't there. I looked back, toward the sound of the party then turned around and walked to the end of the hall. I opened the door to the terrace and there she was, standing alone. Quietly closing the door, I went back to get two glasses of champagne.

As the wind blew her long red hair, I walked up behind her quietly. She was looking up at the stars and I wondered what she could be thinking about. She was a vision, in a long emerald green dress against the background of a million stars.

"Can I offer a beautiful lady a drink?"

"Steven. I didn't think you'd be here. I was just thinking about you."

"Was it good or bad?" I asked, handing her the glass of champagne.

"Good," she said softly, raising her glass toward me before taking a sip.

I leaned back against the balcony to look in her eyes and asked, "So, what are you doing out here by yourself?"

"I was hoping for rain."

"Why do you want it to rain?"

She looked up in the sky, saying, "I just want it to rain, for a long, long time."

"Tiffany, can I ask you something?"

She turned to look at me and softly said, "Yes, you know you can ask me anything."

"What were you thinking about me?"

"I was thinking about the way you say that when you look up at the stars, I'm with you. For the first time in my life, I think I finally understand what you mean."

The silence surrounded us with its thickness as I looked into Tiffany's eyes and she looked away. I could see the years of pain and hurt the world had shown her. If she would have let me, I could have stopped it a long, long time ago.

"I've got to do something to cheer you up, Love." When I called Tiffany by her middle name, she turned sharply and stared at me with wide-open eyes.

"What do you have in mind, Mr. Cross?"

"Let's go dance."

She smiled a genuine smile and sweetly said, "Now that's an offer I can barely refuse."

There was nothing else on earth that could make me feel better, than to see her smile and hear her laugh. I wished I could see her this way everyday, for the rest of my life.

Tiffany slipped her hand under my arm and I put my hand over hers. We reminisced about the first night we danced together as we walked down the hallway toward the ballroom. All these years later, I felt the same nervousness, but my, how the scenery had changed.

As we walked into the ballroom, everyone turned to stare and I knew exactly how they felt. This beautiful woman on my arm could not walk past you without you noticing her. I led her to the center of the dance floor and we turned to face each other. While looking into her eyes, I placed her hand on my shoulder. My hand was on Tiffany's waist, as the band began to play.

We both stood still, as if in a trance, then we magically became the only two people in the room. I slowly moved my fingertips down her arm and took her hand. I pulled her body close to mine as she and I started to dance. Tiffany followed my every move as if we were born to dance with each other. Closing my eyes, I wished this song would never end, if it meant I could hold her in my arms forever.

When the song ended, Tiffany hugged me tightly and with her so close to me; it almost felt impossible to let her go. She was so happy and I could tell her smile came from the heart. I put my arm around her as we walked off the floor and smiled. Everyone was smiling and nodding as if to say they enjoyed watching us dance. But our happiness lasted only a moment because Jared was standing at the door. His eyes were full of anger as he walked over and jerked her away from me.

"What in the hell are you doing with him?"

"I was just coming to find you," she said softly, kissing Jared's cheek.

"I can plainly see you'd rather spend time with your pen pal instead of your fiancé."

"Jared, if you don't lower your voice right now, I'm leaving without you."

My heart felt like it was going to burst as she said the words because I'd never heard her speak in this manner. I wanted to just take her hand and walk out the front door and never look back. There was nothing in this world I needed, except to be with her forever. And I couldn't stop myself from saying; "I think it might be a good idea if you come with—"

Jared stepped forward, looking me up and down saying, "I can't believe you have the audacity to ask my fiancé to leave with you right in front of me. Who do you think you are?"

The smell of alcohol was overwhelming but I stood my ground. "I think you need some time to sober up."

"Well I think it's time for you and me to step outside!"

Tiffany grabbed Jared's arm, pulling him back, saying, "And I think it's time for us to go home. Good night, Steven."

I said good night to Tiffany's back as she took him by the arm and escorted him out. I stood there in shock for a moment, as all the eavesdroppers starting talking amongst themselves.

I walked away slowly, replaying the passing moments in my mind and went to the bathroom. After washing my face, I stared into the mirror. Looking into my eyes, it dawn on me, I had just asked her to leave with me again.

Before I left the party, I knew one thing for certain. I had to get off this roller coaster ride because it was making me sick. Fifteen minutes ago I was the happiest man in the world, now I was the saddest. I could see Tiffany was falling apart and I couldn't do anything to save her. But there was no way I could stick around any longer and watch what was happening. I had to write her one final letter but it was impossible to do it in Los Angeles, so I decided to go back home to Mississippi.

Chapter 50

Over the next few days, Jared and I avoided spending time together. When we were around each other we argued over the stupidest things. The tension was building but it was as if we were prolonging the inevitable, the reality that neither one of us wanted to face.

After a few weeks of pretending to be a workaholic, it was beginning to show on my face. I canceled my last appointment for the day and decided to cook dinner. It was time to make peace and the closer I got to home, the more I thought of how sweet making up could be.

His car was in the garage and I quickly got out of the car and opened the front door. I called out his name but there was no answer. I turned on the stereo and walked upstairs but he was nowhere to be found. I changed into a sundress and touched up my make-up.

As I walked downstairs I could hear Jared making himself a drink. "Hi honey, I'm glad you're home."

He glared up at me and sarcastically said, "Oh, I see your other personality is back."

His words cut me like a knife and I almost wanted to walk upstairs backwards to start over again. But it was obvious that he had been drinking for hours and then I just wanted to vanish. Instead, I took each step down slowly, preparing myself for his bad attitude.

"And where do you think you're going looking like that?"

"I'm going to the kitchen to cook dinner," I said solemnly, walking past him.

He walked up behind me, turning me around and said, "I guess you think, I'll cook dinner, have sex with him and everything will be back to normal. Right, Tiffany?"

"I don't want to argue with you."

"When do you think it's going to be a good time to talk about 'it'?"

"I'm not sure. Right now, I'm going to the kitchen."

He took me by the shoulders, shaking me. "No you're not! Right now, you're going to tell me what in the hell is going on between you and Steven Cross."

"Steven and I are just friends," I said calmly, breaking free from his grasp.

"You should have seen yourself at that party dancing with him."

"I didn't look bad to anybody, except you. You were the one who embarrassed me."

"You embarrassed yourself!" he yelled, raising his hand like he was going to hit me.

Anger rushed through my veins as I yelled, "Are you trying to ruin my career?"

"I don't have to do that either. You'll do that on your own," he said walking back to the bar, fixing another drink.

"That's it, I can't do this anymore. I want you out of my house!"

As I opened the front door, Jared threw his drink at me. It hit the door and a piece of glass stuck in my cheek. I pulled it out and put my hand over the wound as blood dropped to the floor.

Jared laughed loudly, pointing at me. "Maybe that scar will give your face some character."

I ran over and slapped him across the face, yelling, "I hate you! Get out of my house!"

Jared grabbed me by the arm and pushed me to the floor. I looked up and he kicked me in the stomach. As I tried to catch my breath, Jared stood there glaring down at me.

"I was planning on leaving you anyway, bitch! Oh, and about our engagement, forget it. Did you seriously think I would marry a woman like you?" Jared asked with disgust in his voice then walked out the door, never looking back.

On the floor, I felt the pain of all the rejections in my life. I cried for the little girl whose dreams never came true. I cried for the woman I had regrettably become. If I had known the path would lead me here, I would have stayed behind.

Every hand that had ever touched me with the lie of love, weighed heavy upon my conscience. The only person in this world who loved me was a young man named Steven Cross. But he didn't exist anymore, and even if he did how could he want somebody like me?

Stumbling to the bathroom, I washed the blood off my hands. I looked up and when I saw my face, I became enraged. I picked up a vase and threw it at the mirror, breaking both into a thousand pieces.

Running into the living room, I started throwing anything that would break. Somewhere inside myself, I knew I had to stop but I kept looking for something else to throw. I screamed out the questions I had on my mind, knowing there would be no one to answer them.

"Why? Why? Where is love? Where is trust? Why is this happening to me again?"

The moment I stopped, I looked at myself in the mirror hanging on the wall. When I saw my reflection, I couldn't believe what I had become.

The time had finally arrived to change my life forever. I made a promise to myself that from this moment forward, I would refuse to lie. I would never hold back the truth in any situation. I wanted to become more like Tiffany Crenshaw instead of Tiffany Starr.

As I turned to go to the bathroom, there on the floor in front of me were several letters. The one in the middle was in a red envelope and I knew it was from Steven. I fell to my knees and wept as I picked up his letter. I walked to my bedroom, as I had always done, to read it aloud in bed.

My Beloved,

What pain is this I feel when I look into your eyes now? Was it something I did? Was it something I said? Is there any way I can change them back to their original shine? Tell me, did someone take it from you? I will gladly buy it back. I would become a thief if need be. It is harder to breath when I see your spirit broken. Please know I would do anything, to see the light shine in your eyes again.

When you are in pain, I feel it too. I know you think you can hide it from me but this is untrue. Your heart is tied to this heart of mine. It happened a long time ago. If I could have stopped it by now, you know I would.

How can I live with only half of what I need? What will I have to do to forget about you? Maybe your marriage will end it for me.

I am very doubtful; because I'm not sure my heart wants to be free.
Only there is no direction without you, I can make no brilliant plan.
If I cannot be yours forever...that's something I'll never understand.
Never you worry, my beautiful beloved, I will be with you again, after
judgment day. Until that time my love I must bid you farewell, I can no
longer stay.

I will love you forever,
Steven

As I read Steven's farewell, my emotions could not be contained. The reality of what I had done and what I hadn't done flooded my soul with pain. I just couldn't believe it was true. It was me who robbed myself of love, true love. There had been no thief, no evil witch nor poison apple which separated us. Only the foolishness of a girl and the pride of a foolish woman.

Crawling off the bed, I made my way into the bathroom. I took a long look at myself before I washed my face. Then I took his letter to the kitchen table and went back to take a bath.

When I was clean, I put on comfortable clothes and put my hair up. It took me several hours to clean up the mess but it felt good to throw that stuff away. Then suddenly my mind became one-track and nothing else mattered.

The rest of the night, I looked through everything in my house for Steven's letters. They were hiding in the most unbelievable places. It was like finding little pieces of gold between old books or in tattered shoeboxes. I put them on the dinning room table and it wasn't long before there were stacks of them.

The next morning, Diane showed up unexpectedly and I reluctantly let her in the house. I knew she was shocked to see the cut on my cheek by the expression on her face. I took her hand and silently led her into the living room. We sat down and the moment I looked in her eyes, I started crying.

"What happened to you?"

"Jared and I had an argument. It's over between us."

"Are you okay?" she asked, putting her arm around me.

"No, I'm not," I said, putting my head on her shoulder.

"Is there anything I can do to help?"

I sat up and asked, "Can you get them to shoot around me until next week?"

"Sure, I can do that," she said, not sounding too sure. We sat quietly for a few moments then she asked, "Do you want me to stay with you?"

I stood up, reaching out for her hand. "Thanks, but no. I have something extremely important to take care of."

"I can come back tonight and stay. It won't be any problem."

"Thank you so much, Diane. You don't know how much that means to me but I really just want to be alone. Please don't take it the wrong way."

She looked into my eyes, gently holding my chin. "Everything is going to be okay. Jared wasn't the right guy for you."

"I know that now," I said, trying to smile.

"Your face will heal. You'll feel better and he'll regret losing you. It'll happen, trust me, I know."

We hugged for a long time then she followed me to the door saying "Call me if you need anything."

"I will. Thanks."

I watched her drive away then went back inside to finish my search of the house. It was hard to believe how many letters he'd sent me over the years. When I felt satisfied that I'd found most of them, I put them in order by date.

The sun was rising again before I finished reading them all. Some of them made me laugh. Most of them made me cry. All of them left me with a deep longing inside.

Then I drifted off to sleep and had the sweetest dream about the two of us. I was dressed in a sparkling white evening gown trimmed in gold. It looked like we were at an award ceremony because everyone was well dressed and there were lots of famous people there. We were walking to the back of the room and a little boy and girl came running toward me, clinging to my dress. Steven and I looked at each other and smiled. We were so happy together and I awoke feeling elated.

The first thing I did when I woke up was look for everything in my house Steven had ever given me. My promise ring, the pink teddy bear and the ruby ring. His journals were still in the bottom of the box Victoria had given me and all the notes he use to give me in high school.

Then I took a few hours to reflect over every word he had ever written. The floodgate of my heart opened and I was unable to close it. In the moments between sobs I questioned myself repeatedly about which path I should choose. Should I offer him my love or should I go away forever? And then I finally realized it was no longer my choice.

My appetite was completely nonexistent so I took a long hot bath and put on a white lace nightgown. I searched the entire house for every candle and placed them on the dinning room table. After lighting them, I turned off all the lights in the house.

With his letters and gifts in front of me, I sat down and poured myself a glass of wine. Our song from so many years ago, I'll Be There For You, was playing as I began to write Steven a long overdue letter.

My love,

Where have I been? Was I lost in another world? I read your farewell and cannot believe it's true. This is the letter I have waited too long to write. I remember you telling me that life was short. Only now I realize you were right.

Can I say that I have been a fool? Yet if all of these roads can lead me to you, I will never leave you again. This time it is your decision if it will end or begin. I will give to you everything that I have to give. My heart is opened up to you like never before. Your letters have given me the strength, to not live a lie anymore.

I will be standing under the old oak tree waiting for you. Saturday March twenty-ninth, at eleven a.m. If you want to give our love a chance, that is where I will stand. If I don't see you there, I will go on loving you...forever.

Yours eternally,
Tiffany

With a beautiful pale yellow dress on and tiny white daisies in my hair I looked at my refection. I could almost see the girl Steven had fallen in love with. My heart was filled with anticipation, wondering if he would be at the park, waiting for me. I realized that all of the love we had felt for each other was never given the opportunity to grow. In my mind, I knew, I still didn't deserve his love but if Steven was willing, I wanted one good chance to begin.

The wind was blowing lightly and the sun was shining through puffy white clouds. Every time I had dreamed of this moment, it was always raining. Maybe it was because of all the tears I had to hold inside. My greatest fear was Steven had finally found out, I wasn't everything he thought I was. In my soul, I finally knew there was no way for me to be a better person without him in my life. I cursed myself for the stupidity of so many careless decisions. Many times before, we could have risked everything to be together but I was foolish. I couldn't feel love when love was with me all the time. Now I realize it was because I was blind to it. All I ever had to do was open my eyes and live the life I am suppose to live. I closed my eyes and prayed that Steven had found a way to forgive me. At this point in my life, I couldn't see a way to live without him anymore.

Not wanting to arrive too early, I asked the driver to go past the park. I was nervous and worried that he wouldn't show up. I promised myself, I wouldn't fall apart if Steven decided he was better off without me. When I wrote him the letter, I knew it was the chance I was taking. The driver turned around at my request and drove back to the park. Silently, I prayed until he stopped beside the old oak tree.

I got out of the car and told the driver to wait. I took a deep breath and looked around but Steven was nowhere in sight. As I walked over to the oak tree, I held one long stemmed yellow rose in my hand. I reached out my other hand and walked around the roots, just like I had when I was a young girl. As I went around, the words from his letters flooded my mind. One moment I'd feel excited and the next I felt numb. I continued walking, thinking any moment, I would hear his angelic voice. But all I heard were the birds singing.

It had to be past eleven, when I stopped walking around the tree. I leaned back against it and looked out across the park. I closed my eyes as tears began to push their boundaries. If I had missed the opportunity to live with honesty and integrity, not to mention true love, I would leave Mississippi and run away forever.

In my mind, I was begging Steven to be here with me. I didn't know how to do this right but I was willing to try. Even if he wasn't in love with me, I needed to tell him the truth about so many things that had happened over the years. I was determined to let him know everything. I would write him a thousand letters just to try and explain.

Just as I was about to give up and walk away, I felt a hand touch my hand. "You're here," I said, taking his hand.

"I'm here," he said, turning to face me.

"You got the letter?"

"I got the letter," he said, taking it from his pocket.

Pulling him close, I looked into his beautiful hazel eyes. "I don't know how to do this, Steven."

"Let's start with a kiss."

TO BE CONTINUED…

About the Author

Charna Ainsworth is an award-winning poet and was featured on the cover of Poet Forum magazine. The Letter is her first novel, an amazing story which is sure to become part of classic American literature. She resides in a small southern town in Mississippi with her young daughter, Maria.

Website: www.charnaainsworth.com
Email: www.info@charnaainsworth.com
Follow: www.twitter.com/charnaainsworth
Friend: www.facebook.com/charna.ainsworth